Praise for Leslie Dicken's
Beauty Tempts the Beast

"This Beauty and Beast story in a Gothic mode is a feast of sensual tension and secrets with a mystery that pulls you to a surprise ending. From the very beginning it is hard to determine which is greater - the secrets the hero and heroine are hiding or the sensual tension that sizzles whenever they are together!"

~ *eCataRomance*

"If you are a historical romance fan I cannot recommend this book enough. On the Cheeky Reads scale I give it a 4 Heart Review - It really is a fantastic read!"

~ *Cheeky Reads*

"Beauty Tempts The Beast is brisk, fast-paced, and completely sexy...The dark and mysterious atmosphere Ms. Dicken's creates in Silverstone Manor pitch perfect...Ms. Dicken is a talented story-teller."

~ *Long and Short Reviews*

"I was hooked from page one and sat up way too late reading because I couldn't put it down. I found the characters intriguing and well-written....Secrets abound, a mystery is afoot, and romance is in the air: all the makings of a fabulous story that does not disappoint. I can't wait to search for more of Ms. Dicken's work."

~ *BookWenches*

"Dicken's gothic romance has a mysterious villain, a crumbling manor, a scarred hero and a desperate heroine. The mystery is well done, and the hero and heroine engage the reader's sympathies."

~ *RT Romance Reviews*

Beauty Tempts the Beast

Leslie Dicken

A SAMHAIN PUBLISHING, LTD. publication.

Samhain Publishing, Ltd.
577 Mulberry Street, Suite 1520
Macon, GA 31201
www.samhainpublishing.com

Beauty Tempts the Beast
Copyright © 2010 by Leslie Dicken
Print ISBN: 978-1-60504-706-5
Digital ISBN: 978-1-60504-617-4

Editing by Tera Kleinfelter
Cover by Natalie Winters

First Samhain Publishing, Ltd. electronic publication: July 2009
First Samhain Publishing, Ltd. print publication: May 2010

Dedication

I wish to dedicate this book to:

My family, who have always been proud of me and supported my dreams.

Lisa Paitz Spindler, who has been a faithful critique partner and friend for nearly ten years.

Sheila Raye, who begged me to send her a new chapter to read and review each day as I wrote.

Tawny, Trish, Mona and Jenny, who read through this story and offered their feedback.

All members of the Playground (Writers At Play), who have encouraged me and provided me with years of fun and friendship.

And my editor, Tera, and Samhain, for giving me the chance to share this book with the world.

Chapter One

Lake District, Northern England, 1840

Wind screamed over the cliff, rattling the window panes with a phantom's cold breath. Just the way he liked it.

Charles Hansard, Viscount Ashworth, swirled the brandy in his chipped glass, then swallowed it in a gulp. He'd had more than enough. It no longer held a taste. He waited in the darkened room for the clock to tick off several minutes. Let the girl squirm a bit before he entered, then she could flee in gratitude like the others before her.

He would not return to London this year, nor any other. He'd had enough of the ton's whispers and glances. Nay, he'd not give them something else to discuss over tea or at their dreadful balls.

The cracked leather chair squeaked as he stood. It was time to set this next victim free. Despite his mother's attempts at bribing girls with his wealth, Ashworth knew they feared him. He saw the terrified glaze in their eyes. No well-bred daughter wanted to marry The Monster.

He entered the rarely used parlor through the study's adjoining door, expecting to find the girl trembling in the corner. That's what they usually did. Hell, they all looked alike to him. Whether tall or short, dark or light, all of society's debutantes paled at the sight of his hideous scar.

This one stood with her back to him, head angled up at a faded painting, the subject barely distinguishable. Instead of an expensive silk gown and fancy hat, this girl wore only a simple brown dress. Dark hair twisted down her back in a single braid.

"You may take your leave," Ashworth said. He leaned against a column and waited for her to run.

Her spine stiffened noticeably, but she didn't make a move for the door.

"Go on. Leave. I don't take kindly to strangers."

She wheeled around, her eyes, darker than a moonless night, challenged him. "And I don't take kindly to self-pitying eccentrics. Have the marriage contract drawn up. I'm not going anywhere."

He must not have heard her correctly. No one wanted to stay in this appalling, crumbling house. No one wanted to be near him. "I won't hold you to my mother's bargain. Go."

Her olive skin flushed. "I will not go. I have agreed to marry you. Let us sign the contract so that the wedding can take place."

Ashworth shoved a hand through his hair. Who was this girl and what the hell was wrong with her? None of the others had insisted on marrying him. Nay, they all ran like frightened kittens.

Something was driving her to desperation. Her curvaceous frame, obvious even in the plain clothing, did not appear to carry a bastard child. Her stomach looked flat and her breasts were full but not ripened for a babe's hungry mouth. What brought her to him? Whatever the reason, it did not matter; he wouldn't be the one to absolve her of her troubles.

He cleared his throat. "My mother fancies herself a grandmother. She will get those infants through one of her daughters. I do not wish to wed." He went over and opened the parlor door, its creak echoing in the room. "Go."

The stubborn girl stayed put. "From what I understand, you have no choice."

"No choice? Certainly I do."

She crossed her arms under her breasts, drawing his gaze. Ashworth looked away and focused on the clawed branches swaying outside the window. He wouldn't be tempted by her feminine charms. She would not sway his stance. The Monster lived alone.

The girl lifted her chin. Did he detect a tremble of her lip? "You should have a talk with your mother."

Icy fingers gripped his heart. She couldn't do this to him. Yet, his own mother would use anything for her greediness, even an innocent child. Ashworth sucked in a deep breath of air, but his temples still pounded. "What did she tell you?"

The girl blinked, saying nothing. The clock ticked like a noisy heartbeat. Somewhere in the house a bell rang for a servant. At last, she wiped her hands on her skirt. "I only know that you must marry soon. I do not know why."

Did she truly not know or just know better than to admit it? No matter, he could scare this girl away and then deal with his mother's threat later.

Ashworth pulled himself up to his full height. Intimidation. Eventually this girl would submit to it, just like all the rest. Even the boldest antelope eventually fell to the mighty lion.

He crossed the room in long strides and stood within inches of her. She smelled of wild honeysuckle. He narrowed his eyes and scowled, deepening his scar to its most hideous. "You'll not want to be married to me."

She flinched, but only for the briefest moment. "Do not be so certain. What makes you believe you are different from any other man?"

Had she known another man? Is this what brought her to him? "I am not like other men. I have certain tastes. Odd preferences."

"Living in an old decaying manor? Reclusive from society?" She lifted a rounded shoulder. "They do not bother me."

He would learn what bothered her.

Ashworth brushed a finger along her jaw. The caress

startled her, widened her eyes, but she kept her courage and didn't move away. His groin stirred at the soft texture of her skin. "Perhaps I meant in bed."

She swallowed. Her face paled ever so slightly beneath his fingertips. "As...as your wife, I shall obey."

His pulse leapt. He had not dared to dream. To have a wife, a woman to lie beside him at night. It had been so long since he enjoyed the curves of a woman's body, too long since a woman's delicate fingers trailed over his skin.

"What is your name?" The question came from his lips in a husky whisper.

"Vivian."

Ashworth slid his thumb over the small dimple in her chin. He grinned when her red lip trembled. "Have you a surname? Do you come from gentry? Perhaps you are a village girl out to dupe the eccentric viscount."

Ah, that got her temper. Her cheeks flushed to rose-colored circles. "No, my lord. I am a baron's daughter from a day's journey away."

He wanted to ask why she kept her family a secret from him and what caused her to make this trip to be a stranger's wife. But his questions could wait.

Ashworth encircled her fingers in the warm cocoon of his hand. She gasped but still did not flee. "Touch me," he whispered, lifting her hand. "My face. I dare you to touch it."

He brought her fingers to his scar then released them. He knew that at any moment she would recoil in disgust at the deep gash. His heart thumped against his ribs, his mouth dried with the anticipation, but Vivian's gaze softened. No look of revulsion marred her smooth brow as she traced the deep chasm from above his right eye all the way down to his lip. Her finger repeated the trail with an unhurried tenderness, while inside him a fervor blazed.

The man buried inside the monster took over. His flesh throbbed, his lips burned with the need to kiss her. Somewhere, deep inside his chest, an ache swelled with a ferocious possessiveness. He could not let this girl go.

Could he possibly allow her to stay?

Ashworth thrust her hand from his face. "Enough. Why do you not recoil from me? Are you blind?"

Vivian bit her lip, then lowered her eyes so he could only see the black arc of lashes. "No," she murmured. "I am not blind. Nor am I offended by a mark on one's skin."

"Then what does offend you?"

She turned away, then crossed her arms in a self-protective gesture. "A mark on one's soul."

So she revealed a part of her secret. Someone had hurt her, and therein the reason she ran. That's why she agreed to marry him—Lord Ashworth, The Monster of Silverstone Manor.

Vivian listened as the wind screamed and rattled the windows. Only an arm's length away, Lord Ashworth's aroma swirled in her nose, a scent combined of brandy and faint sandalwood.

He did not recognize her. She didn't think he would.

A chime struck from the mantel. It had reached the top of the hour. She had no place to go for supper, no tavern to return to. Every shilling she owned had been spent to bring her to this desolate house. Lord Ashworth could not make her leave.

Martin would kill her if he ever found her.

Hopefully, he would search for her in London. She'd left him a deliberate trail, told just the right people of her supposed plans. Even her mother, hidden away for her own safety, believed her daughter sought a new husband at the soirées of London. Some distant relation provided her with the perfect explanation for where she'd gone. By the time Martin found she'd never arrived, Vivian would be wed to Lord Ashworth. And wed him, she would.

"Are you cold?" Lord Ashworth's deep voice whispered down

her spine.

Vivian arranged a brave smile and forced herself to remember the man she met briefly so many years ago instead of the imposing figure of today. She turned to find him staring at her. "No, my lord, but I do beg you to uphold the bargain."

A vein throbbed on his forehead. "It is my mother's bargain," he said through clenched teeth. "Tell me why it is that you want to wed me."

A light gust of air swept through the room. The drafty chill seeped under her skin. "Tell me why you are afraid to wed."

He laughed then spun away from her and weaved his way through the old furniture to the clattering window. His wide shoulders blocked the remaining daylight, leaving only a lone candelabrum to flicker its ghostly shadows on the walls. "Afraid? I am afraid of nothing. It is others who fear me."

She did not believe him. Everyone had something to fear. "I do not fear you."

"Perhaps you should."

Had he truly changed so much from the hero she once knew? Had this scar transformed an angel into a devil? The cut alone was not the reason. Surface wounds were no indicator of the mortal underneath. She'd learned that lesson well enough. Scars marked painful memories, but true evil lurked within the soul.

If Lord Ashworth had changed it was due the incident which gave him the scar, not the mark itself.

She moved closer to him, yet avoided his post by the window, sensing she'd be intruding. Instead, her fingers traced over the worn wood trim of a high-backed chair, disturbing a layer of dust. "Would you cause me pain?"

She knew pain, still felt it.

At her question, Lord Ashworth dropped his head. His shoulders sagged. "I have no desire to hurt you. But there are times..." He sighed. "I have been here so long."

Wind swept up against the house again, dragging tree branches down the crumbling stones like a witch's nails. Vivian shivered. She wasn't accustomed to this bleak weather, yet it would not chase her away. This marriage would be her salvation.

"I am not afraid," she told him. Dear God, she must make him believe that. She must believe it herself.

He pounded his fist on the window ledge then swung to face her. "You have no idea of this place…of me!"

"I will accept whatever comes my way."

His eyes blazed. "Will you? Do you dare share my bed, dare live in a house with The Monster?"

"There are no such things as monsters," she replied, and, yet, there were…only they disguised themselves as ordinary men. Lord Ashworth was not ordinary.

One long stride brought him before her. "You know nothing." Then he swooped down and captured her face in his hands. Before she could blink, his lips possessed hers.

Vivian's heart trembled. Brief memories tumbled in her brain. Memories of Martin's crushing kisses and urgent ones from Thomas, the man she once hoped to marry.

But then she heard a cracked moan. Not a crushing attack on her mouth with either violence or lust, but a warm, velvety softness.

Lord Ashworth circled her tongue with his, his ragged breathing mimicked the frenzy of her pulse. He tasted of brandy, of dark nights, of loneliness. Her stomach pitched, as uncertainty battled with base curiosity.

He drew her in, inhaled her very being. She was swallowed in his warm breath, overtaken by his wet command. Her veins burned with a curious fire.

Suddenly, it was over. He flung her aside into a faded yellow chair and stared at her hungrily, his scar pulsing. "I do not deserve you."

She struggled to catch her breath. She did not deserve a wealthy viscount. Misfits and wounded souls belonged together to keep the nightmares at bay.

He could not make her go, just as Martin could not make her stay. She'd already lost one chance at marriage to avoid a life of horror, she'd not lose another. Vivian sat up straight and smoothed out her skirt. "Please, do not force me to leave."

He shoved a hand through his pecan-colored hair and groaned aloud. "You have no idea what you ask of me."

Vivian pressed on, biding her time. "If I must truly go, let it be tomorrow. I have no money to hire a coach, nor to stay at the tavern in the village. I can sleep here on the sofa. It matters not."

"Nay." His resigned voice set hope free in her heart. "There are beds aplenty here."

"Thank you, my lord. I shall be out of your sight until morning then. Can you have a servant show me the way?"

"Are you hungry?"

Vivian stood. "Could I have food sent to my room, please?"

His gray eyes halted her. "Would you share my bed tonight?"

Her mouth dried. The taste of his kiss lingered on her lips, but she was not a fool. Lord Ashworth merely tested her resolve.

Although no longer a virgin, she'd never willingly brought herself to another man for his taking. To deny the viscount outright could send her back down his long drive. Vivian chose her words carefully. "Have you agreed to our marriage?"

His lips thinned. "No. But I will agree to this. You can have the chamber next to mine tonight. If you wake in the morning without a visit from The Monster, then I will believe no demon lives here to assault you. I will then send for a special license."

"You cannot scare me from here." She lifted her chin.

Lord Ashworth straightened. The flickering candles cast harsh shadows along the length of his scar. A draft whispered about the room.

He held his hand out to her. "I will not be the one to frighten you away. The Monster will see that you do not stay."

The Monster. He spoke as if it were a specter of demonic fright, not a man possessed by tragedy. "As I have said, I do not believe in such things."

"After tonight you will."

Chapter Two

Pinkley rattled about the room, picking up strewn clothes. "You've no need to do that," Ashworth told his butler.

"Eh? But ye 'ave no valet." With a full head of white hair and a twisted back, the old man resembled a snow-topped ancient oak at a cliff's edge.

Ashworth yanked a shirt from gnarled hands. "I've had no valet for nearly ten years. Nor do I care what state my room is in. Go."

He opened his bedroom door to the hall. A swift river of air embraced Ashworth's skin. Drafts multiplied in this house, seemingly with each cycle of the moon. They, like the sounds of the wind and shapes of the fog, kept him company within the disintegrating walls of Silverstone Manor.

Pinkley shuffled over with an armful of garments. "Will ye be needing anything else, mi'lord? Mayhap yer nightly potion?"

Ashworth swallowed. His pulse echoed inside his skull, his mouth watered for the drink, but he could forego it tonight. There would be no need, not with someone else in the house.

Vivian.

Immediately, his blood pumped hot. A quick glance over his shoulder revealed the adjoining door.

Pinkley shook his head. "Shouldn't be 'ere, mi'lord. She's a stranger, that one. Not safe 'ere. Think of your—"

"Trust me. I think of no one else."

The old man hobbled from the room while muttering to the pile of clothing in his hands.

Ashworth stared again at the wooden door. The keyhole gleamed with an unnatural light. It beckoned him...called to him. He could step through that door. He could claim a bride. He could find salvation.

Candles flickered, the light dimmed. Wetting his lips, he took a step closer. He could hear movement. The scraping of a chair, the squeaking of floorboards.

Then, he heard humming. Vivian was singing. Here, in the most dreadful of decaying manors, the girl sang.

Like a common lecher, Ashworth lowered himself to one knee then peered through the keyhole. He caught a glimpse of her meandering by. Dressed in a white nightgown, Vivian paced about the large room, drawing a brush through her long, midnight hair.

He watched, mesmerized.

Wavering candles illuminated her body, displaying her curving shape through the thin cloth of the gown. Desire sharpened his sensations. His fingers itched, desperate to touch her. His tongue dampened, hungry for a taste. Hot and aching, his erection pressed too tight in his clothes.

He swallowed, then turned away. He would not harm her, at least not by design. If there were a God, The Monster would rest tonight. And finally, after seven years, Ashworth could have more than drafts and spiders to keep him company.

The stench of sewage and rotting food surrounded him. A woman's screams blasted through the air. Fury swirled inside of him, lifting him, charging him forward. Blood splattered, blanketing his hands, its sharp tang filling his nostrils. A roar echoed inside his brain until the window shattered. Then her screams were no more.

Ashworth sprang up from his pillow, sweat dripping down his temples. His heart clattered against his ribcage while a searing pain pierced the length of his scar and blurred his vision.

He'd been wrong after all. He couldn't sleep without the nightmares. Even with a stranger's presence, his past rose up to haunt him.

Naked, he slipped from the bed and opened his door to the hall. The welcome draft slid over his sweat-covered body, cooled his skin and quieted his raging pulse. There, on the floor, sat his glass of nightly potion. With a grateful sigh, Ashworth lifted it to his lips. The drink slid down his throat and warmed his belly.

He returned to his room. A glance at the side wall revealed a dark door. Her lights were out. Vivian slept.

He sank down into the worn sheets again. This time there would be no dreams.

Despite her conviction she'd not be frightened in this house, Vivian burrowed deeper into the musty-smelling bed. Its blood red curtains did little to soothe her soul.

She stared up at the rectangular cut of the window, where an infrequent crimson moon illuminated a spider and its web. Somewhere along the far wall a frayed tapestry fluttered. The drafts were so wretched in this house, they blew across the entire room. Vivian shivered.

Why was she in this dreadful place? How could it be that she'd found no other option?

She rolled away from the window and stared at her fading bruises. Dying embers from the fire flickered, bringing the dark marks on her upper arms to a ghastly life. Martin had promised her death if she were to leave him. From the forceful way in which he violated her body, she believed him.

Vivian could not stay there. Not once her father promised her to that demon. All hope for marrying the local man, whom she thought she was in love with, was lost.

She thought it divine intervention when she heard the

rumor of a remote viscount needing a wife. Once she learned who he was, she had her escape.

Vivian met Lord Ashworth by chance nearly ten years before, when he rescued her from a potentially dangerous man. Could he do it again?

But what of Silverstone Manor and the local villagers' cautionary tales? Could the gentleman she once met have turned mad from isolation? Did ghosts and phantoms lurk in dark corners?

She didn't believe in ghosts, but she did believe the danger awaiting her at home.

The tapestry fluttered again, then slammed against the wall.

Vivian sat up, but in the dark shadows of the room saw no creatures. The wind, the drafts and the poor upkeep of this house were conspiring to stir up terror. She'd not succumb to their taunts.

The warm shelter of the blankets pulled her downward. She pressed herself into the pillow and closed her eyes in the pursuit of slumber. She *would* wed Lord Ashworth. He would be her salvation. Monster or not.

Vivian could not awaken from her dream. The images held her spellbound, dragging her down like a heavy rock under water. In the shadowed darkness of her vision she couldn't see the man who had come to claim her.

She lay naked in a field of flowers, a place she had never seen. A storm swirled far above, darkening the sky to purple. And yet she did not fear. Not even when the man—she assumed it was a man—leaned over her. His head moved to look over her body.

Then he reached a hesitant hand out to her. Unashamed, Vivian arched her back, lifting herself toward him, inviting him. A splintered moan echoed from his throat as long fingers reached from the shapeless overcoat. His hand brushed along her nipple once, then again. It hardened to a tight knot.

Her thighs dampened. Her mouth dried.

The stranger teased her, lightly sweeping his fingertips across her peak until she whimpered.

He shifted across her, grabbing the entire breast into his hand. The kneading sent a shocking firestorm through her blood. She was struck by a wicked urge to pull his lips down to her nipple, have him sink himself between her legs.

No! She could not give herself to another man.

Vivian struggled, twisted away. She plunged into cold water. Like a drowning child, she fought to reach the surface, her lungs expanding with a suspended breath. She couldn't make it. She couldn't awaken.

A door slammed.

Vivian sprang upright and gulped in mouthfuls of air, nerves enshrouded in ice.

The dark room was lit by the random glow of the moon. She could barely make out the posts of her bed, much less see beyond to the far side of the room.

Vivian blinked then stared at the last of the orange embers, her pulse thundering in her ears. Warnings from the villagers rattled in her brain. No one dare spend a night in Silverstone Manor, lest they be attacked.

It was only a dream. Or had she just been visited by The Monster?

Ashworth's pulse skittered as a cool rush of air slipped over his skin. He blinked, but only darkness filled his vision.

He reached around. The cold stone walls brushed against his fingertips, but no window gave him sight to his whereabouts.

The potion. Though it gave him peace from the nightmares, it often caused him to sleepwalk.

Ashworth wiped the sweat from his forehead with his arm.

He must have left his room. Again.

A sudden awareness struck him.

The painful jerk of denied arousal.

Had the luscious and tantalizing dream been real? His palm still tickled with the soft weight of a woman's breast.

Ashworth clenched his jaw. He couldn't be out roaming the halls at night. The villagers already spoke of monsters and phantoms who prowled the halls and hunted for satisfaction.

It wasn't him, damn it. He was only sleepwalking, his mind filled with dreams of desire.

Vivian was unsettling him.

He let the stones guide him through the black veil of mystery. Hopefully he was near to his bedchamber. Usually he did not wander far.

Vivian's door was not far.

The next morning Ashworth entered the dining room for breakfast. The oak paneling had long lost its luster, the blue carpet now threadbare beneath the splintered table. Once the carved sideboard held the finest china, now only a few dusty and chipped saucers sat upon it.

Scrambled eggs, sliced bread and cold ham lay in wait for him, their aromas comforting. It was the same as every other morning. Today should be no different...but it was.

Vivian sat at the far end of the table, her raven hair plaited in a long twist down her plain gold-colored dress. A slant of sunlight streamed from the window behind her.

Scorching blood swirled through his veins, while the memory of her silhouette through the keyhole struck him mute. Thoughts of his dream stirred his groin. He could do nothing but stare at her, wait for her to speak.

"Good morning, my lord," she said, lifting her glass of juice. "Won't you join me?"

He crossed the room, eager to see her face. Though her voice remained even and cheerful, her eyes would relay the events of last night.

She motioned to the chair beside her, but he did not sit. Nay, he would take his food with him in a bit.

Ashworth cleared his throat and found his voice. "Tell me, did you sleep well?"

Vivian blinked, but nothing more. "Does one ever sleep well in a room they've never seen or a bed they've never lain upon?"

"I cannot remember."

"Have you not left this house in so long?" True surprise widened her gaze.

"I've not left the grounds of Silverstone in near seven years." She gasped but he continued. "I have no reason to venture elsewhere."

She took a sip of her juice. "I suppose I can see the finer points of remaining apart from society."

Her words betrayed her. She was on the run. From who or what, he didn't know. Why else would his life seem so enviable? No other woman, fair or not, would find this house a refuge.

Ashworth gripped the back of the chair, his chest tight. As Pinkley so wisely stated, a stranger was not safe here.

Vivian's gaze dropped to her breakfast, where uneaten eggs spread about the plate. She dabbed her lips with a yellowed napkin then set it aside. "Tell me," she began, then lifted her black gaze to his, "will you hold true to your promise?"

"Promise?" He questioned her word, yet his heart raged.

"To send for the license. I have made it through the night unharmed. That was your bargain."

Had he said unharmed? He meant untouched.

Ashworth watched her face, her eyes, for any sign of betrayal, but she was too far away for detection. He reached for her hand. "Come with me to the window."

She placed her fingers within his, and allowed him to lead

her to a recessed nook. Stained glass, remarkably well-preserved, topped the window panes.

The sun skimmed across her hair, reminding him of polished onyx. He wanted to caress it, thread his fingers through it. Instead, he inhaled its scent, heavenly and foreign, like the sweetest of wild flowers.

He bent low, stared at her mouth. "Are you truly unharmed?"

She swallowed. "I am well this morning, my lord. What else would you expect of me?"

"Were you disturbed in any way?"

"Some drafts caused a fright or two, but nothing more."

"Nothing?" His lips moved closer to hers, nearly on their own volition. "No creature molested you?"

Her breath stilled. If he were able to look into her eyes, he might see the revelation, but he could not take his gaze from her vibrant lips.

"Molested?" The word came from her mouth with a squeak. "In what manner?"

He shouldn't do it. Already she'd lured him further than he dared to go. But, oh, how inviting her mouth was, glazed with a touch of the juice, ripened for his taking.

Her fingers fluttered to her throat. Ashworth brought them to his cheek, where her gentleness could soften the hard texture of his skin. "Kiss me," he murmured.

"My lord?"

He took possession of her mouth, nipped at her yielding lips, and tasted the oranges from her breakfast. A cry chimed in her throat then died away. She hesitated, stiffened in his embrace. Slowly, she opened herself to him, allowing access to the sweetness of her mouth.

His blood burned, groin tightened. Every inch of his body begged to feel a woman's skin against his. But he knew so little else of them. Women were a mystery. A mystery he could never unravel.

"Nay." Pulse roaring, Ashworth stumbled away from her to the windows. The sun, warm on his face, added fire to the tempest rampant in his veins. Purple clouds gathered beyond the cliff. Soon they would vanquish the sunlight.

Ashworth wheeled to face her. Her lips glistened still, her cheeks flushed. Those dark eyes shone with an odd hope. He would put an end to that. "We will not marry."

Vivian's face blanched. For an instant, her chin trembled, but then she gathered herself and straightened. "I have heard you must take a bride. Or you will lose something you hold dear."

A knife sliced through his gut. No one should know. It was a mistake that his mother ever found out. "Are you aware of what it is?"

She contemplated lying, but finally shook her head. "If you must marry, why not me?"

"You tempt me," he blurted. He was a bloody fool.

"Isn't that a desirable quality in a wife?"

Yes, of course. But the nightmares...Ashworth gulped the bile climbing up his throat. He could not have her enticing him.

He motioned to Mrs. Plimpton, who waited near the door for his orders. "Wrap up my breakfast, as usual."

Once the servant began on her task, Ashworth turned to Vivian again. His gaze caught the firm curve of her breast, the slender column of her throat. Passion surged to his core. Her very presence endangered his peace. "You may stay one more night. Then, I will provide you with enough coins for your journey home."

"No, you promised me. I made it through the night unharmed."

"But were you untouched?"

Her gaze shifted to the stained glass. "You can't send me back."

"There is nothing here for you."

Her sigh trembled. "Everything I need is here."

"The Monster came to you last night."

"No." Her lowering eyes hinted at the lie. Had he been the one to accost her?

Ashworth forced away the concern, and took the wrapped food from Mrs. Plimpton. "I'll likely be gone much of the day. Do what you like. I will see you again at dinner."

"I see." Vivian angled her chin. The move tempted him again with her lips. "Thank you...for your kind hospitality."

With a short nod at her controlled words, he left her standing alone in the dining room then descended the rear stairs into the bowels of his lair. There was someone he needed to see.

Chapter Three

She would not be dismissed so easily. Vivian turned to stare out the long windows. This isolation would save her life.

Silverstone Manor *was* the answer. Martin would never think to look for her here.

The deep purple gash on Lord Ashworth's brooding face did not repel her. Vivian was no stranger to deformity. Horrible burns disfigured her mother's face.

Vivian's gaze settled upon a square of withering vines and sprawling foliage. It must have been a garden long ago. Tears sparked her eyes. She and her mother spent years planning the beauty of their yard. Nearly every day, they rose in the morning, pruned bushes, weeded beds and planted saplings. The bees and flowers were as much her friends as any schoolgirl.

She would clear the plot below to escape the dark dreary walls of the manor. A bit of fresh air may bring her new ideas.

Vivian left the empty dining room, stopping to peer in a vast, unlit room, what must have long ago been the main hall. An old wooden table stretched from one end to the other and rusty weaponry hung upon three walls. An enormous stone hearth swallowed the fourth wall, its fireplace darkened with centuries of soot and ash.

A cool breeze glided across her skin and chilled her to the bone. Words whispered behind her. She swung around, certain she'd heard a child. But there was no one. Just her and the strange draft.

Shivering, she abandoned the ancient room. She searched for a rear door and finally found a landing after two stairwells and endless dark passageways. The first two doors were locked tight. A light knock brought her no one. At the third, she twisted the knob but the door held fast. Perhaps the wood had swelled and warped in the misty fog.

Vivian leaned forward. She could hear wind whistling through the slats. This was her exit. She had to get outside. She had to be away from this mysterious house, to somewhere she could immerse herself in the happier memories of her life.

"Can't get through there, miss."

Vivian whirled. A cry escaped from her throat. The old man named Pinkley stood at the top of the stairs. She inhaled a shaky breath. "Th-this door leads outside. Why won't it open?"

"Been shut too long."

"No one uses it?"

"Many doors in this house not used. No need to go outside."

A chill crept over her skin again. She rubbed her arms, a feeble attempt at warmth. "I would like to go to the rear yard. How may I get out there?"

"Follow me, miss."

She sighed and followed him up the steps, sweeping cobwebs from her path. The old man led her through several unlit halls, where gloomy portraits hung within tarnished frames. At last, light reached them as they neared the main foyer.

"'Ere ye are, miss."

"But we are at the main door."

"Aye, you can go round the side of the house and eventually ye will find what ye need."

Vivian swallowed the questions plaguing her tongue. Little about this manor made any sense, including why its lord kept himself hidden within its walls.

Making her way around proved no easy task. Between the

knee-high grass and crumbling stones, she faced a hearty walk. By the time she reached the overgrown patch she had seen from the window, Vivian's face was flushed with exertion. At least her effort helped keep the chill at bay.

A quick glance at the sky showed slate clouds rather than the morning sun. She may not have long before rain would drive her back inside.

Finally, Vivian arrived at the tangle of vines and leaves. A hedge must have enclosed the area once, but now it was overgrown and diseased. Without gloves and shears, she began to clear away as much of the dead foliage as possible.

Tiny flowers surprised her now and then as she moved brush aside, more for their resilience than for their vivid color among the gray and molded surroundings. It was a wonder that anything could thrive in this environment. This house.

Vivian glanced back at the manor, to its spires which pierced the bleak sky like ugly tarnished swords. No beauty adorned the exterior, all carvings had worn away. A single unmatched gargoyle jutted from a corner, its partner forever lost to the tangle of thicket at the house's foundation. Ancient, weathered stone, partially covered by rotting ivy, presented itself to any outsiders were they foolish enough to come up the long drive.

Sighing, she turned back to the work at hand but a movement caught her eye. At first, it seemed a hawk had flown from one rooftop to another. She checked again at the top windows.

A face. Her breath lodged in her throat. Was someone watching her?

Thunder rumbled nearby, echoing the boom of her heartbeat. A blink later and the face was gone. Oh God, she had to get out of here or she'd lose her mind.

No. To go home was unthinkable.

For her sake—her mother's sake—Vivian must convince Lord Ashworth to let her stay at Silverstone Manor.

At this point, she was desperate enough to try anything.

Martin Crawford pushed his way past the butler of Suttley House and headed straight for the staircase. The furious pulse of his heartbeat drowned out the servant's cries to have him wait downstairs.

He'd find that double-crossing bastard and strangle him. Baron or not, Vivian's father would pay for this sudden turn of events.

Moans rumbled beyond the wooden door at the hall's end. Lord Whistlebury's bedchamber. Martin wrinkled his nose and bared his teeth, recalling the scene he had witnessed those few months before.

He opened the door without hesitation. Vivian's father stood with his eyes closed and his hands in the hair of a lad kneeling before him. Groans echoed against the mahogany paneled walls, and for a moment Martin considered allowing the act to find completion. But fury stabbed in his core and demanded priority. Lord Whistlebury would answer to him.

"Where is she?"

The baron gasped and drew back. Both of them looked up at the intruder, the young man appearing confused and frightened. Then, without another sound, the lad sprang up from his knees and scurried from the room.

Martin kicked the door shut. "He's different than the last one."

Lord Whistlebury straightened his clothes, then ran a hand through his disheveled gray hair. "You could have waited for me downstairs."

Martin clenched his jaw. "I've waited for my wedding to Vivian long enough. And now your butler tells me she is not here."

"She...she..."

The hesitation pricked the inferno under Martin's skin. "She *what*? Where is she?"

Vivian's father sank into a stuffed chair by the window. Outside a light rain started, and blew its scent into the room. The air cleared of sweat and sex.

"She left a note saying she was going to London. She said she'd never marry you and that she'd find a husband during the season."

Martin balled his hands into fists. Spots whirled in his vision. That careless bitch. He swore he'd hunt her down if she left him. He swore she'd pay. No one abandoned Martin Crawford. Not anymore.

He narrowed his eyes at the baron and swallowed the encroaching violence. "We stopped her attempt at a marriage once before. We will do it again. You'll tell me how I can find her, of course."

The man hung his head. "Maybe...maybe it is better this way. Vivian is not for you. She is a stubborn girl."

No. Vivian was perfect. Her exotic beauty stirred his blood. Her resistance only fueled his desires. His taking of her was a promise of their future. No other man was to have what was his.

"Where is she, old man? You promised me a bride." He nodded his head at the bedchamber door. "Or did you forget our bargain?"

Lord Whistlebury wrung his hands. "Her mother is gone too."

Martin laughed. His gaze drew in the expansive bed with purple silk coverings. "And why should that bother you? Your tastes run elsewhere, obviously."

"People will talk..."

Martin crossed the room and stood over the crumpled man, only a shadow of his true self. These aristocrats all believed they had such power with their House of Lords and acres of land. But they spawned children and then left them behind;

they indulged in perversions and then fretted over the secret. This man was no different and Martin cared not a whit for Lord Whistlebury's sexual preferences, nor for his reputation.

But Martin did care about their agreement. He would marry a baron's daughter. He would have the respect he deserved and he would eliminate whoever got in his way.

Martin narrowed his eyes. "I repeat: where is she? You must know where she has gone."

Lord Whistlebury's mouth twitched. His bulbous nose reddened. For a moment, Martin thought the man might cry.

"Shall I let on about your desire for—?"

"No." The baron wiped his palms across beefy thighs. "She did not tell me where, but I do have a cousin in town. Vivian might have gone there."

Power surged into Martin's bloodstream, He curled his lip. "Now we are getting somewhere."

He sank down into the chair opposite the baron, crossing his long legs at the ankle. Most people eventually saw their way to reason. Martin was not a man to be crossed. Both his mother and Mary Yeardley learned that lesson.

Now it was Vivian Suttley's turn.

Bringing up warm water was an issue in Silverstone Manor. After the sweat and dirt from the garden, Vivian hoped for a cleansing bath. But it seemed impossible for the servants to bring enough water for even a hipbath.

"Me and Pinkley, we's too old and weak to carry it," Mrs. Plimpton had told her. When Vivian inquired as to any other servants, the answer was "none to be spared".

She would have carried the damn water up herself if she knew where to find its source. And if she were able to leave a trail to find her way back to her room.

Vivian was reaching for cloth from this morning's toilet

when a knock resounded on the heavy door. Perhaps they found a servant to spare. "Enter," she called.

"I was told you wanted water for a bath."

Her breath caught. "My lord. I did not expect you to bring the water."

"Ah, but I have." He held out two cans then set them on the scuffed floor. "But where is the tub?"

"I am awaiting that, as well."

Lord Ashworth grinned, his scar softening like the gentle curve of a feather. "It must still be in my bedchamber."

"But—but you can't possibly move that yourself."

Rain tapped at the window as he raised his eyebrows. "Good point. As we've not had overnight visitors in such a long time, I had not thought to your needs properly." After a bow, he said, "Forgive me."

Vivian nodded, a smile playing upon her lips. Something had altered his mood. Or was this his true nature, the one she remembered? Either way, she needed a plan to convince him to keep her here and the sooner she thought of it, the better.

"So—" She took a few steps closer to him in order to gauge his reaction. He did not move. "—am I to bathe or not?"

"To do so would require you to be in my room."

"Does that disturb you?"

His chest rose, straining the fabric of the shirt. "Does it disturb you?"

She gathered up the bathing linens left by Mrs. Plimpton. "Of course, you will not be in the room with me."

Lord Ashworth stared at her for a long, tortuous moment then picked up both cans of steaming water and crossed the room to his adjoining door. "Of course not." He nodded toward the knob. "If you don't mind."

Vivian hurried over and opened the door for him. He led her across the apartment, past his large bed with intricately carved mahogany posts. The black woolen bed hangings had something stitched upon them but its design was no longer discernable. She noticed a walnut cabinet similar to the one in her room as well as an enormous tapestry that took up an entire wall. Obviously the two rooms were created to complement one another with only coloring and small design to differentiate between the sexes.

The sound of splashing water reminded her why she was in his room. The white tub stood several feet from the fireplace, beckoning with its comfort, frightening her with its possibilities. The last time she'd been alone with a man...

"How high do you want the water?"

She glanced inside the basin. His two cans had barely been enough to cover the bottom, and yet she didn't want him going up and down the stairs for her. Not when she needed to convince him she would not cause him any trouble.

"This should be enough."

"Nay, you'll barely get your feet wet."

"I only need to wipe myself off. I certainly do not need the luxury of a full bath."

His eyes locked onto hers. His hot stare challenged her comfort. She could comprehend her fright from Martin's malevolent force, but the viscount's unsettling disquiet worried her.

Finally, Lord Ashworth retrieved the empty cans and moved toward his door. "Once more." Then he was gone.

Vivian did her best not to wander his room and intrude on his privacy. Awkwardness enveloped her as she stood there alone. Yet, other than some clothes strewn on chairs and a glass upon the small table beside his bed, nothing here seemed noteworthy.

Why so many feared the man, she did not understand.

Footsteps sounded in the hall and then he burst into the room. A tall slender boy accompanied him, both of them carrying up larger pails of steaming water.

Once the water had been splashed into the tub, the boy cast a wide-eyed glance her way then gathered all containers and hurried from the room. Lord Ashworth did not seem concerned with introducing her.

"Who was that young man?"

He rekindled the fire back to a vigorous life. "My groomsman."

"But you said you never left the grounds."

"Nay, but my servants do. We do need supplies from town on occasion."

Ah, so there were other servants here she had not seen. In a house such as this, there could be dozens hidden beyond locked doors or on other levels.

"Thank you for your kindness. I will be quick. Have you any soap?"

He stared at her, frozen. Until, at last, he walked to a walnut triangular washstand. "I'm afraid I've nothing for a lady. Only my own soap." He reached into a container and withdrew a bar.

Their fingers touched as she took it from him. A mysterious tingle raced along her arm. "Thank you, my lord."

The shadows flickered along his scar as he stood there, once again immobile. She realized with sudden compassion that he did not know what to do. Visitors were so infrequent here that perhaps he did not entertain mistresses either. And yet, despite the mark along the right side of his face, Lord Ashworth was as beautiful as any Roman god.

He cleared his throat. "Do you, um, need me to aid you with your buttons?"

While she could use his help, the memories of Martin's fingers closing up her dress after he assaulted her kept Vivian from accepting it.

She moved away. "I can do it alone."

A warm hand settled on her shoulder. "Please, I want to

assist."

Vivian held her breath. Again she was tormented by the combination of her needs and her emotions. She must convince him to marry her and yet her most recent experience with a man had been a brutal attack.

Lord Ashworth must have taken her silence as an invitation. One by one he slowly unhooked the buttons until he halted about midway down her back. Before she could step aside, his warm fingers slid the dress sideways and brushed her bare skin.

Unexpected shivers raced. Scorching blood pulsed.

She did not understand her body's reactions. Was it possible for her to break from the cold shell Martin had placed her in and once again embrace another man's warmth?

"Faith, you are lovely." His husky voice dried her mouth, trembled her knees. "I will leave you to your bath. Please call for me when you are finished."

His departure was marked by a blast of chilly air and a slam of the door.

Vivian shook the tumultuous sensations from her body and slipped out of the remainder of her clothes. She sank into the tepid water, quickly unwound her braid, then washed herself with Lord Ashworth's soap. It was his scent. Sandalwood with the hint of berries.

Vivian drew her knees up and wrapped her arms about her legs. Flames cast dancing lights along the walls, reminding her once again of ghosts seeking mischief. If there were such a thing as ghosts, she hoped they were friendly. She was tired of being afraid.

Silverstone Manor was her deliverance, not her damnation. Lord Ashworth must allow her to stay.

You tempt me. The words had slipped from his lips at breakfast.

She could sacrifice her body to buy her escape, but could she let go of those terrible memories? Was it possible to forget one man's cruelty in order to seduce another?

Lord, did she have any choice?

Vivian closed her eyes and breathed in the calming aroma of the soap. She could find that strength and courage again. She had it when she convinced Thomas to marry her, when she gave herself to him before their marriage, when her father tore her from his arms. She had it when she fought Martin, when she devised her plan to escape, when she boldly knocked on the door to Silverstone Manor.

A weak woman would have submitted to the man her father gave her to. A weak woman would have allowed herself to be beaten and destroyed.

Vivian was not weak.

She lifted her chin opened her eyes. Lord Ashworth's room took on a whole new light. The sight of his large bed did not give her tremors, but instead represented a means to an end.

This man would save her from the other. And she would not let her emotions impede that purpose.

Vivian rinsed the bubbles from her body and stepped out of the tub. She wrapped the towel about her middle, leaving her shoulders and legs bare, water dripping down her skin.

A long, deep intake of breath and then, "My lord, you may return now."

The scrape of a chair, footsteps, and then the door swung open.

Chapter Four

He couldn't stop thinking about Vivian naked. He imagined every turn of her muscles, every hair, every freckle.

Her voice called out to him. He expected her to take much longer, but what did he know of women's habits?

Ashworth opened his bedroom door. Then stopped breathing.

Vivian stood before the hearth, a bath linen wrapped around her middle. Her arms glistened, flames creating small drops of fire along her skin. Her knees peeked out from the bottom of the towel, leading the way to long shapely legs.

Lord help him.

Instantly, his erection returned and throbbed intensely against the buttons of his breeches. Parched, he licked his lips.

"It's cold," she said, her voice trembling. "Please shut the door against the draft."

Ashworth bumped the door with his shoulder and it slammed closed. He stared at her, mesmerized, drawing in every inch of her alluring body.

He struggled to find his voice. "Do you need help in dressing?"

Her dimpled chin lifted, exposing the smooth column of her throat. Behind it, her black hair dripped on the stone hearth, the tapping punctuated by the occasional snap of the flames. "I've left my chemise in the other room," she said, "I'm too cold to leave the fire. Would you mind?"

Ashworth blinked. He forced his feet to move. "Where would I find it?"

"In the trunk at the end of the bed. There is a pink ribbon at the top."

Crossing through the adjoining door, the grip in his chest loosened. To see her standing there, her bare limbs available for his view, her skin glistening with water...he could be unmanned without ever touching her!

Ashworth sorted through her clothes, an odd fascination coming over him at the materials he touched. He'd never seen a woman's complete wardrobe before.

By the time he located the chemise, he'd gained control over his reactions. She would dress by the fire, then leave his room. He would be safe from her, safe from any urges or memories.

"My lord," her voice carried through the open door. "A brush also, please."

Sighing, he glanced about the room. It had been decorated many years ago, long before he'd come to settle here. The room was to be a feminine compliment to his room. But now cobwebs spoiled the corners, dust obscured the mirrors.

He found her brush atop the walnut dresser and, with the chemise, returned to his own bedchamber.

Vivian had pulled a stool over and was sitting upon it, warming herself at the hearth. A firm muscle rounded her calf toward the small bump of her ankle. She had pulled her hair over her shoulder and was raking her fingers through the ends. A hint of her breasts peeked above the towel.

Ashworth swallowed.

He held the brush and dress out to her. "I'll wait for you in the hall." Where he could remain harmless.

"Stay."

Her soft plea halted him.

"I would find it much easier if you would brush my hair."

Ashworth clenched his jaw. A spring coiled in his gut, winding him tighter. Desire flushed through every cell of his body, but panic tempered the heat. "I could call for Mrs. Plimpton."

"She cannot be spared."

"Certainly there is a servant here who can attend you."

"Please, I know only you."

Did she realize what she asked? He was a man. A man who had shied away from a woman's touch for too long. What he would give to try again.

Ashworth took the brush from Vivian's hands as she stood, pretending to ignore the unease in her eyes. She turned to face the snapping fire and presented him with her silken shoulders.

He ran the brush lightly through her waist-length hair and forced himself to resist the urge to skim across her bottom. In fact, he had to resist touching her anywhere. But the hunger pounded within him like a violent storm, his pulsing flesh ached for release.

Over and over he slid the brush through her tresses, unable to stop, unable to speak.

"My lord?" Her voice was fragile, vulnerable. She spun quickly, suddenly landing within his arms. Her breasts pressed upon chest. The scent of her tempted his restraint.

She was seducing him. He wasn't a fool. But how could he not react? How could he not take the chance that he might find relief in her warmth? But he would not let her have control.

Ashworth dropped the brush and yanked her hard against him, making certain she understood his desire. Her eyes widened but she did not fight him. He would test how far she was willing to go.

Bypassing her pliant mouth, he grazed her ear with his lips. He licked the curve, inhaled the sweetness of feminine beauty. She tensed briefly, then melted against him.

His hands reached for the cloth wound around her. He wanted to cast it away, lower her to the floor and have his way with her. Why should he not?

Then her arms reached behind him and her palms flattened against his back. It took him a moment to realize that she was embracing him. Ashworth lifted his head and placed a kiss upon her wet hair.

Vivian did not linger. She slid her hands downward, where her fingers brushed the band of his breeches.

Reawakened, he swooped down and lifted her into his arms. Her dark eyes did not leave his. An unfamiliar ache burrowed into his chest. An ache urging him to hold her tight. He'd ignored it. He must.

His breath halted as his gaze traveled the length of her, from her sleek shoulders to her shadowed breasts, past the towel, then down to her well-formed legs.

But those curves which lay beneath the towel...?

He whispered her name then kissed her lightly upon the lips.

She reached for his neck, pulling him down to her.

Passion swelled.

Ashworth ravaged her mouth, suckled on her tongue. He kissed her neck, the hollow space at the base of her throat.

Sitting up, he pulled off his shirt then tossed it to the floor.

She was lovely. Unlike the sheltered white skin of the girls his mother usually sent from London, Vivian's was the color of warm tea.

He nudged her legs apart and settled his hips between them. A draft circled through the air and glided across his back. The candles dipped then brightened again, elongating the shadow between her breasts. He lowered his lips to the valley, kissing her softness, skimming his tongue along the cleft of her delicious skin.

He wanted more. More.

Rain gusted against the rattling window.

A woman screamed.

Ashworth jerked his head up. He stared at Vivian's face. Her head lay upon his pillow, eyes closed, lips slightly parted and swollen from his kisses. Uncertain perhaps, but not terrified.

Resuming his quest, he tugged on her wrap. He must have it gone. But it stuck tight. "Vivian," he breathed. Her eyebrows creased but she arched her back. The towel came free.

Ashworth stared at her beauty, mesmerized. She was beautiful. Incredible. Perfect.

He enclosed his lips over an enchanting pink nipple and it sprang to life in his mouth. He swirled his tongue around the knot, as if he were rolling a small pebble.

Blood.

He recoiled, stared down at her skin. Had he bitten her? But no redness marred her skin. She was perfect. Every place he looked upon her, she was perfect.

Slashes. Screams. Blood.

He blinked, but this time the image did not vanish from Vivian's body. Everywhere, crimson fluid spurted from gaping wounds. He looked down to see his hands covered in it. A nauseating odor stung at his nostrils. Nearby, someone wailed.

Ashworth sprang up from the bed.

"My lord?"

He shook his head, but he still saw her covered in a red haze. Ice choked his veins. Cramps ravaged his gut. Bile burned in his throat.

Vivian sat up, covering herself. "What is it? What's happened?"

Ashworth back away, bumped into a chair. "Leave me."

"I don't understand."

"Go. Now." He spun away from her and braced himself against the window ledge. Rain thrashed at the panes.

Lightening fractured the night.

"Have I done something to upset you?" She came close. Stood directly behind him. He could destroy her with a quick blow of his arm.

Warm fingers settled upon his bare shoulder. "Lord Ashworth?"

"LEAVE ME!"

At last she scurried to gather her things. Hurried footsteps faded and then the door slammed.

He panted, struggled for a normal breath. He'd prayed Vivian would be different, that her innocence and beauty would be enough to heal him. He had been mistaken. He would not be fool enough to challenge his destiny again.

The Monster was doomed to live alone.

Ashworth yanked on the rope for Pinkley.

Vivian tried to slow her frenzied pulse. Her eyes were damp but no tears fell. She was more confused than frightened.

She yanked her chemise on, pushed the bed curtains aside and scrambled onto the blanket. Her hair twisted around her shoulders, knotted and damp.

What had happened? How had he turned so quickly?

She pulled her knees up and wrapped her arms around her legs. Rain gusted.

Lord Ashworth hadn't been violent. No. He appeared frightened. Terrified even. He yelled because she'd persisted and not left when he'd asked.

She was even more puzzled at her body's reaction to his touch. Even now, her breasts tingled from his caress. Her mouth thirsted for his kiss.

Trepidation and dark memories had shadowed her attempt at seduction, yet a part of her found pleasure too. That gave her hope.

Vivian sank deeper into the bed.

Whatever came over Lord Ashworth tonight must not sway her purpose. He wouldn't frighten her from here with a snarl and a shout. She'd endured worse from Martin.

Vivian expected nightmares that night. Instead, she found herself naked again in the meadow of wildflowers.

The heady aroma of colorful blooms swirled in her nose. A shadow fell across her as the stranger discovered her, his form covered by a shapeless coat. He lowered himself to a knee beside her, stroking her face with his warm fingers. She turned away, watching storm clouds collect in the distance.

He refused to give up. Lying down beside her, his arm reached across her shoulders, turning her to face him. She could not see anything but the hood of the coat. And yet, she smiled, surrendering her reluctance, inviting him to caress her.

Hot fingers slid from her shoulders to her waist, then around to cup her bottom. Vivian whimpered, her hips tilting toward him, her body aching to be filled.

"Please." The flowers surrounding her swayed on the breeze of her word.

Trails of fire blazed across her skin as his hand moved up to envelope her breast. His thumb flickered over her nipple, sending spasms to her toes, an inferno to her stomach. She was helpless at his stroke, weightless in his arms.

"Kiss me." Vivian reached out to his face, desperate to touch him. But he recoiled, then stumbled back.

"Where are you going?" She propped up on an elbow.

He disappeared into the sea of flowers. Lightening pulled her attention back to the sky. Lying back, Vivian stared at the rain falling straight down upon her. Coldness bled into her skin, chasing her internal fire.

Thunder exploded overhead.

Vivian awoke, shivering.

Between the flashes of lightening and the dying fire, she looked about the shadowed room. The tapestry quivered, cobwebs danced, but no mortal assaulted her. Somewhere far beneath the chilled skin, her body hummed. But she was alone.

Tomorrow, she would stand her ground. Lord Ashworth could not send her away.

Chapter Five

Ashworth sank to his knees. Though a suffocating blackness enveloped him, he knew where he was. The same spot he'd been last night. With the same throbbing erection.

Damn.

The potion was a wonder drug. It helped him sleep at night, cured him of the devastating nightmares. Every morning he'd awaken to find himself well-rested and free from dreams.

But then Vivian arrived.

Now scorching dreams of desire blazed in his veins. Now he roamed the darkened hallways of Silverstone. But if he denied himself the elixir, he would relive the horror of that London night within ghastly, vivid dreams.

Ashworth pushed himself to stand. He had to send Vivian from here. The Monster must live alone.

Vivian tapped her nails on the dining room table. Lord Ashworth slept late. She'd learned that in two days.

She stared at the dry scone on her plate. Although the strong scent of bacon permeated the air, she wasn't terribly hungry.

Heavy footsteps lifted her attention. Her stomach fluttered as Lord Ashworth entered the room. Aside from his deep scar, his face was as beautiful as ever, though smudges of purple underlined his eyes. It was as if she had imagined his sudden change last night. Dressed in his customary breeches and plain white shirt, he looked harmless. And dangerously charming.

Without a greeting, he sat at the far end the table. She watched him wave to the shadows beyond the door and Mrs. Plimpton immediately poured him some tea. Finally, after a few sips, he looked up and noticed her.

"Sleep well, Vivian?"

Only if dreaming about her body being warmed and caressed by a stranger was called sleeping well. She nodded, but was unable to dismiss the quiver in her belly. "Yes, my lord." She dared not ask him how his night progressed after she left.

Mrs. Plimpton set a platter of scones before him and he reached for one. Chewing, he said, "I have some coins for you. Enough to take you back from where you came."

Her chest squeezed, her lungs stop functioning. He had not changed his mind. "No."

"No?" His gaze narrowed, but his next response was interrupted when the servant named Pinkley shuffled into the room. He carried a tarnished silver platter. An envelope teetered precariously on its surface. "Post came for ye, mi'lord."

Lord Ashworth sighed and took the letter. "Thank you, Pinkley. You may go now."

The old man gave her an evil glare, then hobbled from the room.

Vivian ignored Pinkley and studied the paper in Lord Ashworth's hand. "What is that on the corner?"

He flipped over the envelope. "Ah, this is the Penny Black."

She leaned forward. "Penny Black?"

"Have you not recently mailed a letter? This has changed our world. A sender pays for postage, not the recipient."

If that were indeed the case, Vivian could send her mother letters! She'd not wanted her mother to have to pay for the correspondence, but neither did she want her to go without any communication.

Lord Ashworth glanced at the writing on the envelope, a scowl brewing on his features. His eyes darkened as he slipped out the letter. With each word he read, his face grew ruddier, his scar deeper.

"Bloody hell!" he growled and shoved a hand through his hair. "Damn, damn, damn."

She watched his face carefully. The narrowing of his gaze and flat line of his lips told of anger, not the shocked terror of last night.

He sprang up from his chair and paced the worn carpet before the buffet, his thunderous expression chasing away the sun.

Still angry he would not permit her to stay, Vivian provoked him further. "May I eat my breakfast in peace?"

He stormed over to her and stood above her, his stomach level with her eyes. A vein throbbed on his temple. The purple gash on his cheek blazed with an unnatural light. However, his intent at frightening her did not work. She did not feel the threat of his rage, not the powerful waves of fury or dangerous calm which emanated from Martin at every moment.

Still, Lord Ashworth's size and sheer strength made her pause. He could harm her easily if so driven...but he wouldn't. This was the man who once saved her.

"You will hear my rant. This is my house. You are my guest."

Vivian looked away from the torment reflecting in his eyes. She pushed back from the table. "According to you, I will not be your guest any longer."

He shoved a hand through his hair. "I would like you to stay...until this guest leaves."

Her breath caught, heart kicked up its rhythm. He was allowing her stay? Oh Lord, could it be true that she wouldn't have to run any longer?

Something—or someone—had changed his mind. "Who is this new guest?"

He went to the windows and leaned against them then crossed his arms. No further sunlight graced the walls, only the dim offerings of clouded sky. "Lady Wainscott."

"Who is she?"

Lord Ashworth turned his attention to the yard below. "Someone I once thought to marry, but then..." A sigh, but nothing more.

Vivian fought for a sustaining breath. It was the young woman she saw him with that day. What she thought was an innocent trip to the garden with a friendly duke had been interrupted by Lord Ashworth and his betrothed. At twelve, she did not understand much of the argument between the two gentlemen or why she was warned to stay away from the duke. It was months later when Vivian learned that interruption may have saved her life.

And now the woman he once loved was coming to visit. It would be easy for him to fall for her again, easy to overlook the stranger who had invaded his peace.

She swallowed, her throat tight. "Why is it that you want me to remain during her visit?"

He turned his face so that she only saw the glowing length of the scar. "I want her stay to be as short as possible. I would like for her to believe you and I will marry."

She grew more confused by the moment. "Does this mean we are to be wed as you promised?"

His shoulders tensed. "It shouldn't take long for her to see that my interest is gone. Once she goes, I will give you whatever riches you desire."

So his answer was no. Still, this gave her the opportunity to remain here longer. An opportunity to possibly change his mind.

But could she watch this other woman win him over? How could she possibly compete with a woman he once thought to marry?

"I—I do not know, my lord."

Lord Ashworth said nothing. He still would not turn to her, but stared out the windows. An old clock's soft ticking rippled through the silent room.

Vivian turned back to the table and took a sip of her juice.

"What will it take to get you to do this for me?" The words were clipped, hard, determined.

A real proposal, a wedding, a promise of your love. Something that will guarantee Martin will never find me.

But she said none of those. "I'm not certain what can."

"The garden."

She twisted to see him. "My lord?"

"What if I provide you with new saplings and flowers? Will you stay until there is life out there again?"

Life in the garden. She could finish the project she started, bring beauty to this dead estate. Her mouth dried with the anticipation of once again planting, of recreating the garden her mother designed.

But could she sacrifice her integrity and bear witness to Lord Ashworth's former love? She could easily recall the adoration in his eyes that day. Why had they not married?

Suddenly he was before her, dropping to his knees. Her breath stilled as his finger traced her jaw. A thrill swirled in her belly and thrummed in her pulse.

"Vivian." His voice dropped to a whisper. "Only you can bring beauty to Silverstone. Can you stay, just for a time?"

Lord, she was a fool, charmed by a man claiming to be a monster. She only hoped she didn't regret it later.

Inhaling his sandalwood scent, Vivian licked her lips. "Very well, my lord, I will stay." Where else would she go?

A grin curved his lips, tempting her to brush her finger against them. Instead, she recoiled from his allure and sat back against the chair. "Until the garden is complete."

An unfamiliar quiver raced up Ashworth's spine. He leaned closer to the thickly paned glass, feeling the air swirl between the window and the stones. Vivian cleared the garden down below. Despite that she was little more than a dress and dark hair from this viewpoint on the top floor, he could not take his eyes from her.

"Will we meet her?"

Ashworth glanced at the man beside him, breathing in that ever-present scent of musty books and chalk. Through round lenses of wire-rimmed glasses, warm brown eyes stared back.

"I haven't decided, John."

The man jerked his blond head toward the rear of the room. "He'll learn of her soon."

"I know." Ashworth peered down below again, but could not ignore the incessant tickle under his skin. It was unwise to keep Vivian here. A fool's mission. But how else could he keep Lady Wainscott—Catherine—from invading his heart once more? She had already destroyed it once. He could not allow for it again.

A hand settled on his arm. "Charles."

Ashworth flinched at his given name. Only his friends and his mother called him that. And now he had only John Hughes to call a friend. The others were lost to shame, humiliation...and horror.

He clenched his teeth, then swallowed. His heart hammered wildly, He could not forget the visions of last night, the sights of Vivian enshrouded in blood. Drawing in a sustaining breath, he turned to a man who should have given up on him long ago. John should have his own bride, his own children. But he gave it all up to tutor Harry. How could Ashworth ever repay him such a debt?

"Catherine is paying us a visit."

John's sharp intake of breath spoke of his surprise. "Catherine? After all these years? Why would she come here, didn't she marry Lord Wainscott?"

·"That she did. I assume the man has passed on."

They watched Vivian below as she pulled heavy branches from one side of the garden to a pile on the far end. A slant of sunlight gleamed off her shimmering black hair as she stopped to wipe her forehead.

"I have asked Miss Suttley to remain at Silverstone until Catherine departs."

"You need a shield?"

Ashworth sighed, his chest tightening. He didn't know what he needed. He didn't know why it was so bloody important to have Vivian stay. Perhaps it was just that he could not face Catherine alone.

A chair scraped the floor then footsteps bounded behind them. "Papa!"

Ashworth turned and knelt just in time for a pair of thin arms to wrap around his neck. The scent of jam and soap and a child's sweet breath warmed his heart. Ashworth buried his face in the boy's neck and breathed it all in fully, his throat tightening. What he wouldn't do for this child, what he hadn't done already.

Finally, the boy giggled and squirmed. "Lemme go!"

Ashworth released him with a quick tickle. "Finished your morning studies, Harry?"

The boy nodded, his red hair bouncing. Bright green eyes widened. "Did you say someone else was coming?"

Rising to his feet, Ashworth nodded. "Yes, she should be here tomorrow."

Harry clapped his hands. "Will she bring me a present like grandmother does?"

Spoken like a true seven-year-old. Although, as the boy's grandmother insisted, other lads saw more of the world than a misty moor and ragged cliffs. Ashworth swallowed his growl. The boy had grown just fine within these ancient walls. He had no need for other children, for a finer education. John taught him all he needed to know.

Ashworth glanced about the room. A globe sat in the far corner, among other framed maps. Several desks and tables were set up for different learning tasks. And everywhere, books and drawing tablets for lessons. What else would some fancy boarding school provide for him?

Harry joined them at the window. He rose up on his toes so that his eyes barely cleared the ledge. "Is she there?"

"Whom?"

"The pretty lady with raven wing hair."

Ashworth turned a sharp eye on his last remaining friend from school, his breath halted. "He knows of her already?"

John did not withdraw at the glare. "I cannot keep a watch on him every hour of the day. This boy is as slippery as a muddy creek bank. Besides, he can see her out the window just as you can."

Ashworth glanced down at the bright red hair. Harry was mischievous all right. He longed to visit the lake he saw in the far distance. He certainly gave poor Mrs. Plimpton a few frights. His antics even had Pinkley snickering a time or two. But would he seek out Vivian?

Green eyes lifted up to him. "What's her name? I think she's an angel."

John coughed. Ashworth stared out the window again. "Miss Suttley. But I do not want you finding her."

"Why not?"

"Because she is not staying long."

"But maybe she will play with me."

Ashworth pushed away thoughts of Vivian's long nails trailing down his back, her supple lips tasting his mouth. He wanted to play with her. Again. But he dared not.

"You must listen to me, Harry. Stay to your rooms."

"But what about the other lady coming here? Can I meet her?"

Sharp apprehension halted his breath. "Faith, no."

Catherine could never know about Harry's existence. If he feared Vivian's knowledge, Catherine proved the much greater danger. The boy was a secret that could not leave these walls. His heart quaked at the thought of losing Harry. His son gave him purpose, a hope at a future.

Ashworth tousled Harry's hair. "I realize you are excited to meet new people, but you must stay away from these visitors."

Innocent eyes darted from him down to the grounds far below. "I'll do it...as long as you bring me some sweetmeats from Cook."

John laughed then crossed the room, pretending to straighten the school papers.

"Whatever it takes," Ashworth answered. "You are an excellent negotiator."

Harry's red eyebrows furrowed. "What's a negotitator?"

"Go learn, my boy. You have an excellent teacher."

With an exaggerated shrug of his shoulders, Harry left his post by the window and dashed back across the schoolroom.

Ashworth gave Vivian a last glance, decided she'd need help with her chore, and slipped quietly from the room.

He heard her before he saw her. Soft humming carried on the misty breeze. Her song was punctuated by the occasional caw of a bird or rustle of leaves. In the ethereal fog, her voice could be that of a fairy or a lonely ghost.

Vivian pulled more brush to the pile she'd begun. He watched her work for a moment, savoring the slick shine of her cheek, the ruddy color of her skin. She reminded him of the village girls he saw many years ago while at school. He'd lust for their quiet beauty, their unassuming charm. But his friends swayed him, pointing him down different paths. Ones that would eventually lead to his ruin.

A soft yelp lifted his head. She shook her hand, then rubbed her palm. He should find her the proper tools, gloves and a rake. He should tell her to leave it. This house was meant for misery and neglect.

Instead, he stepped forward. Her tantalizing scent and vibrant loveliness proved irresistible.

"Oh!" she cried, her injured hand on her heart. "My lord."

"You are hurt."

She gave a weak smile, strands of hair blowing about her cheeks. "It is nothing. I've suffered worse."

"Have you?"

Vivian turned away. "It is nothing, my lord. Just some scratches from the thorns."

Ashworth reached for her hand and his fingers accidentally brushed the gentle swell of her breasts. An impulse rose to cup them fully. Drowsy heat breathed life into his groin.

Instead, he brought her palm up to his face for a closer inspection. Indeed, scratches marred her hand. She gasped when he brushed his thumb across them.

"Shall I let go?" he murmured.

"No." Her voice was a whisper, an invitation.

Obliging her request, Ashworth lowered his lips to her outstretched palm, skimming across her cuts with the gentle touch of a butterfly. He meant to let go at that point, but Vivian whimpered, a sound he'd heard from her throat last night as she lay across his bed.

In a flare of a passion, he ran his tongue along the scratches. The sharp trace of blood did not deter him, not when the rest of her hand was so soft, so smooth. Ashworth kissed the damaged palm, then each finger. His lips pressed against her wrist, where her pulse trembled.

"Vivian…" Her name slipped from his mouth as he kissed

his way up her arm. She tasted of earth and salt and wild honeysuckle. All that he longed for, all that he resisted, dwelled here, hot beneath his mouth.

Desire smoldered beneath his faltering control and hardened his flesh.

Then her sleeve blocked his progress.

Ashworth lifted his head and found her gaze fixed upon him with raw emotions. Hunger. Curiosity. Uncertainty?

And was it any wonder with the way he assaulted her here at the garden. The way he took advantage of her in his room and then frightened her away. She must think him a monster.

Ashworth dropped her arm and backed away from her. He was a monster. And she? A beautiful maiden he planned to use for his own agenda. Then discard.

Ashworth stared at the glass in his hand. The house was still, not even the whisper of a draft.

The lone candle flickered a yellow tint onto the liquid as he lifted it to his lips. It was the first time in years he actually considered not drinking it. The first time nightmares seemed more welcoming than erotic dreams.

Those sensual dreams brought him no peace. Only a torturous fire in his groin and no way to relieve it. His hand ended the pain, but not the agony.

The liquid slid down his throat, leaving it raw.

Ashworth locked his bedchamber door then tucked the key into a hidden drawer in his wardrobe. Perhaps that would be enough to keep him to his room tonight.

What other option did he have?

Vivian gripped the candleholder tightly as she turned down a third passageway. The small flame illuminated old stone rather than plaster, a sure sign she was in an unfamiliar and ancient wing of the house. More and more she believed this manor had once been a castle or keep of centuries past.

She lifted the light higher, but saw only a fluttering tapestry and faded oil paintings on the walls. No doors.

Somewhere in this huge, elaborate dwelling there must be a library. Oh Lord, she hoped so. She needed a book to read to help her fall asleep.

Vivian bit her lip and turned back the way she came, searching for other halls or shut doors. Between her concern over Lady Wainscott's arrival and uncertainty regarding her disturbing dreams, Vivian had tossed and turned on her bed for nearly an hour. Even the spiders had fallen asleep.

Nerves taut, she tried a door at the end of long hall. Locked. Another dead-end. Could it be that this place had no library? Did Lord Ashworth not read?

Rounding another corner, Vivian encountered a stairwell. Unlike the grand staircase at the main doors, this small set must be used for servants. It wound upward in a spiral, the walls made of stones, smooth from years of contact.

She doubted she would find a library up these stairs, but curiosity urged her onward. With the candle half-way gone, Vivian climbed the steps, carefully lifting her nightgown to avoid a fall. Once at the top, she came across a single long hall.

The house was silent. Not even the moaning of the night winds could penetrate these walls.

Vivian started to her left, her heart thumping a quiet rhythm against her breast. She was tempted to try the unlit doors until she realized that she had found the servants' quarters. There was nothing here for her.

She turned back the other way. It was unwise to be up here, dressed as she was, so late after turning in for the night.

She reached the staircase when movement down the other hall caught her eye. The form was small, such as a large dog or a young child. Vivian blinked, watched for it again. Her pulse drummed in her ears. It could be a trick of the wind. Maybe it was a phantom or ghost lurking to frighten foolish visitors.

What if it were the monster Ashworth continued to speak of?

Her mouth dried. Knees trembled.

Then, a door at the end of the hall opened and shut. So someone *had* been in the darkened corners watching her.

A strangling vice tightening in her throat, Vivian raced down the stairs to the floor below. But once there she could not remember how to return to her rooms. She had turned so many ways she couldn't find her way back.

The candle burned lower. Hot wax dripped onto her fingers.

Following three dead-ends and two full circles, Vivian finally found the plaster covered walls again. Her stomach ached, her jaw hurt from clenching, but at least she was closer.

Vision blurry from anxious tears, Vivian fought to rein in her panic. As she ventured down another passage, nothing looked familiar. The bitter taste of fear saturated her tongue, but she had to keep going.

Vivian turned another corner, then bumped hard into a large figure blocking her path.

Her flame died.

Chapter Six

Terrifying blackness. Buried alive.

Harsh, deep breathing echoed in Vivian's eardrums. A waft of sandalwood swirled in her nostrils.

She swayed like an open boat in rough seas.

For the first time since entering Silverstone Manor, a true, piercing terror gripped her heart.

She tried to find her voice, to scream, but nothing would come forth. Trapped, paralyzed, she could do nothing but wait.

Without warning, large hands snatched her upper arms. Strong fingers pressed through the gown's fabric, bruising her flesh with a death-like grip. She struggled helplessly against his power, twisting, kicking. The candleholder loosened from her fingers and clattered to the floor.

She closed her eyes, willing the words to form in her mouth. "Wh-whatever it is you seek, please address it now. Else release me so I may find my bed."

One hand came free of her arm, leaving the skin to throb from the crushing grasp. She thought he might release her then but instead a finger grazed her chin. Stunned, she gasped, afraid of what he may do next.

A growl resounded above her head, his ferocity chilling her blood. He released her and thrust her away from him. She stumbled into a wall where the cold stones prevented her tumble.

Suddenly a glimmer of light flashed from far down the corridor, gradually brightening the walls as it came closer. In an instant, her attacker disappeared in the other direction.

Vivian stumbled toward the light, her heartbeat frantic. Now that the mystery had passed, panic rushed up her throat. She bit her lip to keep the hysteria away.

A figure hobbled toward her, his candle illuminating old paintings and chipped murals. At last, she reached him.

The old servant, Pinkley, stared at her with pale, rheumy eyes, shock registering on his wrinkled face. "Ah, Miz, it's not wise to be out at this hour."

Vivian slowed her breath. "I-I know. I merely wanted a book to read."

"Ye should have rung yer bell."

But no servant could be spared for her. She learned that lesson well enough yesterday. Not only with the hot bath water, but anytime she had a request, no one seemed to pay her any mind.

"Could you pl-please show me to my room? I have lost my way."

"Aye." The old man nodded. "Just come from that a-way."

He turned around and headed back down from whence he came. She followed him, glancing at the walls as they went by. But nothing looked recognizable. The house was so unremarkable and gloomy there was nothing to mark her attention.

Finally, Pinkley stopped at a door. "'Ere it is, Miz."

Vivian opened the wooden door and slipped inside the room. Familiar blood red curtains hung above the bed. The walnut dresser and massive, ancient tapestry were as she left them. Oddly, she experienced a slight soothing comfort in their presence.

Vivian shivered. What a fool she was! Who knew what manner of men roamed these unlit corridors. Even without the supposed threat of ghosts and phantoms, real men lived within these walls. Men who could easily attack or injure her. She was not witless enough to believe that Martin was the only such man who thrived by preying on the weaker gender.

But what of Lord Ashworth? She glanced behind her at their adjourning door, ice again in her veins. It was dark. Had he been the man to seize her in a frightening grip?

Vivian unbraided her hair and climbed atop the bed. The heavy blankets calmed her anxious heart like tight wrappings calmed a crying infant.

Still, it would be hours before she could lose herself to sleep.

"I heard you were lost in the halls last night."

Vivian glanced up from her plate of ham and tomatoes. Her midnight eyes measured him, perhaps guessing his questioning. "Yes, I suppose Pinkley told you."

"Aye." Though Ashworth heard it first from Harry. The boy could not wait for breakfast to tell him what he saw late last night. The angel in white had come up to see him, the boy said. Thankfully, Harry had done as he was bid and had not interacted with Vivian.

She dabbed her mouth with the napkin, then set it upon the plate. "Am I forbidden from leaving my rooms at night?"

A muscle ticked on Ashworth's jaw as a distressing feeling settled in his stomach. Relief that she was not harmed, yet anger at her foolishness. He crossed the room, glowering at her. "It is unwise."

"Unwise. But not forbidden."

He leaned across the table, flattening his palms on both sides of her dish. Instantly, the odor of the ham vanished and her tantalizing honeysuckle scent rose to torture him. "I have warned you of this house, yet you disregard me."

Her quick glance away and momentary biting of her lip told him that something else had happened in the late hours of the night. Had The Monster paid her another visit?

A knot formed in his gut. "You are keeping something from me."

Her gaze returned to his. "No."

"I must teach you to lie better or our little folly will be seen through quickly enough."

Vivian lifted her chin, the small dimple mocking him. "I will not allow Lady Wainscott to know the truth of our arrangement."

Ashworth snorted and stood. If he didn't do something this morning, Catherine would see through their charade by tea time.

He waved her over to the recessed nook, where the clouds performed their morning dance with the sun. The sporadic sun shone through the stained glass, sparkling oddly shaped colors on the floor. She followed him, standing in her plain gray dress with her back to the window, hands clasped gently before her.

"My lord?"

"Let me assess how well you can lie."

She nodded. "Go on."

"Do you enjoy my kisses?"

"My—my lord?"

His lips twitched. "Answer the question, Vivian. Either with a lie or the truth, but answer it."

"Very well then." That chin tilted ever so slightly. "I will admit that I do enjoy them."

The truth. And the answer pleased him. "Did you enjoy my caresses?"

Her cheeks flushed. "Is this a test of my abilities or a need to satisfy your opinion of yourself?"

Ashworth grinned, but did not reply to her question. "You will answer."

"Very well. I do enjoy them." Another truth.

He took a step closer, close enough to thread his fingers through her hair if he chose. Instead, he crossed his arms. "Would you like me to touch you again?"

Finally, he broke her. Cheeks blushed crimson. "No. No. No." And yet her pressed lips and averted eyes exposed her lie.

"Vivian, did something happen in the corridors last night?"

She gasped, obviously not expecting the question. "No. Nothing." And yet, her expression had not changed from the previous question. A card player, she was not.

He quirked an eyebrow. "You are not telling me the truth."

She slid him a resigned glare. "Well, I did see something in the upstairs servants' hall. I can't be sure what it was, but something watched me."

Aye, Harry. Still, he was relieved in that she did not recognize the small figure in the shadows. No one other than those living in this house could know about Harry. Ashworth could never risk the boy being taken from him.

"You need lessons in how to lie."

Vivian sighed. "What is it you'll have me do?"

Clenching his jaw, Ashworth braced himself. He must demonstrate what not to do. He must touch her.

"Have you finished with your breakfast?"

"Yes." She fixed her gaze upon his eyes, not gaping at the scar as others did.

"Good." Gently, he lifted her chin, the smooth skin a welcome answer to the rough texture of his own. "You must not look down or away. Keep your face steady, your manner confident."

Ashworth reached for her crossed arms, trying not to brush the tempting swells of her bosom, but was unsuccessful. His knuckles grazed the soft curve of the fabric. The memory of her breast naked and glowing flashed before his eyes. He remembered running his tongue along their valley, tasting her luscious splendor.

Scorching heat blasted through his blood. Like a randy lad, he was instantly erect.

He cleared his throat. "Do not cross your arms or lock your fingers. Remain loose and relaxed." She let her arms drop to her sides. "Yes, like that and always look directly at the person, no glancing away."

Vivian nodded.

Just one thing left to do. He grazed her warm mouth with his thumb, smiling at her hushed intake of breath. "No biting, licking or pressing on your lips."

Ah, those lips! He wanted to kiss them, taste her skin, lick her most feminine treasures. Like any man, he yearned for a woman's tender flesh and sweet scent.

He truly ached with need. But too many horrors had taken over his mind. The other night confirmed it.

Vivian stepped back from him, her eyes shuttering to a quiet reserve. "So when Lady Wainscott asks of our impending vows, I shall answer her with my arms at my side, my chin held high, my gaze directly upon her and my mouth set in a smile."

He nodded, relieved the lesson was over. "That should do it."

A bell rang elsewhere in the house, prompting Ashworth to think of the time. It must be Harry or John calling for breakfast. Catherine would be here before long, escalating his life into further chaos.

"Mrs. Plimpton," he called, never removing his gaze from Vivian's lovely face.

She appeared nearby. "Yes, mi'lord?"

"Clear up breakfast as usual."

"I should wrap it, mi'lord?"

"Yes, then leave us."

Ashworth listened to his housekeeper package up food and scones for Harry, who liked to eat downstairs with the servants.

As he waited for her to leave, he watched the vivid reds and yellows from the stained glass window bounce atop the black shimmer of Vivian's hair. He'd never cared for the sun before, it reminded him of his youth and it shined an ugly brightness upon his scar.

Standing there, amid the dancing hues, Vivian resembled an Italian mosaic come to life. His chest twinged at the sight.

Finally, Mrs. Plimpton left the room and pulled the door shut with a firm tug. They were alone.

He cleared his throat. "What other questions do you have before the Countess arrives?"

Without hesitation, she said, "Why is she coming to visit you now?"

If he only knew. Catherine spurned him after the accident, no longer enamored with a disfigured and scandalous viscount. She pulled her affection for him and found another man to latch onto. Pity of it was, Ashworth had thought he loved her. Her shallowness scarred his heart like the mark on his face.

He could only assume she returned for one thing. His money. And no doubt, Ashworth's own mother had meddled somewhere in the mess.

He sensed Vivian's reservation, her concern. She could easily leave him, walk out the door and force him to face Catherine alone. Ashworth lifted Vivian's hand and placed a kiss upon the knuckles. "I am unaware of her intent. Her letter did not state a purpose."

Vivian's breathing grew shallow. "Oh?"

She did not believe him. Ashworth nodded and flipped her hand over, kissing the raised marks of yesterday's injuries. He should stop. And, yet, he could not seem to let her go. "Any other questions?" he whispered against her palm.

"Um, when would our wedding take place?"

"Good question. We will tell her sometime in autumn."

She pulled her hand from his mouth. "Where? Here?"

Reluctantly, Ashworth let her go. "My mother would want to hold it in London or at our other estate near the coast."

Vivian turned, her head tilted down to gaze out onto the grounds. "Won't your mother continue to find brides for you once I'm gone?"

He stared at her round shoulders, at her straight back with the customary dark braid splitting it down the center. "Yes, perhaps. But eventually she will give up on me."

She gasped and glanced over her shoulder. "You want her to give up on you? To forget about you? What of family?"

Ah, so Vivian missed her home, did she? She had yet to reveal who she left behind or why she needed to run.

She questioned his secrets but would not reveal hers. "Tell me of your family, Vivian."

Her eyes lowered and she turned back to the window. "I cannot go back."

Ashworth took a step closer, his hand hovering over her shoulder for a moment, an impulse to soothe the pain he heard in her voice. He placed his palm on the window instead, the glass cool and uneven to the touch. "Tell me why you can't go back. Have you no family left?"

Her mouth twitched but she did not look up at him. "I-I have family. A mother and a father. But nothing is as it was."

His voice lowered. "How was it?"

Anguish tugged at her lips. "Once I thought we were a happy family. My mother and father seemed in love, my home secure. I thought my father was the most special man in the world for how he treated my mother. It warmed my heart to think of it."

"But now?"

She crossed her arms, as if she could keep the cold memories from invading her soul. "Now I cannot think of it at all. It was all a lie. Everything I believed to be true was not."

Intrigued, Ashworth leaned his shoulder against the

window, angling for a clearer view of her face. "All a lie?"

Her lips pressed together until her eyes dampened. When her face flushed with color, Ashworth realized he'd gone too far. Some secrets she would not tell.

Footsteps and voices echoed in the hall then stopped at the closed door.

Ashworth stared at Vivian's kissable lips, at her midnight eyes. "Have we concluded our questions, then?"

She nodded.

"Then prepare yourself to meet Lady Wainscott."

"My lord?"

He forced a calm smile, inwardly praying Catherine did not intend to stay long. His temper against her could not remain composed for more than a few days. Nor could he withstand the Vivian's unique torture for much longer.

"I do believe the Countess has arrived."

Chapter Seven

Vivian held her breath, her nerves afire. The door swung open and she sucked in a deep, calming breath. Mrs. Plimpton hurried in, her face more flustered than normal. "Mi'lord. The Countess of Wainscott awaits you in the parlor."

"Thank you, Mrs. Plimpton. I will go meet with her."

Lord Ashworth's piercing gray eyes glanced down at her and dared her to question him. "Return to your room, Vivian. I will send for you within the hour."

She watched his large, imposing frame maneuver past the housekeeper and out the door. His heavy footsteps faded into the distance.

Wait in her room. Whatever would she do there? She had yet to find a book to keep her busy and had not brought her sketch pad from home. No supplies were about for stitching, nor any tuned musical instruments to play on.

She could do nothing but lie upon her bed and stare at the bed coverings! She could not sit idle now if her very life depended upon it. Distraction would prove her closest friend.

Vivian poked her head out into the hall. All was clear.

To be certain she avoided the parlor, she twisted her way down the other corridor and past the Great Hall, then down the set of rear stairs. She could get that back door open somehow and save herself the lengthy jaunt around the outside of the house.

Descending the creaking stairs, Vivian pushed cobwebs out

of her way. There, at the bottom, stood the door she'd seen a few days ago. Light filtered through the slats, freedom whispering to her. Passing this door from the outside, she'd noted that nothing barred it from opening, no debris or nailed wood. It was merely warped into the frame.

She would open it.

Vivian banged on it with her shoulder, then pushed with both hands. The wood groaned and cracked under her pressure, but the door stuck firm. Any minute now Pinkley would come and shoo her away again.

Instead, one of the other locked doors in the hall opened. Vivian gasped and pressed herself back against the wall when a stranger emerged from the dark.

The man's bright blue eyes stared at her, as if he were shocked to find her there. He had blonde, disheveled hair that told her he did not expect to be seen and a strong jaw that spoke of a man still in the prime of his life. In fact, she expected he would be of a similar age to Lord Ashworth.

Vivian waited for him to speak, to introduce himself or even ask who she was. But he said nothing. Stunned by her presence, he remained immobile. And so they watched each other like wary tomcats until something startled the man into action.

"Kick the bottom," he whispered. Then, just as quickly as he'd shown himself, the man retreated behind the door and yanked it closed. Vivian was once again alone in the shadowed landing.

She blinked, watching and waiting. Other than the wind whistling through the slats, all was quiet.

Vivian turned back to the stuck door. Glaring at it, she thought to give it one more attempt before moving onto more fruitful endeavors. Using the stranger's advice, she kicked the door repeatedly. The wood splintered beneath her shoe, but she felt it pull away from the frame. With a good, hard shove, Vivian pushed it open.

Light spilled into where she stood, along with a shower of dust fluttering into the air like sparkling fairies. The cool, misty air greeted her as she stepped onto the soft earth. Finally, she was free.

Clouds rose up the cliff and built upon themselves over the roof of the house. The light color of beach pebbles, Vivian did not expect rain from them today.

She waded through the tall swaying grasses and weeds, stopping to assess her progress on the garden. So far she had only managed to pull off overgrown vines and dead vegetation. Much remained to be done. But now was not the time to do it. And it wouldn't be wise for her to return to the house looking disheveled.

So Vivian carried on past the garden, walking further than she'd ever ventured. A row of trees impeded her path, their growth heavy and unkempt. At one time these specimens must have bordered the rear yard with a regal bearing and upright snobbery. Now they appeared as withered old men, their clothing loose and ill-fitting on their once proud state. Much like Pinkley himself.

Vivian walked along the line of trees until she found a clearing to pass through. Branches snagged her hair and scraped her dress. She should turn back. This walk had been a foolish adventure to soothe her boredom and nerves, but now she would appear a disaster.

Gull cries filled the air. There must be a body of water she had not seen from the house. Oh, she could chance another few minutes and still have enough time to return and clean up.

Vivian scanned the horizon, finding crops of rocks and green hills bordering the water. Of course, a lake. The cries of the birds and whispering of the water calmed her nerves. Ducks and swans glided toward her. Who knew such beauty and tranquility lay within such a short distance of the decaying manor?

She closed her eyes as the breeze, like a lover, gently

caressed her face. The scent of sandalwood and berries arose from her memories and tormented her with their sweetness. It was as if Lord Ashworth stood beside her, tracing his finger down her jaw, murmuring in her ear. A surprising delicious shiver skated down her spine.

She could stay here all day. She could—

A soft rustle of leaves broke her from the fantasy. Vivian opened her eyes and glanced around the rocky beach. The noise came again, between a large bush and boulders. Vivian took a step in that direction and a fox darted into the thicket. She quickly pushed branches aside to see a lone egg within a nest.

Gasping, Vivian gently scooped the egg into her hands. She didn't want to leave it for the fox's lunch and yet she didn't want to take it if the mother planned to return.

Sitting atop the boulder, she tucked the egg into the folds of her lap and waited. Lady Wainscott be damned.

Vivian would not take an offspring from its mother. Neither would she permit a young life to fall victim to a predator. She would not repeat her father's sins.

Ashworth set his face in a scowl. He had no desire to appear handsome for Catherine. If she thought him too ugly to marry seven years ago, he would make certain her mind had not changed.

He stepped into the parlor. Immediately his chest tightened at the sight of her standing near the carved marble fireplace. Her golden hair and flawless skin brightened the dim room like a vibrant lamp. Dressed in an expensive dark purple dress, Catherine was the embodiment of fine London society.

Her hazel eyes lifted and stared at his scar, revulsion lurking behind the polite mask. Then, finally, her gaze locked onto his. "Ah, Charles, how nice it is to see you again."

For a moment, he was back in London, holding her on a polished dance floor. But then the pain of her rebuke crashed through his senses. "Lord Ashworth," he corrected, not tolerating familiarity with her.

Her lips curled. "Oh, really, must it be that way?"

He'd not bother with a pretense of politeness. "Why have you come, Lady Wainscott?"

"You must call me Catherine."

Nay, he detested even saying the name. "What has brought you to Silverstone Manor? My mother, perhaps?"

Her gaze darted to the floor. "I thought a visit was long overdue."

She thought she could fool him with a lie. There was no need to visit him other than for his wealth. "And your husband, is he well?"

"The earl died last year." Catherine pressed her lips together. "I am alone now."

Ashworth did not believe her sorrow, nor would he allow her to use it to her advantage. "Have you no children?"

"I have a daughter. Still in the nursery."

"Did you bring her?"

Her widened gaze lifted to him. "Of course not. She is at home with her nanny."

Wind swept up against the house, screeching tree branches across the stones. He noticed Catherine shiver, but he made no move to warm her. Instead, he pointed to the sofa. "Sit, I will call for some tea."

She glanced at the furniture, her nose wrinkling. "Your servants have not been doing their duty."

His lips twitched. His servants did exactly as they were told. "Silverstone is a very old manor."

She sniffed. "That is no reason it cannot be kept properly."

Ah, this was not what he needed, a woman like his mother telling him how to keep his house. He was lord of this manor. He could keep it any way he pleased. The dusty furniture gave him no pause, and yet it did wonders to dissuade anyone else from staying.

Leslie Dicken

Other than Vivian. She never once mentioned it or seemed disturbed by it. Suddenly, he longed to have her here with him.

She wouldn't turn right around and leave. He knew that well enough about her. Catherine was quite purposeful and stubborn when she wanted something badly enough. He would have to endure her until she tired of the pursuit. "I will have someone prepare a room for you. Did you bring a maid?"

"Of course."

Ashworth turned to go.

"Wait." Her gloved hand settled on his arm. Once he experienced warmth in her touch, now only a hollowness in his chest.

"Nothing is left to be said." He watched the tree sway outside the window. "You should rest until dinner."

"I have not stopped thinking about you."

Ashworth winced at her husky voice and obvious lie. Did she think him a fool? "Whatever we had has long been over, Lady Wainscott."

Catherine took a step closer. The scent of lavender swirled in his nostrils. "I was young then. My father worried of the scandal. I didn't know what to do..."

He snorted. She did not seem so innocent and naïve that day she sent him away from her doorstep. Horror and revulsion were not given to her by her father. "You made your choice."

"You left London within days."

He had to. For Harry's sake. "I could have explained it all to you then, but you never gave me the chance."

Her hand touched his cheek, his unblemished cheek. "You could enlighten me now."

Like hell he would. Ashworth pushed away from her clutches and narrowed his eyes. "It is too late for explanations. It is too late for us."

She reached out for him, undaunted. "But time has—"

"Too late," he said, closing his hand around the cold

72

doorknob. "I am engaged to another woman."

Without listening for a reply, Ashworth left the parlor and headed straight for Vivian's bedchamber. With each step, the prickling under his skin eased, but his blood burned. Vivian both comforted and plagued him.

Ashworth reached her door, his pulse brisk. Knocking, he called her name.

No answer.

Perhaps she had fallen asleep. His knuckles rapped louder. "Miss Suttley?"

Again, nothing.

Ashworth tested the handle and found it unlocked. He quietly pushed it open but found no one inside. Her bed was still smooth from the servant's straightening, the fire dim. But the scent of her lingered. Even with the ever-present odor of musty dampness, he could smell her honeysuckle sweetness. If he closed his eyes he could imagine her standing before him, a vision of glowing skin and shapely legs.

Where had she gone if not here?

Ashworth retraced his steps down the main corridor. Drafts swirled past him, fluttering tapestries and cobwebs. A few turns brought him to the library, the place Pinkley had said Vivian sought last night. But the dark room was empty.

He shoved fingers through his hair, his heart beating a whisper of concern.

"Charles."

Ashworth's swung around at the sound of his name. John stood at the end of the shadowed hall, his frame half-concealed in a doorway. "What is it?"

"Miss Suttley. I thought you would want to know..."

Ashworth's long strides brought him quickly to his son's tutor. "Where is she?"

"Outside."

Relief percolated through his blood. Ah, of course. Vivian

used her time to work on the garden. He should have known. "Thank you, John. I'll go collect her now."

"Wait." A hand settled on his shoulder. "There is something you must know."

A breath hesitated in his throat. He waited for more.

"She saw me."

Ashworth's gut twisted. "Did she see Harry?"

"No. But she certainly saw me. I was coming upstairs from breakfast and she was on the landing, trying to open the rear door."

Ashworth swallowed. "What did she say?"

"Nothing."

"She didn't ask who you were or why you were there?"

John's hand slipped off, his cheeks slightly flushed. "No. She said nothing. Perhaps she waited for me to speak. But then I heard Harry coming up the stairs, so I quickly withdrew and shut the door."

"She will assume you are a servant. I appreciate your honesty." Ashworth straightened his coat. "I'll find her in the garden."

But Vivian was not in the garden. He'd found the door still slightly ajar from when she left from it, but she was not anywhere in the rear grounds. Ashworth searched behind the overgrown boxwoods and even within an old outbuilding, dangerously close to collapsing.

He sank upon the cracked pedestal of a fallen statue.

Why would Vivian leave? It was she who insisted she could not return home. It was she who promised him anything if they married. It was she who seduced him.

Ashworth licked his lips, wishing he could taste her on them. He wanted her. He needed her. The very essence of her feminine scents and textures stirred something within his soul.

Ducks quacked as they flew overhead, bringing Ashworth to his feet. With no other direction to guide him, he followed their lead. Past the fallen stone wall, Ashworth climbed the wooded slope of Briar Fell, his pulse tapping at his throat.

He'd followed this trail many times through years, especially as a boy, when he would wander off to fish. He would be gone hours before any noticed his absence. He wouldn't have minded the punishment so much if he'd actually caught any fish. But Briarwater never gave him any of its riches.

Gull cries died away as Ashworth stepped through the willow thicket. Geese and ducks crowded along the rocky beach, but he did not see Vivian.

He crunched his way toward the clump of towering oak trees, forcing away the panic. What if she had drowned? What if she were lost on the slope? What if he allowed her to come to harm?

Despite the cool air, sweat formed on his forehead. He would not fail her.

Wind whistled through the oak leaves, bringing with it the sweet sounds of a woman's hum. Ashworth's long strides brought him to a large rock, where Vivian sat calmly. His heart surged forward, his limbs weakened. Her dress was dirtied, her face smudged, but she was safe.

Vivian did not see him approach, her dark, uncovered head angled down to something in her lap. Her song rippled over the water like the lightest mist, airy and comforting.

Ashworth swallowed. "Vivian..."

She looked up, her eyes drawing him in like a hidden treasure cove. His throat closed up with the intense trembling within his chest. She was a mythical mermaid perched along the seashore. "Isn't it lovely here?"

He blinked, stunned into silence.

"Those pretty little flowers."

Ashworth looked over to where she pointed. Wild thyme nestled within the crevices of the boulder, the tiny purple flowers a sharp contrast to the gray stone.

Heedless to the worry she had given him in her disappearance, Vivian lifted her closed fists to him. "Look."

He knew she meant for him to bend close, to inspect whatever riches she discovered, but he was immobile. Desire for her drummed in his blood, crashing against his veins like water upon the pebbles. And yet, he feared touching her. He feared wanting her too badly. He feared the haunting agony of what she did to him.

"It..." Ashworth cleared his throat. "It is time to go. Lady Wainscott awaits our return."

"But I am not sure if the mother will return." Vivian slowly opened her fingers to reveal a duck egg.

"Leave it." He could not be concerned with hatching an egg. And he was certain Vivian did not plan to have it for breakfast in the morning.

Vivian rose to her feet, her eyes bright with temper. "I will not leave this orphan to be lunch for a hungry fox."

Ashworth crossed his arms. "Leave it. You were to remain in your room but I had to climb hills to find you."

She lifted her chin. "I will not remain a prisoner in my room, nor that house. You may choose to, but I will not."

"I stay inside because..." He swallowed the reasoning in a bitter lump. He stayed inside because he was marked. The villagers believed him a monster, why should he not believe it of himself? Besides, no one could know about Harry. If he ventured away from Silverstone Manor for too long, eventually his secret would be out.

Vivian brushed past him toward the path, her honeysuckle scent eddying through his senses. "The air is chilled," she said, without looking back. "I shall hurry back and change my dress. And find a home for this lost soul."

Ashworth waited, letting her go ahead of him. Chaos churned within him like the building of a storm. His life had been predictable, clear, serene before Vivian arrived. How had it derailed into such disorder?

And why the hell had Briarwater given her a treasure at her first visit and never once offered one to him?

Chapter Eight

She was narrow.

Vivian tried not to stare down her nose at the woman perched at edge of a chair. Lord Ashworth's former love was the tightest person Vivian had ever seen. Straight, thin nose, long neck and slender form hidden beneath a deep purple dress.

"You hail from the south," Lady Wainscott asked again. Even her voice was stiff, controlled, constricted.

Vivian nodded. "Staffordshire, my lady."

"Your father a baron, you said?"

Clearly, Lady Wainscott did not recognize her either. It was just as well. She did not want either of them to have the ability to contact her father.

Wind rattled the windows as she lifted her chin. None of this was a lie. "Yes, he is a baron. I have been presented to the queen."

The woman arched a blonde eyebrow. "Ah, have you?" She then shivered. "Do you not feel those drafts in this wretched room?"

"I do. They are all over the house." Perhaps they alone would send this woman on her way.

"Lord Ashworth has been neglectful in his upkeep of the manor."

Vivian smiled. She knew that Lord Ashworth did not care for the upkeep. She rather thought he wanted it to go to hell, to appear as dreadful as he suffered inside.

Lady Wainscott tilted her pointed chin. "How is it that you found no husband during your seasons in London?"

The direct, sharp question struck like a knife through her stomach. Her cheeks heated. But she could not allow for weakness. She promised him she would stay on. At least until this vixen had left.

"My father had chosen a husband for me at home instead."

"Oh?" A wicked gleam flashed in those hazel eyes. "Then what are you doing here?"

What the heavens was taking Lord Ashworth so long? He said he had pressing matters to attend to. Thus, Vivian had to face the jaws of the lioness alone as they awaited their evening meal.

She stood and wandered over to several large windows, never having been in this formal dining room before. All other meals had been taken in her room or in the breakfast room. This space must have once been glorious, with an intricately carved ceiling and ornate plasterwork around the fireplace. But now, despite having been tidied for the dinner, the room appeared as neglected as the rest of the house.

Vivian stared out the glass into the encroaching darkness. Whispers of cool air breathed across her skin. This room faced the front of the manor and she could see beyond the long drive to the village lights far in the distance.

Finally, she sighed with her response. "The man my father chose for me was unsuitable." As if one could call a violent manipulator merely unsuitable.

"Ah," Lady Wainscott sneered behind her. "But the Viscount Ashworth is suitable for your liking?"

Vivian had no answer.

"I'd say you were after his money."

Lord Ashworth's money would be enough to send her far away, to the continent or America even. But Vivian didn't want to go that far. She didn't want to live among strange cultures. No, she didn't covet the viscount's wealth, only his hand in marriage. With the bad history between he and Martin and his isolation, Lord Ashworth was indeed her perfect match.

Vivian traced her finger along the cold window ledge, unsettling a layer of dust. "As you can see, Lord Ashworth does not care to spend his money." She lifted her finger to show Lady Wainscott. "I do not believe I can change him. Do you?"

A rustling of skirts and the strong scent of lavender brought the countess before her. Sharp, hazel eyes narrowed. "The two of you may think you have an engagement, but I am not conceding."

Vivian swallowed the truth dancing on her tongue. There was no engagement. Only this morning, Lord Ashworth wanted her gone. How could she hold up the obvious lie with such an intent predator? She lifted her chin, forced the courage. "What makes you think he will prefer you?"

Lady Wainscott curled her lips. "He loved me once. Tell me, Miss Suttley, does he love you now?"

಄

Her whimpering made his skin crawl.

"I thought you said you'd played rough before."

Martin slid the trousers up his legs and rolled off the bed. The smell of sex and sweat permeated the air. Outside the window light rain tapped on the gutter. The small room had no French wallpaper or deep cushioned chairs like the places he used to visit, just a worn bed and ripped lace curtains.

He didn't even remember the whore's name.

Martin dug in his pockets, pulled out an extra coin, then flipped it on her pillow. "This is for you. A little something extra."

She groaned, but then her hand snatched out from under

the blanket and the coin disappeared.

Martin chuckled. She may be sore now but she seemed to be enjoying his rough handling earlier. "Come now, I told you I'd compensate you."

He glanced over her back, smiling at the circular shaped welts. A little nip or two couldn't be making her moan so much. Perhaps it was the manner in which he drove himself into her.

The whore rolled onto her side, long yellow hair falling over her shoulder and covering her ample bosom. "Yer the devil."

Martin arched a brow. Her opinion of him did not matter. "I'm not the only one of those here in London."

"Aye." The candle dipped, drawing shadows along her ruddy cheeks. "'Tis true."

She stared at him with glazed eyes, as if she just saw him for the first time. And perhaps she did, since they never did face each other. Already his cock, though raw, throbbed for more attention.

Martin stood and pulled on the rest of his clothes. Now that this wench had tempered the rampant lust clouding his mind, he could begin his search for Vivian. He would need to be invited to a few balls and soirees.

Just knocking on the door of the baron's cousin wouldn't do. Not if Vivian had told the world why she'd run.

No, he'd dealt with that before. Other girls he'd chosen to be his wife had either been pulled away from him due to his lack of historical title or some whimpering prattle the girl told her parents.

Vivian was perfect. Her father's indiscretion gave him the ammunition he needed to secure the beauty as his wife.

But she was gone.

Anger tightened his gut and sharpened his focus. He'd find that bitch and make her pay. She should have believed him.

"I knew ye looked familiar t'me."

Martin forced his pulse to calm and laced up his shoes.

"Don't all men look the same to you?"

Her eyes narrowed and then she laughed. "Aye. But ye look like someone from many years ago."

He shrugged, already itching to be out of this whorehouse.

She tried to sit up, winced, and dropped back to her elbows. "I-I was a young girl then. Just come ter London." Her hair slid over a large, peach nipple. "And me only friend had a regular customer, a true lover. I'd swear ye were 'im."

Martin swallowed, his mouth suddenly dry. "You must be mistaken."

She nodded. "Aye, could be."

He gathered his hat and coat. No need for concern. No one would believe this streetwalker's word over that of a gentleman like himself.

"But ye do look like 'im."

Her incessant chatter combined with the constant tapping on the gutter vexed Martin's nerves. He clenched his teeth. "What was her name? Your friend?"

Instead of answering his question, the whore sniffled, her eyes and nose reddening. "'Twas awful how she died. And the baby..."

Martin froze. *The baby.*

He tried to remember, tried to piece together the moments of that night, the sounds that reverberated in his skull. "She had a baby, this friend of yours?"

"Aye, but he went missing after that night. We think the killer took 'im."

His gut clenched. Mary had a baby? Could it be possible? Could it have been his?

He shook his head but the memories would not return clearly. He remembered the blood, the suffocating heat, the screams. But no baby.

No, if Mary had his child, she would have told him. She knew his desire for a son. She would have never kept his child from him, even if she'd found another lover.

This whore didn't know of what she spoke. Calm once again, he pulled on his hat.

She sighed. "Aye. Ye must not be the man I remembered."

Martin straightened, closing his hand over the cool knob of the door. He'd seen enough of London's underbelly for one night. "What did you say her name was?"

The whore wiped her nose on her arm. "Mary Yeardley."

Æʒ

Odd as it was, the sun brightened with each step Vivian took down the long drive. By the time she'd reached Silverstone's gate near the village, the air was clear and colors vivid.

She glanced back to the manor to see its ugly spires hidden beneath a heavy layer of clouds. Was it possible that impending doom actually lived above the very structure?

Vivian shook her head. No, 'twas just her imagination. Still, she'd been smart to get away from there today, away while Lady Wainscott rested in her rooms.

The jaunt to the village was still a bit of a walk, and at her brisk pace, she'd warmed up considerably from the drafty chills of the morning breakfast.

Mrs. Plimpton had told her that the post office was only a few streets once she reached the village.

This errand brought a smile to her lips. Ever since she learned that she could send a card and not worry if her mother could pay for it, Vivian had set her mind to dashing off a note as quickly as possible. Lord Ashworth had even given her the penny needed, but tried repeatedly to have a servant complete the task.

But Vivian was not a prisoner in that house. She'd not allow his self-pity or reclusive behavior prevent her from interacting with others. Especially not when she could enjoy a hearty walk and see new sights.

Vivian started down the main street. Memories of her brief visit to the tavern flickered in her mind like wary ghosts. The village was dark then, her fear and determination heavy. Over and over, people warned her not to enter Silverstone Manor, not to proceed with her mission.

They had nearly swayed her. In fact, she'd planned to pay Lord Ashworth a call the next morning, but feared her mind would be changed if she waited that long. And so she'd gone up his long drive that very evening.

Much had changed in those few days. Much, and yet the crumbling house still held so many mysteries.

Vivian saw the sign for the post office and crossed the street. Only then did she realize people were gaping at her. Stares, whispers, pointing fingers. Everyone knew she was the foolish woman who'd ventured up the hill.

What could she do but lift her chin and continue onward?

Vivian entered the door next to the Post Office sign and came to stand before a worn, wooden counter.

An older woman stood at the back wall, her back to Vivian as she sorted letters into various compartments.

"Pardon me," Vivian said. "I'd like to purchase a stamp and mail this letter."

"Be with you in a moment."

Vivian turned back to watch the villagers go by the window. There was a time she was as carefree and untroubled as they appeared. There was a time, before Martin entered her life when she could smile and dream of a future. Now her future depended upon a secluded stranger agreeing to marry her.

"You're the girl staying up at the manor!"

Vivian swallowed, forcing a grin on her lips. "Good morning, I'm Miss Suttley. I'd like to post this letter."

The plump woman adjusted her glasses, squinted her blue

eyes. "You are the girl up at Silverstone, aren't you?"

"Yes, I am staying at the manor. May I purchase a Penny Black, please?"

But the postmistress made no move to either take her money or get the stamp. "You haven't married him yet, have you?"

Vivian lifted her chin, straightened her back, but did not answer.

"I didn't believe so." A thick hand waved through the air, as if brushing off the absurd notion. "No chaperone up there with you either, is there?"

"A stamp, please."

"My son works up there. He's the groomsman. Told me about you, he did."

The groomsman. That was the boy who helped Lord Ashworth carry up pails of water. No wonder this woman looked at her as if she were nothing more than a streetwalker.

The woman leaned across the counter. "You heard the rumors about that house? They're true, I tell you. Something isn't right up there. Not right at all."

A chill skated down Vivian's spine at the memory of the confrontation in the dark halls. There *was* something going on in that house, but whether monster, ghost or foul play, it would not sway Vivian from her purpose.

"As you can see, I am in fine spirits and excellent health."

The postmistress raised an eyebrow. "That may be, but how is your mind? Have odd dreams haunted you at night? Have the drafts and noises stirred you from slumber?"

Vivian sighed. Perhaps next time a servant should mail her letters. "My mind is still alert and sound."

"And the master? Lord Ashworth? He's not frightened you with his behavior or terrifying face?"

Terrifying face? Vivian could only think of the roughness of his chin, the sensual curve of his lips, the intensity of his eyes.

His scar was a groove upon a spectacular stone, not diminishing its luster but adding to its uniqueness.

"I am perfectly well. Thank you for your concern. Now, a stamp, please."

"Eh, you've only been there a short time." She reached into a drawer and withdrew the same small stamp Vivian had seen on Lady Wainscott's letter. "You'll regret staying in that house, mark my words."

Vivian slid the coin toward her. "I see no reason why I shall."

Once the stamp was on the letter, the postmistress glimpsed at it then slid it into one of the lower slots. Still facing the wall of compartments, the woman glanced over her shoulder. "Keep a sharp eye out, Miss Suttley. You may think we only speak of rumors, but even gossip usually begins with a bit of truth."

In her room that evening, Vivian set the brush down on the dresser and blew out the candle. Wind gusted, tossed clouds around the sky and gave the moon little chance to illuminate her room. Only the subtle glow of the fire led the way to the bed.

She pushed aside the bed curtains when a knock came from Lord Ashworth's room. "Vivian?"

He wanted to see her at this hour? With no robe nearby to cover over her nightgown, she climbed into the bed and pulled the blankets over top. "Yes? Come in."

The door separating their two rooms creaked open. Lord Ashworth crossed the room toward her in a pair of breeches and nothing else. The shadows cast dark curves along the angles of chest. Dark hair sprinkled upward from his stomach.

Vivian swallowed as shocking heat pooled between her legs. She still could not comprehend what this man did to her. Thomas's kisses had stirred hope in escaping Martin, nothing else.

Lord Ashworth shoved his hand through his hair and stood at the end of the bed. "I'm sorry to disturb you this way but a thought had occurred to me."

"Yes. Go on then."

"I realize I know very little about you. That if I were asked about your life, I could not answer."

A breeze blew across the bed, bringing with it his unique scent. Her mouth watered. "And—and you think to do this now?"

"There will not be much other time when you and I are alone."

"Very well," she sighed. "What is it you wish to know?"

"First, have you any brothers or sisters?"

"No. I am an only child."

"I have two sisters, both married, neither one will speak to me."

Vivian caught her breath at the emotionless manner in which he spoke of his family. It could not be true that they dismissed him from their lives only due to the scar upon his face. And yet, he seemed resigned to their actions, as if he could not care any less.

He pushed the bed curtain aside and sat down on the far end of the bed. The mattress sank beneath his weight. "You father is a baron, yes? What is his full title?"

She did not want to talk about her parents, especially her father. The recent memories were still too raw and implausible. She drew in a shaking breath. "He is Lord Whistlebury, a baron."

Vivian waited to see if he recognized the name from that one garden party all those years ago. But his expression did not change. "And you come from Staffordshire. A village there?"

Her stomach knotted. Would the village name stir his memory? Would he have any knowledge that Martin Crawford now lived there? She couldn't chance it. "Does the name matter?"

Lord Ashworth leaned forward, his hands down on either side of her legs. Heat radiated from his skin. His eyes narrowed. "You are hiding something."

"We both have tales to hide, do we not? Do you wish to share what caused the demise of your relationship with Lady Wainscott?"

Immediately, his jaw tensed, scar pulsed. "No."

"Then I do not wish to share the name of my village."

"Nor why you ran from it?"

"I love animals, children and flowers. What else do you need to know?"

Lord Ashworth leaned closer. His scent caved in her reserve. In an instant, her breathing turned shallow. A debate stormed within her blood. The disquiet under her skin yearned for his warmth, yet the uncertainty of his reactions, his behavior, those damn rumors, troubled her soul. Who was this man? Was he a threat to her?

"My lord, I really do not think—"

"Vivian." His gaze shifted to her mouth. "I want to taste your lips, feel your skin."

Awareness quivered between her legs. "But you..."

His hand lifted from the bed and slid its way over the blankets, beginning at the apex of her legs, skimming over her breasts, and then up to her throat. Vivian clenched her teeth, but a whimper escaped into the night air.

He halted, paralyzed by the sound. She could hear his harsh breathing, see his jaw tighten.

Her gaze drifted from the agony written across his furrowed brow down to the rapid rise and fall of his chest. Curious, she glanced below his waist, glimpsing a shadowed rise in his breeches. The sight didn't frighten her, but shot a dizzying spasm to her toes.

Lord Ashworth caught her stare. "Faith, Vivian..."

He bent forward, pressing her further into the mattress, trapping her with his kiss. His lips nibbled at her mouth, set free any restraint she had left. Vivian opened herself to his invasion, tasted the desire on his tongue. An unbearable pressure climbed inside of her.

She brushed her palm along the hard muscles of his arm, feeling warmth and light sweat on his skin.

Lord Ashworth shifted, leaning his body across her chest, freeing one hand to caress her hair. He lingered there only briefly before his fingers explored her throat. With a gentle tug, he loosened the bow at her neckline. Cool air swept across her shoulder. Wet fire spread from her neck down to her breast. He circled the nipple with his tongue.

Her body came alive and freed her from any lingering fear or revulsion.

Arching her back, Vivian pressed herself into his suckling lips. She squeezed her eyes closed, but even without the view of his lips on her body, moisture swelled between her legs. Somewhere deep inside a pleasurable torture arose, pushing her past decorum and into desperation.

"Please..." she whimpered, her fingers skimming across his strong shoulders and into his thick hair.

Lord Ashworth lifted his head only long enough to scoot his entire body onto the bed. He lay alongside her, one leg entwined with hers, his unyielding erection pressing insistently against her hip.

His palm cupped her other breast, kneading it, massaging it. He flicked her nipple with his thumb, while his tongue did the same on the other side. Vivian threw her head back, her mouth parting with a guttural sigh.

Lord Ashworth's large hand pushed down the blankets, then glided atop the nightgown, past her stomach to the aching flesh between her legs. He lifted the material, finding the dampness with efficient ease.

Coyness fled. Vivian raised her hips, reaching for

something, anything, to assuage the throbbing so deep inside. His fingers danced over the sensitive nub, winding her tighter with each stroke. "Oh Lord, please..."

He captured her lips with his, thrusting his tongue inside as one of his fingers slipped within her folds. He swallowed her gasp, forced her to ride the wave swelling with each breath she took.

Vivian rocked against his hand. Showers of tingles raced down her legs, up to her nipples. Each flick of his finger pulled her taut. She pointed her toes, arched her back, strained for a release that seemed beyond her grasp.

He left her mouth again and dipped his dark head to her breast. She watched him lap the stiff knot, swirling his tongue over and around the straining peak. Vivian whimpered, moaned, then cried out into the darkness above her.

"Vivian..." his strangled voice accompanied a sudden thrust of his hips. Two fingers plunged deep inside.

She broke.

Not pain. Ecstasy.

Waves of pleasure crashed upon themselves, rippled outward from her center. Her hips rose from the bed, lunging into the air, deepening his stroke.

Vivian turned her head to the pillow and attempted to muffle her cries against the fabric. But the clamor from her throat didn't fade away until the last surge receded.

She turned to Lord Ashworth, but he leaped up from the bed with her next heartbeat.

"What...what is it?"

He had that same look as before, the horrified eyes, the blanched skin. One would think he saw a terrifying ghost lying before him rather than his false bride. "No, no," he choked. "Not again!"

He blinked once then backed away from the bed. Before she could call out to him, he was gone from her room with a slam.

Chapter Nine

Vivian was not a virgin.

Ashworth slumped on his bed, his heart raging, his arousal pulsing. Her body accepted his fingers too easily, although he sensed her reaction surprised her. If another man had taken her, he had not given her pleasure.

Passion clearly simmered beneath her cool exterior. A passion which inflamed his lust and brought on the visions.

He took a deep breath. Thankfully, the horrible images were gone. Vivian's cry of delight had become a scream of terror in his brain. Instead of her lush, inviting skin, he saw her covered in blood. Bile had clogged his throat.

Even as he ran from her, his desire had not dimmed. His blood scalded, knees shook, pulse hammered. He could still smell her essence on his fingers, taste her skin on his tongue.

A draft whispered about the room, cooled his skin. But not his need.

Ashworth dropped back on the mattress. His heartbeat echoed in his skull. Vivian's pink nipples graced his daydream as he closed his eyes. He recalled running his tongue across their pert loveliness. She tasted of the wild honeysuckle growing on the hillside. Inside her folds, slick warmth swallowed his finger. And as he thrust it over and over, he imagined his erection in its place.

Ashworth clenched his teeth, but it was no use. He unbuttoned his breeches and fisted his pulsating shaft.

Instead of his fingers on his erection, he imagined her damp tunnel enclosing over him. He'd sink deep inside her, filling her, driving her.

Yes, he could envision it all so clearly! Her hips rocking against his. His hands squeezing her breasts, thumbs rolling her nipples. Sharp fingernails tracing down his back, reaching lower...

Tingling raced from his spine, circling his toes, tickling his nipples. Ashworth threw his head back, tightened his grip.

In his fantasy, he could hear her whimpers rising to moans. Finally she'd cry out while her spasms wracked his slick flesh. It would drive him deeper. Faster.

Ashworth moaned and pumped his erection to a hot release.

He slid his hand away and stared at the dark canopy above his head. His breathing shattered the stillness of the night.

Vivian...Vivian!

She tortured him so blessedly, so exquisitely, his whole life was in chaos. Did he want her to leave him to his tightly controlled world or stay and absolve him of his delusions?

He wanted her warmth, yet feared her intimacy. He yearned for her body, yet refused her tenderness.

Suddenly parched, he turned to his nightstand. Pinkley had left his nightly potion, a watered-down laudanum concoction. Without hesitation, Ashworth swallowed the liquid in a gulp.

He needed to find peace. Pray God this potion brought him peace tonight.

CR

Martin avoided looking at the brick manor as he walked up the drive. A wave of fury rippled through his blood. The entire trip over he attempted to control the rage he knew would surface. With this hunt for Vivian already gnawing at his nerves, facing his mother would only incense him more.

But he had to come. He had to see her. After all, his mother was the reason he'd become who he was.

It was as if he was to blame for her careless mistake in getting pregnant. She never would answer why she didn't abandon him when he was a baby instead of a young lad.

A crisp breeze lifted Martin's hair as he walked around to the back of the house. He'd not knock on the front door, allow a servant to turn him away. No, Martin would see his mother today.

She always sat on the back porch, staring at the trees. Even as a small child, he remembered her watching the branches sway out their tiny flat window. Usually she retreated to her private world after kicking him for ruining her life by being born.

The ground squished beneath his feet, the sky swarmed above his head, building to a storm. He didn't plan to stay long. Just enough time to get what he needed.

Martin slowed his walk as he approached the rear of the manor. He heard voices chattering. Servants. He pressed himself against a large statue and waited for them to pass.

Finally there was no one but himself and the cool air. Himself and the first woman to abandon him.

A set of steps led up to the terrace, where his mother often drank her tea in the afternoon. He'd come here enough over the years to watch her, to sense her movements and patterns, to decide what to do about her future.

The clank of a tea cup told him she was up there. Just as he suspected. Habits did not change much in the old. The infirm.

A few silent footsteps brought him up the stairs and to her side. Her eyes widened at the sight of him, then dropped with resignation. Shoulders slumped, hands knotted, mouth tensed. Whether it was guilt at what she'd done to him or fear at what he could do again to her, she always reacted to his presence in the same manner.

"Mother." He looked at her gnarled hand, but didn't touch it. "It has been a year since we've talked."

"Go away. I will yell for someone."

Martin grinned at her hoarse threat. Without access to a bell—which he blocked from her reach—no one could hear his mother call.

"Why don't we take a walk?"

Her dark eyes glared. "You've seen to it that I can never walk again."

He straightened. "I meant we can take a stroll. I'll push you along the pond. I have something to speak with you about."

"Let go!" She tried to twist around from her chair, but she was too frail and weak to reach him.

He took a hold of the handles and steered her toward the ramp. It had been built a full year after she fell down the terrace steps. Her husband had some strange belief that his wife would get up and walk again. But the woman had not worked hard for anything in her life. Why would she start then?

"You want something from me. You only come when you do."

A wheel squeaked as he drove her down the ramp and started across the lawn.

"Shall I visit you more often?" His pulse jumped, fire tipped his ears. "Perhaps I should come to see you as often as you came to see me twenty years ago."

He could see her tense. "I—I told you I tried to find you. I asked all the neighbors where you'd gone. No one knew."

Rage boiled below the surface of his skin, threatening to crumble his composure. "I waited there six months for you to return. Six months! As winter approached, I grew too cold to sleep in alleys and steal food."

The wheelchair bumped over dips in the grass, jostling his

mother in the seat. She cried out, but then settled when they at last reached the pond's edge.

"You left me to fend for myself. I was still a boy. A child." He let go of the handles and walked around to face her. She wouldn't look at him. "I made my own way. Whatever way I could." Martin narrowed his eyes. "And *I* am the one who finally found *you.*"

"And then ruined my life when you did!" She gasped at her outburst. Her face paled.

His hand shot out as reflex, but he stopped just short of making contact. "I ruined your life from the moment I was born. How often did you tell me that? How often did you kick me to make me pay for your sin? Finally, you just walked out and left me behind." Martin crossed his arms to keep his impulses in check. "But you found a way to marry yourself into wealth and status. And now I will do the same."

"What...what do you want from me?"

As a mother, he could give her nothing. He'd long lost the opportunity for kindness and comfort. Now, she was only worth the money and connections she could provide him.

Voices startled him. People were gathered on the porch. He didn't have much time.

"I need invitations to balls, parties and the like this season."

"Why?"

"Why doesn't matter!" Martin squatted before her, not to become less intimidating, but to hide from the onlookers. "Just find a way to get my name on as many invitee lists as you can."

"And if I don't?" A tremble lurked beneath the words.

He peeked around her to see three people coming down the steps and looking this way. "Send the cards to Crawley's Hotel." He stood, backed away toward the trees crowding the banks. "You should know better than to cross me."

Martin did not wait for a reply, nor to hear what was said to his mother by the servants. He knew enough of this land to skirt around the pond, through a path in the woods and to follow it to the road a quarter mile down.

Now he had only to wait a day or so for the invitations to arrive at the hotel. Then, he would find Vivian Suttley and bring her back home.

He would have the wealth and status he deserved. He would not be cast off again.

"What is she doing?" Catherine's pungent lavender scent assaulted Ashworth's nostrils.

He tensed, taking a step away from her. "I believe she and Pinkley are finding a way to keep the egg warm."

"The egg?"

Yes, the bloody egg Vivian had saved from a fox at Briarwater. Now she tried to build a warm nest for it, keep it secure until it hatched.

He turned away from the window, though he yearned to watch Vivian longer. "Tell me," he said as he poured a splash of brandy. "Why are you really here?"

Skirts rustled as Catherine crossed the room to join him. "I've missed you. You've not returned to London in all these years and..."

"And?"

"And I was curious as to what kept you away."

He swallowed the liquid and set the glass on the table. "Surely you were able to talk with my mother."

"I did see her now and then."

Ashworth nearly snorted. At this point he wasn't sure which vixen sought out the other, but he was certain it was more than now and then. "So what did my mother tell you of me?"

Pray God, not Harry. His jaw tightened. His mother

promised, on every ring and jewel she owned, not to divulge the secret of her grandson.

Catherine's eyes revealed nothing. "The Dowager merely told me of your continued refusal to return to the city. I could not imagine it was merely the shame of your face which keeps you away."

Shame. Is that what she thought kept him within these walls? His motivation was far more agonizing than that.

Resisting the urge to return to the window, Ashworth wandered the parlor room. It was here that he first laid eyes on Vivian. He knew so much more of her, and yet so little, since that fateful day.

"Shame is not what keeps me from London."

"Oh?" Catherine sat on the deteriorating sofa, her back erect, chin forward. She was an elegantly cut gem set within an utterly flawed setting.

"I have no reason to go back. Nothing is there for me."

"A bride?"

He nearly had that. Until Catherine slammed the door on his face. "Why go there for one? I have my bride here."

Her lips pursed. "Yes, Miss Suttley. What do you know of her?"

Branches swept up against the manor, scratching the stones with an ear-shattering screech. Ashworth watched Catherine's reaction. Her eyes widened, face blanched. He hid his grin.

"I know enough of Miss Suttley to know she will not desert me."

Catherine stiffened. "Are we back to that? Doesn't it say something that I've journeyed all the way out here to see you again?"

"After your husband has died."

"You certainly didn't think I would come while he lived, did you? I could not do such a thing."

"But you thought of me then?" He knew better, but he enjoyed seeing her indignation. Perhaps he would draw enough ire to have her stomp out of Silverstone.

She glanced away. "At times I did. I regretted my decision to end our engagement."

"You told me yesterday it was your father who put a stop to it."

She caught her breath, then recovered. "I've made a mistake. I see that now."

Lies. All of her words were lies. He went past her and back to the window. Down below, Vivian was arranging straw in a box. Shifting rays of sunlight danced upon the black strands of her hair. He wanted to join her.

Instead, he crossed his arms. "What do you see now? A man still marked, a house in disrepair. I have nothing for you, Lady Wainscott."

"Yes, you do." She remained on the sofa, her voice carrying through the dust. "You have our memories. We once loved one another."

Ashworth stared off at the approaching clouds. The pain of her rejection had long since been replaced by emptiness. Now only Harry could fill that void. "No. *I* once loved *you*."

He would not get the truth from her today. "I have business I need to attend to."

He started for the door but Catherine blocked his path. Her gold hair and pale skin appeared fragile in this harsh environment, yet her lips glistened a vibrant red. "I did love you."

If she loved him, his scar and the mystery of that horrible night would not have deterred her. But there was no point in telling her.

Catherine raised her chin, her lips curving as a gloved hand touched his chest. Green eyes sparkled with overt seduction.

Though Catherine had matured into a woman, her bosom larger after pregnancy, she held little appeal for him. He once coveted her fair, unblemished skin, her lithe body. But now he coveted nothing.

Catherine traced a finger along his shoulder. "Things are different now."

His jaw clenched as a storm raged in his blood. He wanted her gone from his sight, but his anger yearned for revenge. "You are not safe here."

She lifted her chin, her face so close to his own. "I am safe anywhere with you." Then, her lips touched his.

She had seen them at the window.

Lord Ashworth and Lady Wainscott in the parlor looking down as she worked. Despite what Lord Ashworth told her of his feelings regarding Lady Wainscott, Vivian could not stem her fear that he would return to his former love.

But what of last night?

Vivian rested against a boulder, her knees suddenly weak. What he had done to her, the passion he had brought from her lips...oh, she scarcely slept afterward. Even now, her nipples ached, heat gathered between her legs.

She wasn't a virgin. But she had never known true desire. And now she desired more. Her dreams each night left her quaking for release, Lord Ashworth's kisses left her breathless.

There were times when she could think of nothing but having his large hands on her skin, his mouth on her breasts. She considered how hard the muscles on his legs were, how long he could control his urgent needs.

Above all, she wondered what it would be like to be loved with tenderness.

And yet, what had started last night with gentle awareness then progressed into passion, ended in an abrupt mystery. Once again he left her cold and alone, once again he would not discuss what had transformed him. He did not trust her.

She should not trust him.

Vivian swallowed the sting in her throat and finished cleaning the straw. She carried the last of it to her garden, covering the seeds she recently planted.

Leaves and twigs crunched behind her. Vivian waited, expecting Pinkley to return. But there was only silence.

She grinned, her heart fluttering. Perhaps it was Lord Ashworth who had come to disturb her peace. Vivian straightened and turned. "My lord."

But no one was there.

She shrugged it off to the movements of a fox. But then the rustling sounds came again. This time in the tangle of bushes at the base of the house. Perhaps the animal was trapped.

Rain splattered about her, daylight rapidly waned. The storm had come over the cliff, but she could not bear to think of a hurt animal trapped in the thicket.

Vivian reached the overgrown bushes, several feet deep, but found nothing other than leaves and branches. She would have to either wade in or crawl in on her knees.

Wind pushed at her skirts and blew her hair from her braid. Several fat raindrops landed on her shoulders. She wouldn't have long before the full fury of the tempest was upon her.

Vivian dropped to her knees, heedless to the damp ground, and crawled into the brush. Branches scratched her face, but the sounds increased. Rustling of leaves, whimpering.

Thunder clapped.

A squeal. Or was it a scream? Her heart lodged in her throat. She had to get back there.

"Shhh, it's all right," she called.

The undergrowth thickened so that Vivian had to flatten to her stomach. She pushed through the wood, the dirt and crawled over stones.

She had just about reached the manor wall when the deluge began. Even through the dense leaves, the rain pelted her back.

The crying intensified with the strengthening of the rain. Vivian tried to hurry but she couldn't crawl any faster. Twigs snapped just beyond her reach. She saw a flash of color—was it clothing?

Good Lord, was it not an animal, but a person? A child?

Frantic, Vivian pushed harder, her dress tearing, her face smeared with damp earth.

A clap of thunder. Another scream.

Her heart ached. "I—I'm almost there."

Finally, her head was out of the branches. Twigs snapped. Water sloshed.

Scrambling from the underbrush, Vivian pulled herself up against the wall and into the tiny clearing.

Chapter Ten

Catherine watched Charles leave the room, the dust floating into the air as he slammed the door to his study.

She surprised him with that little kiss, did she?

It took her the entire night to get up the courage to do it. Part of it was the hideous scar on his face, disfiguring a once handsome man. But she was also afraid she still harbored some feelings for him.

Luckily, she did not. The kiss did nothing for her.

Thunder clapped overhead, startling her. This wretched weather. It forced her to remain inside this miserable house. True, it was large, even grander than her late husband's estate.

But it could not be saved. Too many years of neglect had reduced it to disaster. Catherine had no intention of living in this despicable place, but she would marry Charles.

Rain gusted against the window, prompting her to peer outside.

Was that ordinary Miss Suttley still outside with her duck egg? Catherine chuckled as she scanned the yard, but saw no figures foolish enough to be out in the storm.

She did not believe their lies.

He had yet to hold Miss Suttley the way he once held her. He did not take her hand or watch her speak. He may have affection for the girl, but more than likely he offered her money in exchange for his deception.

A draft circled the room, sending chills down Catherine's spine. She hated this manor. She could bear it only a few more weeks. That should be long enough for her seduction to work, to have their charade exposed, and secure Charles's hand in marriage.

Then, with his wealth to pay off the debts Wainscott left behind, Catherine would return to London. Without Viscount Ashworth at her side.

Why had Catherine invaded his life now? Ashworth was accustomed to the long stretches of silence here at the manor, the small group of people who inhabited this isolated place. Harry was growing and learning, his staff was loyal. Everything was just the way he wanted it.

He had to get Catherine out of Silverstone. And then he must see that Vivian left. The chaos she created went much deeper than an extra plate at breakfast.

Vivian! Was she still outside?

Wind howled and thunder cracked, rousing his nerves. He had no other choice but to check the rear yard, though he clearly did not see her through the window from the parlor.

Ashworth followed the trail Vivian normally took, descending the rear stairs to the splintered wood door. Even with her repeated use, cobwebs still hung from the ceilings. The steps were slick beneath his shoes, the air damp and musty.

Cool air greeted him at the landing, where the warped door stood ajar. Rain blew in, creating a small puddle on the worn stones.

"Vivian?" he called. The two doors behind him were shut tight.

He pulled the door open, the wind whipping his hair. Sucking in a deep breath, he plunged out into the yard, heading for her garden.

Silver sheets of rain blew across the hills and against the house. Instantly wet, Ashworth headed up the slope. Thunder rumbled overhead.

"Vivian!"

"Here, my lord."

He raced to the top of the hill and saw her not at her garden, but against the crumbling walls. She was trapped between the stones and a tangle of underbrush.

As he got closer, his stomach plummeted. Her dress was ripped, her hair in wet disarray. That beautiful face was smeared with dirt and marred with bloody scratches.

She'd been attacked!

Ashworth stood at the other end of the thicket, his pulse crashing like thunder. He wanted to go to her, to hold her in his arms but he may as well have been miles from her.

"You're injured." He could not bring himself to say his other thoughts.

She sniffled and he just noticed the drops on her cheeks. He'd assumed they were rain, but now he suspected tears.

"It's gone," she said, looking on either side of where she stood.

"Gone? What's gone?"

Vivian brushed hair from her forehead, smearing blood across her skin. "I—I don't know. I saw something and now it is gone."

Ashworth saw nothing but green brush and gray walls. Had she gone mad? Had the desolation of the manor so quickly driven her insane?

He stretched his hand out, though it fell far short of reaching her. "Something has hurt you, Vivian. Come inside."

She blinked. "No, I heard crying. An animal or a...a child. I-I crawled under the brush to rescue it..." Her voice broke. "But it's gone now."

A child? *Harry?*

Ashworth's gut burned, his temples pounded. Had his son been outside? Did she see him?

He had to get inside and find Harry. First he needed to get Vivian into a warm bath and under heavy blankets.

Glancing her over, he realized that her torn dress and scratches could have easily been made by the thicket between them. The ache in his stomach eased, but he still worried for her health. She must come inside now.

"Whatever was there before is now gone. You must come out of this storm."

Rain dripped from her hair as she stood there, immobile. But then she nodded and lowered to her knees.

"Wait." There must be a better way than having her crawl back under the bushes. He'd force his way through the branches before he let that happen again.

Vivian shivered as she rose again to her feet. Her lips had turned blue and she nibbled on the lower one. Yet her eyes, blacker than the clouds overhead, shimmered with distraught tears.

Pain stung his throat as if he'd swallowed a handful of thistles. Breathlessness tightened his lungs. What was she doing to him?

Ashworth pointed at the wall. "There. Follow the stones downhill to the door."

She nodded. Using the solid surface for support, Vivian followed its path to where Ashworth waited for her.

He wasn't quite sure what possessed him to do it, but he opened his arms the moment she was free of the thicket. She collapsed against his chest. An urge to brush his lips across her wet hair flared through him. Instead, he resisted and stared out into the dark, wet afternoon.

They stood there in the downpour, the sky rumbling. His blood flowed like warm wine. With a troubled sigh, Ashworth pushed away the very peace he'd been seeking.

Ashworth descended the several flights to where he knew

he'd find Harry. Being spoiled by Cook.

He found him on a wooden chair in the warm, dark kitchen, his face glowing, his red hair damp. Rage and dread mingled in Ashworth chest. Damn this boy and his curiosity. Damn the circumstances that forced him to be hidden away in a crumbling manor.

Ashworth clenched his fists, forcing his anger into the squeeze. He'd not lose his temper in front of his staff, nor frighten his son.

"Harry," he said.

The boy turned and grinned. "Papa! Look!"

He ignored his son's request. "Were you outside Harry? In the storm?"

"Yes, but just for a moment, I—"

Ashworth sank to his knees. "You must keep to the house, Harry. I've told you this time and time again."

"But—"

"I won't take any replies from you. Miss Suttley nearly spotted you. What if it had been Lady Wainscott? Do you want to be taken from me?"

Harry started crying. "No, Papa."

Ashworth pulled him into his arms. The gentle warmth of the boy did not cause him the distress he experienced while holding Vivian. There was no vulnerability, no feeling of utter helplessness with his son.

He kissed his forehead and stood. "What did you want me to see?"

Harry sniffled, then his smile returned. He pointed to a wooden box next to the oven. "It was out in the rain, so I brought it inside."

Ashworth knelt beside the box and pushed aside the straw. A small, dull egg lay nestled in a dry cocoon. A sudden dawning came up him. "You went outside to bring in the duck egg?"

Harry nodded. "I didn't want it to get too cold."

So if that were the case, then Vivian must not have seen him. It must have been an animal, perhaps wounded, that scampered away just as she reached it.

Relieved, Ashworth gave his son another hug and headed upstairs to change from his wet clothes. Vivian should be out of the tub in his room and back into her own bed.

Unfortunately, he didn't think she'd be well enough to join them for dinner. He'd have to suffer through it alone, facing Catherine like the adversary she was.

Warmth. Finally, the chill in her bones eased but now flames spread along her skin.

Vivian kicked off the blankets, yet sweat still soaked her. Groaning, she pulled off her nightdress and tossed it to the floor. Her face stung from the scratches. A bandage irritated her forehead.

Vivian reached for the glass beside her bed and gulped the water. The heat would not ease.

She dropped back down to the pillow and fought the invasion of sleep. She had to be up. There was something she had to do, some unfinished business she must resolve. But her brain was foggy, her concentration lacking.

The egg. It had something to do with the duck egg. There was a box and some straw...

Unable to stave off the encroaching slumber, Vivian closed her eyes and sank into the depths of a fever-inspired dream. She was on a boat, lying on her back, staring at stars in a darkening sapphire sky. Her stranger, familiar enough to her now, rowed them to the center of Briarwater. The water gently rocked her, like a babe in a mother's belly. Secure, safe, protected.

The stranger leaned toward her, his face still shadowed, but his musky scent ignited a liquid fire in her veins. She spread her legs, lifted her hips. Her nipples peaked, begged for his caress.

The last rays of an orange sun dipped below Briarfell. Vivian smiled as the stranger placed his hands upon her legs. Slowly, he lifted her dress, pushing his way higher and higher up her legs. Cool air slid across her skin. She wore no stockings or petticoats.

Vivian sat up on one elbow and reached her hand out to him. "Come to me." She wanted to taste his lips, suckle his tongue.

But he shook his head and trailed a warm finger down her shin.

She shivered. "What—what are you going to do?"

But she may as well have been asking the moon, for the stranger would not answer her. He never spoke in her dreams. But his touch elicited a passion she could not control, a craving she could not deny. He settled himself between her legs then rubbed warm hands over them, kneading and pressing along her skin.

Vivian sighed, relished the sensuality of his touch. The stars winked, the boat swayed. Contentment drifted like rose petals through her bloodstream.

Then his lips touched her skin.

Vivian lifted her head, gasping.

The stranger did not notice. He continued to kiss her thighs, alternating between the two of them. She wriggled as impatience spiked.

Soon enough, his tongue traced damp trails down from her knees to the apex of her legs. He licked the crevice of her hip.

Vivian moaned as the sweet tension built. She reached down and grabbed a hold of his hair. She needed more, something more.

His tongue flicked over her sensitive nub and she shook with an instant release. But he would not let her go; no, it seemed he was only beginning. Like a starved man, the stranger tasted her. He lapped her essence, thrust his tongue inside her willing body. Vivian closed her legs around his face as the pressure grew once more. She rocked, reached, yearned for more than just his wicked mouth.

He was relentless.

He kissed her thighs, her hips, her mound. He licked her core until she had to shut her eyes and block out the twinkling sky.

Pleasure rose to an unbearable pitch. She had to find release, she had to let go. Lord, she needed him inside her. So very deep inside...

A finger slid in her damp flesh and she shattered.

Intensity burst her tranquility, shocked her awake.

Vivian sat up in her bed, panting. Her pulse thundered in her skull. Or was it the storm still raging outside?

Naked, having tossed her nightdress off earlier, she stared down at her flushed body. Instead of the shame Martin brought, Vivian suddenly felt beautiful. Desirable. Her breath hitched, sensuality bloomed, as her gaze floated over pointed nipples, a smooth stomach and fuzzy, dark hair.

She stretched, like a purring cat, then reached for her blankets.

A wooden floorboard creaked.

She was not alone.

Chapter Eleven

Vivian sat up, her blood chilling.

The far corner of the room was too dark to see if someone stood amongst the shadows. But there had been a noise. She was certain of it.

She swallowed the fear expanding in her throat. There were no monsters. No ghosts. No demons. Only mortal souls who conspired to rouse terror in her heart. Was one of those souls Lord Ashworth?

"Who's there?" She pushed the bed curtain aside.

The floor creaked again, a draft of cool air spun through the room, then the tapestry slammed against the wall.

Vivian glanced at the shadows at the door to the hallway, then the door to Lord Ashworth's room. Both were closed.

"Make your presence known."

The fire snapped. Wind whistled. No one answered.

She had enough. She'd been terrorized in the hallway, but she'd not allow it in her bedchamber.

Vivian slid down from the bed and reached for her gown. She quickly pulled it over her head then straightened her shoulders.

"I'll not sit idle while you spy on me." She took a step forward. "Be known that I am making my way toward you, so you may as well show yourself."

But the air was still. The sense of eyes watching her was

gone.

She crossed the room with only the light of the fire to guide her, now certain she would find no one standing in the shadows.

The room was empty, save for sleeping spiders.

Someone had been here. She was not going mad. Drafts may whistle about the room, draperies may flutter, fires may dip and brighten, but floorboards did not squeak on their own.

Vivian paced before the tapestry, the wood creaking beneath her feet. Chilly air slipped under her nightdress, blew strands of her hair.

She crossed her arms, nearly shivering, and stopped where the air blew the hardest. How could air blow with such force if she were on the opposite wall from the window? Not only that, the window was closed.

Vivian reached a tentative hand out to the tapestry. The frayed weave was rough against her fingertips as she pushed and poked the fabric. She felt nothing but sturdy wall and then...

"Dear Lord, of course!"

Vivian lifted the edge of the wall-hanging and a blast of air rushed against her skin. The thin, black rectangle in the stones must be an opening to a secret passageway!

A knock at the door startled Vivian. She dropped the tapestry and stepped away from the wall.

"Vivian. May I come in?" Lord Ashworth.

She glanced around for her robe. Where was it? She'd been weak and half-faint when she was brought to bed earlier.

The door latch clicked as Vivian bent to lift open the trunk lid.

"Faith..."

Her knees weakened at the seductive purr in his voice. She rose and turned to face him. A bottomless hunger darkened his stormy eyes, desperation lurked in the tightness of his lips.

Despite her fright of a few moments ago, a dizzying tingle raced down her legs. Her dream came rushing back and the memory of her shattering release stilled her breath. The air between them sizzled, snapped. Drafts surrounded her skin like a lover's caress, tightened her nipples and dried her mouth.

Vivian stared at him, at the rising chest under his white shirt, and the precise cut of cloth on his muscular legs.

Lord Ashworth cleared his throat then thrust a hand through his hair. "Vivian, I came in to check on you. I heard voices. I..."

His voice trailed off as his gaze swept down the front of her nightgown. She glanced down to see her nipples poking through the thin white fabric.

She crossed her arms over her chest and glanced away. "I heard a noise. Someone was in my room, watching me."

"Surely not."

Vivian lifted her chin, challenged his stare. "I am not hearing things. I know someone was in here."

He clenched his fists but kept his face unreadable. Something flickered in his eyes. Was it disbelief, anger? She'd not tell him she knew about the secret passage, not until she found out where it led.

"So you are feeling better then?"

His quick change of subject proved his uneasiness in her words.

Vivian nodded, her cheeks warmed. She'd just had the most sensual dream of her life. How would that not make anyone feel better? "I am quite recovered, thank you."

Lord Ashworth crossed the room and stopped before her. His sandalwood scent surged through her bloodstream. Desire and tension crackled between them. Heat infused her body, scorched her skin. She held her breath and waited for his touch. Her pulse crashed against her eardrums like waves upon a shore.

His hand brushed at her forehead, across the bandage. "Shall I remove this for you, Miss Suttley?"

Down between her legs, a desperate yearning swelled.

Dear Lord, she couldn't take this any longer. Lord Ashworth had somehow taken away her fear of a man's touch and now drove her mad with desire. Was she only to find relief in dreams under the cloak of mystery?

Gently, he peeled back the bandage. Vivian studied his lips, the dip in the center, the brush of whiskers along his jaw.

"Ah, there now." His warm breath sent shivers down her spine. "The cut wasn't too deep. You shouldn't have a scar."

Vivian shrugged. "Having a scar would not bother me."

Darkness clouded his features, narrowed his eyes. "What do you know of it?"

He spun away but Vivian moved after him. She didn't intend to offend him, she merely told the truth as she knew it.

She reached out to his face and cupped it with her palm. He was about to brush her off until her fingers traced down the gash on his cheek. He melted.

His eyes fluttered closed, his lips slackened, his breathing went from harsh to calm.

Vivian stroked the line, proving its existence did not give her pause. He was not a monster for it. Indeed, it only proved he was as mortal as anyone else. And the ripeness of his pain, coupled with the defensive anger, proved he was a man.

Lord Ashworth opened his eyes. His gaze devoured her like a man starving in the desert. He swept down and enveloped her body in his, nudging his leg between her thighs, his mouth slanting upon hers.

Vivian accepted his tongue, tasted a hint of brandy. His kiss was hungry, firm, and yet vulnerable. She gave herself over to his demands, to his quest for control, knowing he yearned to forget his loneliness as she did hers.

His arousal pressed against the curve of her hip. Her inner

core throbbed, hurt for his fulfillment.

Lord Ashworth cupped her bottom, pulling her firmly against him, moving her along his shaft. Quivers scattered through her blood, pinched at her nipples, sparked in her groin. Dear Lord, she was ready to strip herself bare for him.

He rubbed her along his unbending iron, his kiss passionate and dangerous, his tongue plundering her mouth with a hazardous urgency.

One hand left her bottom and snaked its way up her gown to capture her breast. He squeezed it, flicked his thumb across the nipple. Vivian moaned.

His pull on her hastened, his grip tightened.

A wave rose within her, lifted her on her toes, pressed her against his straining erection. She thrust her hips forward.

Lord Ashworth broke off the kiss and nuzzled behind her ear. His tongue lapped at the curve of her neck.

She reached around his waist, holding on to him, feeling his strength and power under her fingertips.

His hands lowered to her hips and yanked her nightdress up her legs. Vivian shuddered as warm, thick fingers caressed her bare thighs, then cradled her bottom. Fingers kneaded her skin, urgent and desperate.

Pain suddenly sliced through her burning hunger. She gasped.

"What is it?" His voice was gruff, yet alarmed.

She clenched her teeth, tried to will the tenderness away. But when he pressed upon the spot again, she could not withhold her whimper.

Lord Ashworth did not ask again. He spun her around and lifted the gown, exposing her flesh to the drafty air.

"Vivian! What's happened?"

Shame clogged in her throat. Hot tears stung her eyes. "I—I thought they would be gone by now."

His fingertips glided across the various marks on her

bottom and waist, an unexpected sensuality blooming at the gentle caress. The cuts and welts must have diminished to bruises.

He let the gown drop and turned her back to face him. The room stilled, heavy with raw emotion. Fury contorted Lord Ashworth's features, deepened his scar. His gray eyes narrowed, dark and perilous. "Who did this to you, Vivian? Tell me and I will see to it that he never injures you or anyone else again."

But she could not tell him. She could not let Lord Ashworth know of her connection to Martin Crawford. She used their association to find a safe harbor. Admitting to the relationship would only destroy her sanctity, bring peril to this refuge. Ruin her chance at escape.

His jaw clenched. A vein throbbed at his temple.

Finally, he turned and paced away from her, a tense power caged in his stance. He stopped at the door separating their rooms and cast a glance over his shoulder. A surprising mixture of concern and despondency lurked in his gaze.

"You've known a lover, haven't you?"

Vivian held her breath. Would that be her ultimate dismissal? Would he only wed a virgin? But she could not lie to him, for certainly he would one day learn the truth. Vivian nodded, saying nothing more.

Lord Ashworth's face relaxed slightly and yet his eyes remained uncertain. She knew not what he thought at the moment, whether her wounds and confession had proved an aid to her cause or thwarted it.

He whispered good night and disappeared into his bedchamber. The click of the door extinguished the low hum pulsing in her bloodstream.

Catherine watched the gloomy sunrise from her window, a troubling abyss widened in her stomach. Despite being given the "best" room in the manor, she still could not grow accustomed to the peeling wallpaper and fraying tapestries. She had not slept well since she arrived.

Desperation did bizarre things to people. Who would have thought it would lead her back to Charles, back to the man she forced herself to forget?

She once loved him, or loved the thought of being married to him. He had status, prestige and good looks. Her friends were jealous of their courting. He'd been the perfect man. The perfect match. Until that night.

Catherine drew in a shuddering breath and banged her fist on the cold window ledge.

Mystery still surrounded the events of that day. She'd heard various reports from different sources, including Charles, on what occurred. None made much sense. But a few things remained clear in the end.

A prostitute had been killed. Charles was found covered in her blood. A huge gash destroyed his face.

Catherine doubted he had actually killed the woman. The magistrate seemed to believe him, as well. Yet, the scandal spread through London's elite faster than the latest fashions. By all accounts, Viscount Ashworth was ruined. In every sense of the word. Catherine and her parents did not want to be connected to the downfall in any way.

And yet, here she stood, in his remote manor. She was not only willing to seduce him but to marry the man. She quite possibly could one day bear his children.

Desperation.

Damn Lord Wainscott and his failed business ventures. Ironic that her first intended husband lost all but his money and the man she married kept all but his money.

"My lady?"

"Come in, Martha."

Her maid scurried in and did a quick curtsey. "Are you ready to dress, my lady?"

Catherine nodded and stood. She sighed as Martha retrieved her dress for the day and set about preparing the toilet.

She missed her morning rides in Hyde Park, the afternoon calls, the evening dances. She should be making the rounds this year, hunting for the perfect husband to give her what she deserved.

Instead she was in Silverstone Manor, in God-knows-where northern England. The weather was dreadful, the house wretched and her prey resistant.

Damn the dowager, who had made this trip seem like an effortless endeavor. Rekindle Charles's love for her and capture his hand in marriage. Neither of them anticipated his opposition or that this supposed fiancée would still be present. The Dowager was certain the chit would be long gone by now.

Catherine pulled her gaze from her reflection in the window pane. She did not like who looked back at her. Already the gray dreariness of this place had cast its shadows upon her skin.

"Tell me, Martha, what do you think of Silverstone Manor?"

The girl blanched, her lip trembled. "It-it is right nice, my lady. Very grand indeed."

"Don't be concerned you will displease me. I want your honest thoughts. I find it quite dreadful myself."

Martha's shoulders relaxed. "Yes, my lady. I shivered as we came up the drive and have suffered no peace since we arrived."

"It has quite an imposing appearance."

"I-I fear the ghosts." Martha averted her eyes.

Catherine herself had wondered at the noises echoing in the halls, the drafts wandering through each room. But she did not believe in the mystical.

"No ghosts, Martha, only the poor upkeep of what was once a grandiose manor."

"Yes, my lady. But there are the rumors..."

"Rumors? Do tell, please."

Martha bit her lip, her young face puckered in what was either fright or embarrassment. She looked down at her hands. "I've heard there is a monster who roams these halls at night."

Catherine chuckled. "Does he look for supper?"

"No, my lady, he looks for a woman."

"A woman? Any woman?"

Martha nodded. "They say if he cannot catch you, he will instead invade your dreams. He will either frighten you away with his evil or shock your feminine sensibilities."

Feminine sensibilities indeed. Catherine lifted an eyebrow, not at all concerned of a monster within these walls. Likely they were the rumors started by Charles himself to dissuade any visitors. This information only proved that her intended husband was determined and a bit mad.

But it did give her an idea.

"Did you learn these from the servants here?"

Martha shook her head. "When we stopped in the village to rest the horses, a lady at the tavern issued a warning."

And her maid must have kept it silent fearing that Catherine would see nothing amiss at the manor upon the cliff.

"Have you confirmed any of these rumors with Lord Ashworth's staff?"

"No, my lady, they tend to keep to themselves. I do not even know some of their names."

Catherine would have to change that. She had no qualms about using whatever means necessary to get her way. If she journeyed all the way out here, subjected herself to the misery of this house, she would get what she came for.

Charles would bend to her will. If seduction did not succeed, she had other ideas. Blackmail usually worked miracles.

Catherine nodded at the rose dress and stood while Martha dressed her. The sun had risen to the tip of the nearest hill, spreading sunshine amidst the gathering clouds. Sheep dotted the highest pastures, lakes scattered throughout the peaks. Summer did not seem so unpleasant here.

She would not stay for winter.

Martha finished lacing the stays and Catherine took that moment to turn to her maid. "Tell me, do you wish to be away from this place shortly?"

"Yes, my lady. I am very unsettled here."

Catherine smiled. "As am I. Therefore I could use your help in this matter."

"My help?"

"Do what you can to get to know the servants here. And learn all that you can about the home's master."

Martha's lips flattened. She clearly did not like being put in the role of a spy and yet the girl wanted out of this house as soon as possible.

Catherine patted her shoulder. "Don't you see? The sooner you tell me something of note, the sooner I can use it against Lord Ashworth and the sooner we can be on our way back to London."

The girl finally nodded. "I will do my best, my lady."

"Ah, that's what I wanted to hear." Catherine turned again, preparing herself for the remainder of the dressing. "Now, let us continue with our chore so that I may present myself at breakfast. There are other mysteries I must unravel."

Chapter Twelve

Ashworth stood out in the stables, where the mists crept up the cliff and enveloped him like a dream. He wished this were a dream, one where he could lose himself to tranquility. One where he could end this perpetual loneliness.

He had not ridden in weeks, content to entertain himself with Harry or books or other matters of keeping the manor running. But now he wanted to be free of the house. Freedom beckoned to him with the call of seabirds. Catherine's presence unsettled him, ruffled his feathers a bit. Vivian's presence disturbed him, troubled his every movement and thought.

He climbed upon Demon, a chestnut stallion who should be ridden much more frequently. They took off behind the manor, the wind blowing through his hair. Demon knew the paths well enough, freeing Ashworth to exercise his suppressed energy. He must release this agonizing force somehow or he'd use it to knock down every stone in the manor.

Fury, lust, doubts and frustration roared in his veins. He knew not a moment's peace since these women had invaded his house. Nay, his troubles multiplied daily. By the minute, even.

He slowed Demon's pace as they neared Briarwater. They approached the rocky shore where Vivian found her treasure. She sought to protect an innocent from a hungry fox.

But who protected her?

His jaw clenched at the memory of the bruises on her backside. Their circular shape led him to believe they had once been bite marks.

Vivian's confirmation that she had lain with someone eased the deepest concerns that The Monster—himself?—had caused those injuries. Part of him still feared he had. The other part of him raged at the bloody bastard who would inflict such damage on her.

Ashworth stopped near the water to calm his furious pulse and clear his mind. He watched the ducks and geese paddle their way across the lake. As a child his father would take him out on Briarwater in a small boat. He loved the lazy movements, the gentle rocking to soothe his bitterness. He had dreamed then of being the captain of a ship, to live forever on the water.

That foolish dream didn't last long.

He turned Demon around. Harry would like it here. But too many others were about to ask questions.

They trotted the paths of Briarfell until the unspent vigor dissipated within his blood. This was what he needed. A good, solitary ride to sort his thoughts and dispel his restless energy.

The morning's last rays of sunlight guided him toward Silverstone Manor, the light breeze gusting into a strong wind. He welcomed the approaching rain, the rousing storms. It kept Harry inside and visitors away.

As he neared the house, he saw a woman riding sidesaddle upon another of his underutilized horses. For the briefest moment his heart clenched, breath paused in his throat. But then he saw a glimpse of gold hair beneath the hat and his stomach tumbled.

Not Catherine. Not now.

Ashworth trotted Demon down the slope toward her, steeling himself for her company. She had stopped near Vivian's garden, eyeing the tangle with look of disdain.

Her chin rose as he approached. "Ah, Charles, lovely morning, isn't it?"

"Most mornings here are, but the weather shall be upon us soon."

He started past her.

"What is this? I saw Miss Suttley working here the other day."

Ashworth stopped, glanced at her, squeezing his gloved hands. "Miss Suttley has asked to restore this flower garden."

She raised a delicate eyebrow. "Ah, that would explain the delivery I saw arrive on a cart this morning." Her gaze traveled beyond Vivian's garden to the overgrown yew trees and crumbling statues. "I am to assume then that you do not employ a gardener?"

He shifted back in the saddle and crossed his arms. "Nor a scullery maid, nursemaid, butler, footman...need I go on?"

Humor twinkled in her eyes. "So if Miss Suttley is your gardener, does that leave me with the work of a nursemaid?"

He'd much rather see her toil as a scullery maid, but he kept his opinion to himself. "Miss Suttley rather enjoys the work."

Catherine quickly cleared away her smirk. "I see."

Ashworth gave her a slight nod. "Enjoy your ride, Lady Wainscott."

"I need a companion...a guide, don't you think? I'm not familiar with these hills."

"I'll send my groomsman out to accompany you." He turned his back to her, nudging Demon to a canter.

"Charles!" The word sliced through the swirling air.

He was tempted to continue forward. Eventually Catherine must be dissuaded by something. The weather, the house, his rudeness...

She rode up beside him. "You were not at breakfast this morning."

He didn't look at her. "I often take my breakfast elsewhere."

"And Miss Suttley? Was she with you?"

Vivian did not come down? Since she had come to Silverstone, she had always eaten in the morning room whether he joined her or not.

Ashworth swallowed, a sudden compulsion coming over him to check on Vivian's welfare. "I can only assume Miss Suttley was still feeling too ill to leave her room."

"Ah, yes, and what was it that made her so ill again? Crawling under bushes in the rain to chase a phantom?"

He tensed, gripped the reins. "Pettiness does not become you, Lady Wainscott. Have a good day."

Sending Demon into a full run, Ashworth left Catherine far behind and prayed the impending storm would swallow her in its fury.

Vivian held the candleholder firmly and slipped behind the tapestry. Darkness immediately engulfed her, save for the small glow of the flame. She swallowed, straightened her shoulders and forced herself to continue on. If someone was using this passageway to spy on her then she would brave the darkness to see where the trail led.

She first turned to the left, seeing the hint of light a bit further down. Only a few paces and she was at another cutout in the wall.

Vivian gently pushed a heavy fabric aside and peered into the room. It belonged to Lord Ashworth. She recognized the black bedcovers, the walnut triangular stand. Her gaze fell upon the tub by the fireplace.

Her breath caught, as she remembered his touch, the way in which he was able to transform her hesitation into desire.

Quickly she withdrew into the passageway. So now she had Lord Ashworth at the top of her suspect list. It would take him only a matter of minutes to go from his room over to hers and back again.

It could very well be him who entered her room as she slept. He could be out in the halls at night. Would he terrorize her in the dead of night?

Should she fear him or seduce him?

Vivian sighed and withdrew from his room. A dead end greeted her just behind his entryway, so she retraced her steps past her bedchamber.

Her candle illuminated multiple spider webs, dust and crumbling stones. She'd not be able to go far with it if she wanted light for her return journey.

Vivian rounded a corner and poked her head into a few empty rooms. Mostly unused bedchambers and dressing rooms. At the very end she came upon a set of stairs leading up to the highest floor.

She glanced at the candle, then back at the rickety, wooden steps. Noises sounded above. Footsteps, deep laughter.

Curiosity edged her onward. Using one hand to hold the candle and the other for the railing, she began the climb.

Her dress caught under her foot on the third rung. Vivian slipped, but caught herself before landing on the floor. The loud tear of her skirt echoed in the small space.

The noises above her stopped.

Dear Lord, had someone heard?

She gathered up her skirt and hobbled back into the darkness, the candle now dripping onto her fingers.

"Don't!"

The shout stopped her cold. She stood stark still and pressed herself against the cool stones. Vivian held her breath, waiting.

"Please..."

The plea came from a child! A child lived here in Silverstone Manor? One of the servant's offspring? But if so, why would they be upstairs where the nursery or schoolroom must be?

Her pulse roared in her eardrums but she didn't move.

"No," answered the firm, male voice.

The child whined, then she heard footsteps carry them

away.

Vivian lifted her skirt again and hurried down the long passageway back to her room. She had to poke her head through several openings before finding the right one.

She slipped past the tapestry to hear hard banging on her door. "Vivian, I insist you open the door this moment or I will have Mrs. Plimpton arrive with her keys."

Lord Ashworth!

"Just—just a moment." She glanced down at her dress, which was not only torn but covered in dirt and cobwebs. She wouldn't have enough time to change, nor was she ever accomplished at quick thinking.

"Are you still ill?"

Damn him and his concern right now. But she was certain that the voice she heard upstairs was not his. Even Lord Ashworth could not have moved so quickly from that spot to her door.

Vivian smoothed out her dress as best she could and unlocked the door.

The room diminished in size when he entered, filling the space with the breadth of his shoulders and heated emotion of his gaze. His eyes, at first dark with concern, widened the moment he actually saw her.

"What have you gotten yourself into this time?"

For the second day in a row, she stood before him scratched, torn, and blemished. The thought of her becoming a viscount's wife suddenly seemed so ludicrous, she giggled.

The corner of his lips turned up, relief breaking over the tenseness of his shoulders. He came before her and started picking things from her hair.

"I do say, Miss Suttley, you have quite the knack for dirtying yourself."

She seized the chance. "Rather like a little boy, I suppose."

Lord Ashworth immediately stiffened, but then quickly

released his tension. She bewildered him even more. "I think you may be worse than I ever was as a boy."

He brushed his hands over her shoulders. Her mouth dried at his touch. His hands moved lower then stopped at her breasts. Vivian waited, her nipples suddenly pebbling and begging for his caress.

She heard him gulp. Then his gaze shot up to hers once he noticed the skirt.

"What *were* you doing in here, Vivian?"

Would he believe she was crawling under the bed for something? Reaching out the window? Dusting out the fireplace? She never was good at coming up with lies or excuses.

Instead, she must distract him. She glanced down to his waist, then to the swelling between his legs. Her mouth watered, heat swelled deep inside. Why was it that awareness pulsed so cruelly anytime he was near?

Vivian reached for his hand and brought it to her breast. "I believe you have missed something."

Chapter Thirteen

Ashworth's hand seized the treasure she offered. His growl reverberated in the room. His flesh throbbed with a reckless hunger.

"Vivian."

But he did not remove his hand. Instead, his thumb drew circles around her nipple. Her eyes lowered, cheeks flushed. She melted, fire upon ice.

Ashworth nudged his leg between hers, drawing her close to him, enraptured by the sweet scent of her hair. Covered in dirt, scratched by thorns, it didn't matter Vivian's appearance. He lusted for her like a hound after a fox.

Passion roared through his veins. His fingers cupped her breasts then moved around to her slender waist. Her breath hitched, back arched.

Pulse rampant, Ashworth pushed her backward until she was against the bedpost. He trapped her between his arms then lowered his lips to feast upon her neck. She tasted of flowers and dust and feminine beauty.

He lifted his head and stared at her, breathing wildly as Vivian opened several buttons at her throat. She was seducing him again. What did she want of him? Could she possibly know that he would give her just about anything to find relief in her warmth?

When the white lace of her chemise peeked from beneath the buttons, Ashworth snatched her wrists and raised them above her head. Pleasure buzzed in his head, fear tore at his heart, rage pounded in his gut.

"Why, Vivian? Why do you torture me this way?"

Her dusky eyes blinked at him. "Because you equally torture me."

He thrust his hips against her stomach. "Do you feel that? You tempt me into danger."

She bit her lip, her breasts rising and falling with rapid breaths.

With his free hand, he traced a line down her jaw. "You don't know what you ask of me, why it is impossible for me to deliver what you seek."

Her gaze sharpened. "Nothing is impossible. You make your choices as it pleases you."

"You still want to wed me, Vivian?"

She lifted her chin. "Yes."

He let her hands drop but did not back away. Her lips were mere inches from his, enticing him beyond reason. But he must have the answers he sought.

"Why?"

The word hung in the air, twirling with the wind gusting at the window.

Vivian sighed, lowered her eyes. "I cannot go back."

"Because of those marks on you?" His jaw tightened at the thought of the pain she must have endured.

"I left much misery behind."

"You came to me as an escape?"

"This seemed the perfect place to hide."

But what or who did she hide from? Ashworth swept several black strands of hair from her face, stared at her mouth. "Yet you've no idea what you've found."

"Perhaps not."

Her vibrant lips lured him into temptation and he nibbled

at their succulence. She relaxed against him, pressing her mouth to him with a desperate fervor. Ashworth cupped her jaw in both hands, controlled her every move.

He plunged his tongue inside, sweeping against her in a fury of strokes. Liquid fire erupted in his bones, weakened his knees.

Vivian's fingertips tickled up his legs like butterfly wings. He moaned, then gasped, as her hand reached in his trousers and closed around his shaft.

Ashworth reared back, clenched his hands into fists. With an intense curiosity, he glanced down at her caress. Her slender fingers moved across the rise in his breeches, stroking the length, then circling him at the tip.

He shuddered. All coherent thought fled.

Immobile, he dared not move away from the excruciatingly sweet sensation. Instead, he watched, his pulse thumped madly in his throat, sweat collected at his collar. When he could bear it no longer, he squeezed his eyes shut. Tension built within him like a powerful storm. A tingle raced throughout his limbs, curled his toes, then sparked into his groin.

The memory of her pink-tipped breasts rose in his mind. He saw himself licking them, imagined his fingers plunging inside of her.

His breathing lurched, his hands gripped her waist.

Vivian moved faster, fondling him with just the right amount of pressure. He wanted to pound himself into her but he dared not move.

"Oh, Vivian..."

Through the crashing of his heartbeat he heard her whimper. She was denying herself in order to please him. He looked down to see her lips bright, her skin slick with sweat. Her arousal impaired his thinking.

Ashworth needed to stop this torture, but he couldn't. He'd let it go too far, found himself struggling at her mercy. It had been so long since a woman touched him. So long—

Vivian's fingers tickled the tip of his flesh and he exploded with a moan. Scalding fluid emptied from his body in glorious release. He tried to catch his breath and slow his heart.

Finally, he glanced down at her face, surprised to notice only a blank stare in her eyes.

Ashworth blinked, looked again and saw pale, pinched skin. Then blood. Pungent, red liquid. Everywhere.

His gut cramped, bile rolled in his stomach.

No! Not again.

He stumbled back from her and shook his head. Lungs seizing, he quickly glimpsed at her again.

But this time Vivian was normal, with a flushed face and distraught gaze.

Her hand reached toward him then slowly dropped back to her side. "It happened again, didn't it?"

Ashworth said nothing, but gulped in mouthfuls of air.

"Why won't you tell me about it?"

His temples pounded. How could he tell her when he didn't know himself? Was he a killer? Had he once murdered a woman in the crest of passion? "You...you are not safe here."

Her eyes softened. "I won't be frightened of you."

He swallowed while his heart beat furiously against his ribs. "You—you've run from one misfortune to another perhaps far worse. I'll not let you stay."

"But Lady Wainscott—"

Ashworth wiped his forehead with the back of his arm. "I'll have her gone from here shortly. And you will be directly behind her."

Vivian stared at him with those mysterious eyes, her lips set and determined. She would challenge his command. Her motivation to remain was as strong as his was to have her go.

Damn her.

She was an angel. She was the devil.

Vivian sent him to heaven and then plunged him back

down to hell.

Cʒ

The chandeliers blazed too brightly upon the floor, casting the dancers in an eerie glow. Martin tensed with the rage knotting his stomach. This was the sixth ball he'd attended since his mother sent him a stack of invitations, yet he'd not found Vivian or the baron's cousin.

The burn of a heated gaze pulled his attention over to the far corner of the room, where a woman stared at him without scruple. Her large breasts peeked above the deep blue bodice of her gown and she raised a dark eyebrow at his interested grin. He licked his lips. His groin tightened.

Martin surmised that his voluptuous, middle-aged admirer was a widow on the prowl. Just what he needed to dispel this gnawing frustration.

He crossed the room as the sounds of the waltz came to an end. Stopping at the refreshment table, Martin pretended to look for something to quench his thirst. What he needed quenched was something entirely different.

The woman slid beside him, her heady scent warmed his blood, aroused his cock. Her gloved hand brushed against his elbow.

"Good evening." He kept his voice light and pleasant.

"Evening to you, sir." She opened up her fan and waved it against her face. She was not the most beautiful woman he'd ever seen, but she was enough to satisfy his hunger. "I'm amazed I have not seen you before."

Martin curled his lip. "I am not often in town."

"Oh?" The answer seemed to interest her more. She moved slightly so that her breasts now pressed against his arm.

He steeled himself, clenched his teeth. He'd not had a woman since that whore a week ago but he also did not want to be swayed from his purpose. Vivian Suttley was somewhere in this city and he would find her.

"Have you pledged yourself to dance the whole evening?" Her sultry, blue eyes winked at him. "Or do you have the time for a walk in the garden perhaps?"

Martin took a swallow of tart lemonade as if he couldn't care less for her offer. "Actually, I was looking for someone."

"Someone? And old friend?"

"You could say that."

She skimmed her tongue across her lower lip. "I believe I am acquainted with everyone worthy of knowing. Perhaps I can help you."

Martin straightened his shoulders, finding it odd that she had yet to ask his name. He cared not for hers. He used people the way a farmer used his horse. They could plow his field or take him to town, it didn't matter to him.

He slid her a sideways glance. "Perhaps you can. Rather than the gardens, are you intimately knowledgeable of this lovely house? The architecture is quite striking."

His companion smiled, her eyes sparkled. "As a matter of fact, I am. Follow me."

With the crush of the crowd, Martin doubted their absence would be noticed. Not that he cared for that either. As a man, he was permitted to seek his pleasures, as long as they held within the boundaries. He could not rape a debutante, but he could fornicate with a willing widow.

She proceeded to point out several rooms, none of which he took much note of. A few things caught his eye if he had a mind to pocket them for profit. But right now he had other more pressing matters on his mind.

Achieve pleasure. Locate Vivian.

At the far end of the dimly glowing hallway, the widow opened a door and shut it quickly behind him. The room was dark, save for the glow of the moon through the windows. The smell of dust and leather told him he was in a library.

"I simply must be the first to have you," she cooed as her fingers crawled up his chest.

Martin snatched her wrist and slammed her back against the door. Her breath hitched, his cock throbbed. He plundered her mouth, greedily suckling her tongue until she writhed against him.

"You know of everyone you say?" He squeezed her breast.

She whimpered. He didn't know if it was from tenderness or desire. Nor did he care.

"Yes," she breathed. "Whom do you search for?"

"Vivian Suttley, the daughter of Lord Whistlebury, baron."

She reached around and grabbed at his ass, pinching him with the same strength he'd done her. Reckless fire blazed through his veins. He bent low and licked the tops of her breasts.

"Oh my!" She gasped, bucked her hips. "I think I recall that...that name. When was her first season in London?"

Martin couldn't remember. His brain was fuzzy. He pressed his lips against her ear. "Last year. No, two years ago."

The widow reached for his cock. His whole body shuddered as his arousal pulsed in her hand. "Take it off. Oh, please hurry."

He snatched her wrists again and clenched them behind her back. "Vivian. Tell me where to find her."

"I...I don't know. I don't recall seeing her this year." Her hips thrust out to him again. "Please..."

Martin reached under her skirt and yanked at the petticoats and other annoying garments blocking his quest. "What about Lady Ethington, Lord Whistlebury's cousin? Do you know of her?"

She threw her head back, panted. "Yes, damn you. I know of her."

He let go of her wrists and unbuttoned his pants. His pulse

crashed inside his skull. "Which homes does she frequent? Will she come here tonight?"

"No. She won't be...here...tonight."

Martin dropped his trousers, pushed her skirt up and out of the way. He lifted her leg then slammed his way inside her waiting heat. He pounded her relentlessly, the ravenous passion welling up to an excruciating fervor.

The widow cried out, her channel convulsing around his cock. But he wasn't finished.

"Tell...me...how...to...find...Lady...Ethington."

Martin pulled out of her and in a swift movement, borne from years of practice, bent her across the arm of the nearest chair.

"You'll not...not find her at the balls."

Martin licked her bare cheeks, then bit them. She squealed and trembled, excited at the pain he created for her. He nipped the soft skin several more times then straightened. "Where is she?"

"At...at home. She's an invalid. Hasn't—hasn't come to her London house for years."

Bloody hell! Sharp fury hurtled through his bloodstream, dimming his sight. Which one of them had lied? Vivian or her father?

Wrath merged with sadistic craving. He plunged inside her wetness for lubrication and then forced his slick cock into her tight hole. She screamed, then moaned.

Martin thrust, oblivious to anything but intense rage and blinding lust, until he collapsed in satisfied exhaustion.

Chapter Fourteen

Could a flower grow in the shadow of such a menacing structure?

Vivian glanced over at the manor. It stood as severe and daunting as its master. The afternoon sun set on the other side, leaving long shadows to slither through her garden like a wary snake.

If this garden grew, survived, matured, then certainly there was hope for Silverstone Manor. And for its master.

With the majority of the vines and dead brush cleared away, Vivian could now begin her planting. She'd secured a shovel from Pinkley, resisted his reluctant offer of help, and set out the seeds and saplings.

The temperature was surprisingly warm with only a scant breeze to cool her skin. Vivian glanced upward. No clouds rolled over the cliff, no hint of rain spiced the air. Normally she'd relish such a delightful change in the weather, but today rain would help her garden.

She brushed the hair from her face with the back of her hand and sighed. She'd best get started on her next chore of digging.

"I could have someone out here to help you with that."

Vivian sucked in her breath, her nerves afire. Without looking behind her, she began to dig her third hole. "Mr. Pinkley offered but I declined his aid."

Lord Ashworth chuckled. "And yet that does not surprise

me."

Her lips curved but she continued her task. "About Mr. Pinkley offering or me declining?"

His hand captured her elbow, warmth spread to her fingertips. "You refusing, of course." His voice shimmied down her spine, stealing her breath. "Pinkley does surprise me, however. He told me he didn't like you."

Vivian straightened then wheeled around. "He told you such a thing? Why, I've been nothing but kind since I arrived."

Lord Ashworth's laughter danced through the branches and across her heart. "Pinkley has said nothing of the sort. But I did get you to look at me, didn't I?"

Vivian's lips twitched. So perhaps she had been avoiding him for the last day. Not that she'd been rude exactly, just a somewhat shy. Something about what transpired a day or so ago in her room left her feeling a bit uneasy, distracted. For just the tiniest moments, he'd lost control. He'd allowed her to guide him, to bring him pleasure.

Feeling her cheeks flush, Vivian turned back to the hole. "You are devious, my lord."

"Yes, perhaps. But I do what's necessary." He took the shovel from her hands. "Now tell me what is necessary."

She lifted her eyes to his face, startled at the genuine shine of concentration upon it. His gray eyes held determination and a slice of amusement.

"Certainly you aren't asking to help me turn up this garden."

"And why not?" His lips bowed, softening the line of his scar. "Do I not look capable of yielding such a tool?"

"Well, yes but—"

"Perhaps you think I lack the skill or the strength to lift the heavy clumps of dirt as you do."

"No, not at all—"

He drove the point into the soft earth. "Then it must be that you think me too full of myself to sully my hands and clothes."

Vivian laughed aloud. He was more capable than any man she'd ever met, stronger than any man she might ever meet again. As for getting himself sullied…

"You told me the other night that you did not get dirty as a child."

The muscles of his shoulders and back flinched beneath his white shirt as he tossed a bit of dirt onto the pile. "I said no such thing."

"Yes, you did. You told me that I got dirty far more than you ever did as a boy."

His gaze raked over her dress. Awareness eddied through her bloodstream. Her mouth dried.

"And today you are yet again dirtier than I ever was."

"But boys are rough and tumble. They like to climb trees and hunt for frogs." She twirled around, her mind alive with possibilities. "If a boy lived here he would climb that trellis near the kitchen. And he'd find himself at Briarwater each afternoon looking for tadpoles. I'm sure he'd—"

"Miss Suttley."

Vivian turned back at the whispered words. Pain—and was it sadness?—lurked within his eyes. For a moment, she could see through his careful façade to the vulnerable man underneath. He spoke volumes to her without saying a word. Whether the boy she heard had any relation to Lord Ashworth or not, he had once experienced the overpowering love for a child.

She waited for him to continue. He looked as if he debated telling her something, but then decided against it and went back to his digging.

Vivian eased off the topic of the mysterious boy. "So you spent most summers elsewhere then."

"No." He grunted as he lifted a heavy yield of dirt. "I spent many summers here. But I wasn't permitted to do most things you mentioned. As the oldest son, the only son, I had far too much to study."

Vivian's throat tightened. She put her hand on his arm and stilled his movements. "You weren't permitted to be a child."

His gaze met hers. She gasped at the rawness she saw within. She brushed his cheek tenderly. "There must first be the boy before there can be the man."

His dirt-covered hands cupped her jaw. "Vivian..."

"What is it, my lord? What are you afraid to tell me?"

The light breeze blew a scented ribbon of her new flowers between them. Concentrating, he stared at her, struggled within himself.

She wanted him to tell her of the boy, for she would not mention it unless she saw or heard him again. But Vivian knew that the child was only one of many secrets lurking within the stone walls of that house. Eventually she would uncover them and bring them to the light of day.

"I do say you lied to me." The frigid voice of Lady Wainscott ruined Vivian's chance for the day.

They turned in unison to find her standing at the edge of the upturned garden like an elegant flower. Her delicate pink stripes and vivid green bows must be the essence of London fashion yet it couldn't be more outlandish for Silverstone Manor.

Lord Ashworth tensed beside her. "In what manner have I lied, Lady Wainscott?"

"You said you did not employ a gardener. But it appears that you do. You are not only the master here but a servant, as well." The woman tried to lift her voice with humor but iciness weighed it down.

"Have you come to join us?" Steel replaced softness. Where a moment ago Lord Ashworth was quiet and vulnerable, he once again returned to the gruff man she'd first met.

Lady Wainscott gave a small snort. "While I'm sure it may

be fun to dig in the mud now and then, I'm afraid I'm not wearing the appropriate dress." Vivian cringed as a pair of chilly blue eyes perused her clothing. "But I see Miss Suttley has come abundantly prepared."

Embarrassment surged into anger. "I have others if you'd care to borrow one."

The other woman's face paled at the mere suggestion of it, but she recovered quickly and lifted her chin. "I think perhaps, Miss Suttley, it would behoove you to borrow some of my dresses. As a matter of fact, I have some I was ready to give my maid. I'll have them sent to your room instead."

Vivian clenched her hands. The nerve of this woman. It wasn't as if Vivian didn't own any nicer dresses or know how to present herself in the proper situations. But when she ran from her home during the night, fear replacing the blood pumping through her heart, she did not have the time to plan or pack everything.

"Miss Suttley." Lord Ashworth's voice rang out like village church bells.

She turned to look at him and drew in a sharp intake of breath at the distant mask he now wore. It was as if the previous moments never occurred. She cleared her throat, moving aside the sudden welling of defeat and emptiness. "Yes, my lord?"

"On this point I must agree with Lady Wainscott." His gaze held hers, not shying away from what appeared to be sudden betrayal. "You are in need of new clothing."

Vivian clenched her teeth to withhold her ire. Even if that were the case, was it necessary to say it in front of her conniving adversary? Had the man any sense at all or was he starting to feel something for his former love?

She set her chin. "I'll not wear her cast-offs." She doubted they would even fit her. And as she said it, she realized that the uptight woman was only goading her. She probably never intended to pass along her clothing.

"Of course not. I can have a dressmaker come to the manor or you can go into town, whichever you choose."

If the other villagers believed as the postmistress did, Vivian doubted a dressmaker would set foot upon this land. As long as they didn't lock the gates after her, she saw no other choice than to venture down to the village.

However, she would not let Lord Ashworth get away with injuring her pride so easily. She took the shovel from his hands and stabbed at the dirt.

"I am hopeful, my lord, that you will not expect me to continue working in this garden in a dress such as that." She lifted the shovel handle to point at the frilly pink and green costume. The sudden motion sent dirt soaring into the air and raining over both people standing behind her.

Vivian stifled a giggle. Lord Ashworth forced his grin into a frown. Lady Wainscott screamed, glared at her with murderous intent and then stomped back to the house.

He brushed the soil from his shirt, still struggling to keep his rigidity in check. "I believe that would have been even more amusing if you had done it deliberately."

She lifted her eyebrows. "How do you know I did not?"

He swept wayward strands from her face. "Because for all the fire you have burning inside of you, malice is not part of your character."

Despite the urge to brush her finger across his lips, Vivian remained immobile. "How do you know who I am?"

"You saved an egg from a hungry fox. You saw the possibility of beauty in a patch of dead vines." His voice dropped. "You touch me without revulsion."

She tightened her hold on the shovel, attempted to ignore the frantic beat of her heart. "Yet I do not know who you are."

His eyes hardened. "You do not want to know."

"Oh but I do."

"I—I believe I've done something horrible in the past. I don't want you to be a party to it."

Could it have something to do with the horrified looks that crossed his face after he touched her? It didn't matter. He needed tenderness and she needed to give it.

Vivian gave in to the impulse and traced her fingertip down his scar. "Sometimes we are the egg and sometimes we are the fox."

With the slightest shift, he leaned into her hand. "What I did is more terrifying than any fox, Miss Suttley."

"Every soul can be saved, my lord."

His eyes bored into hers, hope and uncertainty transforming pewter to brilliant silver. "Do you truly believe that?"

Every soul? Could Martin be saved or was he truly evil, not a man but a monster? Or was there a reason for his actions? Had something happened to him once to make him so loathsome?

It was not her place to judge, only to survive. Suddenly she wanted more from life than survival alone.

"Yes," she said at last. "I believe that. And now you must too."

"Tell me..." His voice hardened as he turned away from her. "Tell me why I must believe."

For the child she heard upstairs. For the pain reflecting in his gaze.

"Because I'll not leave this house until you do."

She meant, of course, that she'd not leave the house for good. Vivian made her trip to the dress shop that very afternoon. If Lord Ashworth wished to have her dressed more fashionably and he would pay for it, why should she resist?

Yet, as the carriage dropped her off at the corner, Vivian started to wonder if coming to the village again was a mistake. At the sight of the viscount's emblem, every person on the pavement stopped to look. Every eye watched her take the few short steps from the vehicle to the shop door.

What reputation did Lord Ashworth hold? Did his terrible act occur here among these people? Or did they only embrace the rumors and feed upon them like starving rats in a trash heap?

Vivian entered the dress shop and her shoulders dropped with a release of tension. The store held feminine, flowery scents. Although the room was no bigger than the dining room at Silverstone Manor, the smells alone were a welcome change.

A customer brushed past Vivian, giving her a quick glare on her way out the door.

Vivian glanced over the fabrics, alive with vivid colors and subdued pastels. How would she know what to choose? It had been so long since she'd had a fancy dress made. After her season in London, there seemed no real reason to spend money on nice clothes. Especially when her father declared he'd found her a husband.

She shivered. She could be Martin's wife now. Had she not run, she would be in his clutches. Morning would find her bruised and beaten. Nights would sink her into devastating darkness.

Yes, she'd made the right decision. Lord Ashworth was no monster like the man she'd left. He would keep her safe.

"I'll not take his credit."

Vivian looked up to see a shrewd woman with fierce brown eyes staring at her. "Pardon me?"

"The viscount. If'n he sent you without coins, I won't put your dresses on credit."

Stunned, Vivian could not bring herself to answer. She merely nodded, knowing the carriage driver held the money necessary to pay for her bill.

Those eyes drew up and down Vivian's body. "So, what'll he have you wear?"

"I—I don't know. A fine dinner dress, I suppose."

The dressmaker circled her. "Any particular color?"

"No. I mean, he didn't specify. What do you suggest?"

"For the mistress of a monster?"

"Mistress? Monster?" She wasn't sure which appalled her more.

The woman fingered a deep red silk. "You've heard the rumors, no doubt, and yet you continue to stay at that...that house."

Vivian lifted her chin. "I am in no harm in that manor, nor am I his mistress."

The dressmaker snorted. "Lord Ashworth isn't hiding himself up there for nothing. If he hasn't done something worth hiding for, then why haven't we ever seen him?"

"But everyone speaks of his scar. You must have seen him at some point."

"There's enough who work up there who've spoken of it. Looks like a monster, I've heard."

Looks like a monster. Done something worth hiding for.

Was she the fool not to believe as so many others did? Did she have a real reason to trust Lord Ashworth? Vivian's stomach plummeted. Every time her confidence soared something else came along to shake it up.

The woman lifted the blood red silk higher. "He refuses to marry, I hear."

"I am not his mistress."

"No?" Dark eyebrows rose. "Then why are you there?"

To marry him. Even to Vivian, it sounded hollow. She could give no other answer. In fact, she couldn't answer at all.

The dressmaker's smile did not reach her eyes. "Perhaps you'd care for something in green instead."

Vivian's throat suddenly tightened. With a sigh, she nodded.

"Green it is."

Chapter Fifteen

"I'm not fooled, you know."

Ashworth glanced up from the large stack of paperwork on his desk to see Catherine standing in the study doorway. Having cleaned up from the shower of dirt, she appeared as polished as any fine silverware. Hell, as any emerald or sapphire.

Silverstone Manor held none of those treasures within its walls.

He looked down with a sigh at another letter from his mother. She continued to insist he rekindle his love affair with Catherine. She was damned determined to give Harry a mother and bring them all to London. She would not master him. No matter what idle threats his mother issued, he would not marry.

"Charles. Did you hear me?"

"Yes, I heard." He still did not look at her. Maybe if he ignored her she would go away.

Instead she swept into the study, bathing the room in her lavender scent. "You can't pretend I am not here."

Growling, Ashworth crumpled the letter and tossed it into the fire. "Can't I?"

"I am more determined than you realize."

He lifted his gaze to find her nose wrinkled, hazel eyes staring at his scar. His gut clenched like he'd been dealt a swift blow. "You do not seek my love, you seek my money."

Her lips pursed. "Are you so certain?"

Rain gusted against the window. The candles dipped, drawing long shadows on the wall.

He shrugged then stood. "Whatever the reason, you waste your time."

"Because of Miss Suttley?"

At the mention of her name, Ashworth had the urge to see if she had returned. Instead he straightened his shoulders and poured himself a splash of brandy and ignored her question. "I feel nothing for you anymore."

With a rustle of her skirts, she was behind him. Her gloved hands moved down the sides of his arms. She leaned against his back, but the feel of her breasts did not tremble his heart or stir his groin. It was true: he held no passion for her.

"Oh, Charles, you loved me once. I'm certain there must still be something for me inside of you."

He lifted the cup to his mouth and swallowed the liquid in a gulp. "I don't believe you'd spend more than one extra day at Silverstone."

"Once we are married, why would I need to?"

Ashworth moved away from her clutches to the rain spotted glass. "Because this is where I live."

"You can come back with me to London."

But even as she said it, he saw the panic in her eyes. Catherine didn't want him. He curled a lip. "I'm not fooled, you know."

Her cheeks bloomed scarlet. "Fine then. Marriages do not have to be for love. There can be a mutual benefit for both of us."

"Oh? Do tell."

"I am in need of funds. You are in need of a bride. It's as simple as that."

Ashworth crossed his arms and leaned his shoulder against

the mantel. "You forgot one thing in your simple plan."

Her delicate chin lifted. "Oh? Do tell."

"Miss Suttley. We are already engaged."

Her laugh tittered in the dark room. Wind moaned around the corner of the house. "Yes, that's what you said. But she has no chaperone, no family, no decorum. I cannot fathom why she is truly here unless as your mistress. But I do not expect her to become your wife."

Ashworth wheeled around and faced the small window. With a shuddering breath he inhaled the cool draft. He wanted to say that, yes, Vivian would be his wife just to prove Catherine wrong. And yet it would only further the lie. He'd not wed Vivian. She deserved far better.

"I see the truth." Her voice was softer now, not scornful. "She was only a ploy to keep me away. If that is the case, why do you not force me to go?"

Because he needed Catherine here to remind him what happened when he gave his heart to a woman. He needed Catherine to remind him what people outside of the manor still believed about him.

Ashworth caught sight of a carriage climbing the wet drive to the manor. His nerves danced, mouth dried.

He shrugged a shoulder. "I've no need to force you to leave, Lady Wainscott. As I said, it is only your time you are wasting."

"Can't you remember the times we shared?" Desperation crept into her voice. "Remember when your friends John and Martin bet on whether I would snub you that first night we met? You told me about it months later, laughing at how sure you were of yourself."

He watched the vehicle lumber over the ruts and puddles until it disappeared to the front of the house. "I have done my best to forget those memories." Ashworth turned to look at her. She was still beautiful, like an exquisite china doll. "There must be a number of men in London who would gladly have you."

Her lips flattened. "As a wife? You forget I have a child

already."

"And debt?"

"Yes, and debt. I'm not quite the prize I was as an eighteen-year-old virgin."

"You think too little of yourself."

She rushed over to him and pressed her cheek against his chest. "Then why do you deny me? We can live together or apart. Certainly you'd not turn me away when I have a child to raise."

A child. Yes, he knew all about raising a child. What would Catherine think of his son? How welcoming would she be to the truth of Harry's real parents?

Catherine could find herself another husband, but he must not take a wife. Harry meant more to him than anything or anyone else.

Besides, as he'd learned well enough, The Monster was doomed to live alone.

Vivian requested dinner be sent to her room and collapsed on the crimson bedspread.

Each trip she took to the village brought more and more turmoil to her thoughts. She believed with certainty that Lord Ashworth would cause her no harm. And, yet, the villagers were so sure he was a menace.

Was she truly such a poor judge of integrity? Certainly the young man who had risked his reputation on a stranger could not be evil. Despite what gave him the scar, despite years of isolation, his true character must survive. Lord Ashworth was once her hero. He would be so again.

Vivian slipped off her shoes and removed her bonnet. If she didn't have dinner arriving soon, she would strip off everything to find comfort in her nightdress.

A rustling sound pulled her attention to the tapestry. Did

someone lurk behind the wall? Vivian tiptoed across the room, her stomach prickling. She pressed herself against the far wall and waited for the fabric to move aside.

Finally her mystery would be solved!

Cold air swirled from around the frayed edges. The fire across the room dipped then brightened. Vivian held her breath. She waited.

Impatience and curiosity overtook her fear. She reached a hand out and pushed aside the cloth.

Darkness.

No. A flicker of light. A flame.

The light cast its illumination on a white shirt.

Vivian gasped. Someone *was* there!

In an instant the light disappeared and blackness consumed its void.

No! Vivian pushed aside the tapestry and slipped inside the opening. The glow moved down the dark hallway, vanishing around the corner. She could never catch up in time, especially if she turned back to get her own candle.

Damn!

Darkness swallowed the dim light and Vivian was left with nothing but the crushing blackness of inside a tomb. Her throat closed, lungs seized.

Pulse roaring, she patted the walls surrounding her until she could find the opening of the stones. Pushing the tapestry aside, Vivian stumbled into her bedchamber and gulped in mouthfuls of air.

She'd been so close to uncovering the mysterious visitor. Perhaps in even discovering if there was a child in the house.

Vivian headed toward the bed but stopped midway across the floor. She was never told not to go upstairs. No one forbade her from exploring the house.

Without bothering to put her shoes back on, Vivian left the bed chamber in search of the rear stairwell.

Ashworth fidgeted as if he'd been sitting on an ant hill all throughout supper. His knees bounced, collar itched, fingers tapped. He could not have sat there another minute.

A few weeks ago he ate alone or with Harry or with John. His meals were simple and without pretense. There was no need to dress, no formality to entertain.

Then Vivian arrived. Suddenly with a visitor in the house, he had the need to eat in the dining room, have dinner prepared with several courses.

And then came Catherine.

She sat across the table tonight dressed in a fine mint-green gown, her hair piled high and curled. She commented upon eating turtle soup back in London and the delicacies she enjoyed at her late husband's estate.

Ashworth wouldn't have minded so much had Vivian been present. But she never came down. Mrs. Plimpton finally told him she was exhausted and requested dinner be sent to her room.

Exhausted from being fitted for dresses? Women confused him more than he was willing to admit.

Especially when Catherine insisted he stay to hear her play the piano. He wanted to dismiss the thought and disappear into the hidden rooms of his lair, but he also knew the piano was out of tune and so it amused him more to watch her grow infuriated.

Catherine tried to play a few notes but her cheeks grew more flushed by the minute. Ashworth held his grin as she wheeled to face him.

"I am assuming that no one has tuned this piano in years."

"Nor has anyone played it."

Her hazel eyes flashed with fire. "Why do you let this house go to ruin? Do you not have a care for anything beautiful anymore?"

He crossed his arms. "I do not have a care for *anything* anymore." Except Harry.

Her lips curled into a smirk. "Not even Miss Suttley?"

Ashworth yanked at the collar tight around his neck. Damned woman had caught him in her trap. Did he care for Vivian? If he did, he must stop. He had nothing to offer her. Just a man marked as a monster.

Catherine smoothed down her dress. "I am curious, Charles. You do not wish to spend your income on the upkeep of this house, nor on servants, nor do you travel. What do you do with it?"

Some he saved for Harry's future. Some he sent to a certain London charity. He didn't see the need to keep servants who had no purpose or keep a house presentable for visitors.

"Lady Wainscott, you have plainly seen where I do not care to spend my money. And I guarantee you I won't spend it to forfeit your late husband's debts, nor to buy you new dresses."

"As you bought them for Miss Suttley." She was like a bloody hound on the hunt today.

"We are engaged."

Catherine brushed a layer of dust off the piano. "Yes. And you are planning to marry her because she does not ask you to spend your funds?"

What was she looking for? For him to proclaim an admission of love for Vivian? Is that what it would take to have Catherine leave Silverstone? If so, he must lie.

What did he know of love? His parents barely paid him any mind as a child. His sisters never had much to do with him. The one time he thought he found love, it was ripped away from him in brutal force.

Ashworth clenched his teeth against the twisting in his gut.

Vivian intrigued him, aroused him. But he did not love her. In a few short weeks, she would be gone from here and he would not think of her again.

Just as he'd not thought of Catherine. Until she barreled back into his life.

His mouth watered for brandy. Instead of satisfying the thirst, he stared into Catherine's scathing gaze. "What transpires between Miss Suttley and me is none of your business."

She laughed and the sound echoed off the walls. "I find it hard to believe anything transpires between the two of you." She stood and made her way across the room to him. "Since I've arrived, it seems that I've spent more time with you than she has."

True, Vivian had once again not come to dinner. She had not made it to breakfast for a few days either. In fact, she spent more time out in her garden than inside the manor.

Still, Catherine had no idea what else took place up in Vivian's bedchamber. When night fell and darkness invaded the house, somehow he ended up in Vivian's arms.

"There you are wrong." He glanced down at Catherine with a raised eyebrow. "I see Miss Suttley *far* more than you realize."

Her blanched face brought a grin to Ashworth. "And now I must check on the welfare of my betrothed."

Chapter Sixteen

Waning daylight still struggled to find its way through the manor windows. As Vivian climbed the spiral staircase to the third floor, the lit candelabras danced with the drafts.

Her nerves jumped as she reached the top step. She looked both ways down the long hallway but found she was alone. All doors were closed.

Certainly there must be a schoolroom up here. She'd heard a child. It was not a trick of the wind or the cry of a cat. Unless ghosts truly roamed these grounds, a child lived in Silverstone Manor. And what child would live here other than the master's own?

Instinct told Vivian to turn left. She was certain it was the way the hidden passage had gone. And it would also make sense that the windows facing her garden would be at the center of the house.

Without shoes she could quietly tiptoe down the hallway. The first door on the right, just past the small alcove with worn chairs, had light shining from beneath it.

Vivian pressed up against the door. A chair scraped along the floor. Then, she heard the rumble of a man's voice. She could not make out the words, but she did not think it was Lord Ashworth. No, the tone and inflection were different. Yet it was definitely a grown man. Was it the one she'd seen on the landing by the warped door? The man who'd told her to kick the bottom?

Her heartbeat thudded in her ears, palms grew sweaty. Who was the man talking to?

More movement of chairs and other sounds she couldn't recognize. She held her breath and prayed they would not come to this door. There would be an adjourning door to the nursery, wouldn't there?

The man's voice called out again, this time farther away. He must be over near the windows.

"Yes, sir, I understand."

Vivian's heart stopped. This voice was clear, loud, beside the door. And it was clearly a child. A boy, perhaps about seven or eight.

Dear God, she had been right. A child did live here. The man must be his tutor.

Vivian moved back from the door and ducked into the alcove in case they came out into the hallway. She should be running down the steps but she couldn't force herself to go yet. Too many thoughts raced through her brain.

Who was the boy? Was it Lord Ashworth's son, or perhaps a nephew? Why would he keep him hidden away, never speak of him? Lord Ashworth had never married, so who was the boy's mother? Certainly it wouldn't be Lady Wainscott. Or was that the real reason she came? Did they share a son? No, she didn't believe it. Wouldn't believe it.

Tingles raced up her spine. Goosebumps sprouted on her skin. Outside, rain tapped gently at the window, reminding her of the day she heard crying against the outside wall.

Had that been the boy, after all? He might have slipped from her grasp just seconds before she arrived.

Vivian curled up in the chair, where shadows sprawled across her like a warm blanket. She stared across the hall to the opening of the spiral stairwell.

Somewhere around here was the opening to the secret passage. Was it in the schoolroom?

Dear Lord, was it the boy who had entered her room the other night? She blushed, remembering lying on the bed naked and flushed from her release. The memory curled heat in her belly but also brought shame to her cheeks. It couldn't have been the child. Please, no.

She must find out who entered her room that night. Had they come other times? It could be anyone. Lord Ashworth, the tutor, even old Pinkley.

A door down the hall opened. The loud squeak sent apprehension slithering into her heart. She pressed herself harder against the cushion and prayed the shadows would conceal her.

"Go on and get settled, Harry." The man's voice echoed down the corridor. "I'll collect your father while you ready."

His father!

Vivian held her breath as the same blonde, spectacled man she had seen by the rear door passed in front of her and disappeared down the stairwell. He did not see her in the alcove.

Her pulse chattered, stomach pitched, as she waited to hear the boy. She expected him to return to the schoolroom and pass through to the nursery. Once he did so, she would run down the stairs and back into her room.

Instead, she heard footsteps coming closer.

She gripped the armrests of the chair, clenched her teeth to keep silent.

The small boy, red hair glowing under the flickering candles, passed before her in the passage. He continued toward the other end of the hallway.

Vivian trapped the air in her lungs, waiting for him to be out of her sight before she would let out a breath.

He stopped.

She could do nothing but watch as he turned to her and stared at her with large, round eyes. Instead of the fear she expected, a smile spread across his adorable face.

"You are the pretty lady with raven wing hair."

Vivian didn't know how to answer. Catherine's hair was a yellow as a daffodil so the boy—Harry—must mean her. She finally nodded.

He looked around then whispered, "I'm not supposed to talk to you."

"Oh?" Vivian uncurled from the chair. "And why is that?"

Harry bit his lip and looked down. Clearly he did not want to tell her what he'd been instructed. "I—I think it's because you aren't staying very long." He blinked. "You won't tell, will you?"

The genuine concern in his voice tugged at her heart. She didn't think she could promise such a thing but she didn't want him worrying either. "All will be fine, you'll see."

Voices and footsteps echoed on the stairs.

"Papa!" His eyes widened. "Hurry, go into the school room." He pointed to the door where she'd listened earlier.

Vivian rose from the chair and came to where he stood. She chanced a caress at his baby face, brushing her finger along the freckles covering his cheek.

His skin reddened, then he leaned against her. He behaved as if he never had a mother, or any woman, to hold him tight.

The chatting on the steps grew louder.

He stepped away. "There's a secret passage." His voice dropped, "Behind the panel near the globe."

Then Harry scampered down to the far end of the hall and turned back to wave, his face alive with a huge grin.

Vivian slipped inside the schoolroom door and shut it just as the sounds reached the top step.

The voices of Harry's tutor. And Lord Ashworth.

Ashworth stood in the center of the hallway. Something was amiss. He couldn't place his finger on it or name it in any way. But something was different. A scent lingered in the air, faint and elusive. For just a moment he thought it might be honeysuckle.

But he had to be mistaken. Vivian would not be up here. She had no reason to be. Nor could she find her way around the manor without getting lost.

"Is something wrong?" John's blue eyes blinked at him behind the spectacles.

"Did anything out of the ordinary happen tonight?"

"Out of the ordinary? What do you mean?"

Ashworth shrugged a shoulder. "I'm not certain. I have an odd feeling."

John raised his brows. "Perhaps because there is no wind tonight. The rain taps softly on the glass rather than its usual thrashing."

Ashworth grinned. "That could be it. Still...nothing got broken? No one unusual came up to this floor?"

"I know of nothing." John patted his shoulder. "You must be tired. Or at least tired of those women disrupting your life."

"Yes, of course, it must be that."

They walked down the hall and into Harry's room. John gave a quick goodnight then left for his own bedchamber.

Harry had moved into this room at his last birthday, claiming he was too old to sleep in the nursery. It wasn't true, but Ashworth did not care if the boy wanted his own place away from the schoolroom. He chose the corner room at the end of the hall, with deep blue furnishings and multiple windows. With John and other servants on this floor, Ashworth did not worry for his son's safety.

And yet, that distressing sensation still lurked in his gut.

Harry had changed into his nightclothes and climbed into his bed. Lying back with his head upon the pillow, his son stared at him solemnly. He was typically a very happy child, didn't complain much or question his situation. Tonight his green eyes told a different tale.

"Papa?"

Ashworth swallowed, sought a way to distract his son. He reached for the book they had started reading last night and sat on the edge of the bed. "Shall we begin where we left off?"

"No. I want to ask you questions. May I?"

"Questions?" Never before had the boy asked anything other than if he could have a sweet before bed or why the sky was blue. What happened tonight?

Harry sat up and crossed his arms. His lips tightened, eyes narrowed. "Where is my mother?"

"Your mother is dead, Harry. You've asked me that before."

"Well, then, who was she?"

The dry taste of dust filled Ashworth's mouth, his palms broke into a sweat. What could he tell his son about the woman who gave birth to him? About the woman who did not ask for the responsibility of another life but did what little she could to care for him?

Ashworth cleared his throat. "Your mother was very pretty. She had long red hair, just a little lighter than yours. She had freckles, too, and the brightest green eyes I had ever seen."

Harry relaxed, a smile graced his lips. "Did she love me?"

"She loved you as much as she could. Did whatever it took to keep you healthy."

"Can I have another mother in her place?"

Ashworth recoiled, a stab pierced his heart. "Another mother?"

"What about the lady who works in the garden with black hair? Can she be my new mother?"

"No, Harry—"

"What about the other lady here? The one in the fancy dresses?"

"No. Absolutely not." Ashworth stood up, paced the room. His stomach burned with a gnawing emptiness, a pain he did not know how to end.

"Why not, Papa? Why can't I have a mother too?"

Because Ashworth could never love her, because a monster could frighten away her mind, because a wife to him would insist her own son inherit the family wealth. He could not explain any of these to the boy. "You are too young to understand..."

Harry crawled to the end of his bed and rose up on his knees. Ashworth had never seen his son with such intent, such desperation in his eyes. "I have one more question."

Jaw clenched, shoulders tense, Ashworth nodded.

"How did my mother die?"

The room blackened as Ashworth gasped for air. Memories of that night assailed him at a harrowing clip. The glint of a blade, the sharp tang of blood. Screams. Cries. Moans.

"Papa?"

He fought through the choking visions, stumbled back into a dresser. Blinking, he focused on his son, who stared at him with the same wide-eyed look of curiosity and terror Vivian often wore.

He wanted to lie but the words wouldn't form in his mouth. "Someone kill-killed her."

Harry began to cry. "Why would they do that?"

"I—I don't know."

His son stared at him with large tears slipping down his cheeks. "Who did it, Papa?"

Ashworth swallowed the agony. Razors slicing his throat. "A monster."

Chapter Seventeen

Vivian tucked stray hairs behind her ear, watching the large evergreens sway in the wind. There was a unique peace and beauty out amid the trees that she'd never witnessed before seeking out Lord Ashworth.

"Eh, Miz Suttley."

Pinkley's voice carried out across the yards of brown earth. She rose to her feet and turned to him.

"Ye wanted to see the master?"

She asked to have a word with him nearly two days earlier when she learned several of her new saplings were infested and disease-ridden. "Yes, is he able to meet me here in the garden?"

Pinkley's white hair blew about in the breeze. "Nay. He asks that you meet him in the study."

Vivian glanced down at her old brown dress, once again covered in wet dirt. She was not finished with her chores out here and she wasn't about to go upstairs to change for him and then have to change once again.

"Why can he not come out here? I want to show him some of the plantings he purchased."

"He requested the study, Miz. Immediately." And with that he turned and hobbled back to the house.

Of course, on his time only, however it suited him best.

She snapped off several branches and leaves of the affected plants and marched around to the front of the manor. No sense tracking her muddy shoes through the house when she could get to his study easily from the main door.

Despite the daylight filtering in through the window, the study whispered with shadows. Two candelabras sputtered, wax dripping over the sides. The room smelled of him. Sandalwood with berries. It also reeked of brandy.

Lord Ashworth stood in the far corner, his back to her, and gulped the liquid in a glass. His hair curled carelessly over his collar, his firm jaw darkened with unshaven whiskers. The scar glowed hideously in this wretched lighting, as if reflecting gloom from deep within.

"Close the door."

His words were not slurred and yet Vivian could hear a distinctive tone within them. Something she had not heard from him before. Her stomach pitched, anxious of his true reasons for meeting with her.

She latched the door closed and lifted her chin. She would state her business with the plants and then leave him to his moods.

"Lord Ashworth." She marched forward to stand by his massive desk. "I asked to see you because some of the—"

"It does not matter."

Vivian set the cuttings atop a stack of papers. "I beg your pardon, my lord. But I believe it does matter."

He swung around to face her.

She gasped, brought her hand up her heart.

What had happened to him in these last few days? His eyes pierced her like the deadliest of swords, but were rimmed with anguish. He had fallen into an abyss of which he had yet to be saved. Something occurred that night she met Harry. For it was after then that Lord Ashworth withdrew from everyone's presence.

He marched over to her, his face in a snarl, teeth bared.

No doubt he expected her to recoil, to run. But Vivian stood fast, swallowed against a tight throat. A rapid heartbeat pulsed at her temples.

He stood over her with the ferocity of a deadly lion. "I have decided this all must come to an end."

She blinked. "An end?"

"Your presence. Lady Wainscott." He gripped her shoulders. "I cannot take this disruption any longer."

Tears pricked the back of her eyes. "I won't go."

"You deserve better, Vivian. I am a monster, not a man."

She wanted to caress his face, but his grasp on her arms prevented it. Instead she lifted her chin, slanted her face. "You are not a monster. You are every bit a man."

He closed his eyes. Growled. "Leave, Vivian. Find your refuge elsewhere."

She stiffened her back, ready for the challenge. "You can't make me go."

"I can..." His voice was low, hoarse. Silver eyes opened, hooded with smoldering need. "I can make you do whatever I want."

With her next heartbeat, his lips were on hers. She could sense his hesitation as he battled against his desires. But he was a man, after all.

Vivian opened her mouth to him, stroking his velvet tongue with her own. He tasted of the brandy, of emptiness, of sorrow. She gave him what small amount of pleasure she could. Even if passion was fleeting, he could at least indulge in its bliss for a short time.

Lord Ashworth ravaged her mouth like a drunk gulping his ale. He crushed her against him, forcing his erection upon the softness of her stomach. Her nipples tightened, heat spiraled to the deepness of her core.

He lifted her up and sat her on the desk, nudging her legs apart. Breathing erratic, he brushed the hair from her face. "You are dirty again." His fingers traced a line down her cheek.

"It arouses me."

Hands, large and powerful, cupped her breasts. Her breath hitched, dampness flooded her upper thighs.

"Vivian..." Growling, he captured her lips again with a raw intensity. She reached up to encircle her arms about his neck but he captured them with his hands and held them above her head.

"I will prove to you that I am a monster." Each word sizzled, wicked and seductive. "You won't want to stay here."

Vivian did not struggle. She licked her lips, raised her eyebrows. "You forget that I know the meaning of a true monster. I cannot be fooled."

His eyes narrowed, lips flattened. "I do not refer to the scar."

"Nor do I."

Lord Ashworth watched her. A vein pulsed on his shining forehead, lips flushed from brutal kisses.

Then he released her hands and pushed her back on the desk. Papers crumpled under her shoulders, the leaves she brought in scattered to the floor.

Shadows stole across the length of his face, darkening the strong curve of his jaw. His eyes pinned her with a wild stare.

She should feel afraid. It was what he wanted to provoke within her. But only desire and compassion mingled in her heart. She acknowledged that this man made her feel wanton, sensual, alive with feminine beauty.

It was his obvious pain which brought out her compassion. His inner rage drove him to desperation. But he would not succeed in frightening her away.

Lord Ashworth thrust his hips against the aching spot between her legs; his hard arousal rubbed her sensitive nub. A longing cry rose up her throat but she swallowed it.

He reached under her skirts and smirked, "This is what a monster does—" He yanked on her petticoats, "—takes whatever he wants."

Vivian rose up to her elbows, set her chin. "You cannot take what I freely give."

Lord Ashworth stopped cold.

His hands dropped then he spun away from her. He braced himself against the decaying mantelpiece. "Why? Why do you want to give yourself to me?"

Vivian slid off the desk and moved to the other end of the fireplace, where sputtering flames did not remove the ever-present chill. "Tell me of what happened when you got your scar. What has turned your world into such loneliness?"

What made a carefree man who once rescued strangers into someone who believed himself a monster?

His hostile glare spoke of cloaked secrets, best left to hidden recesses of the mind or prayers to God. He would not tell her today.

His jaw tightened. "You tell me why you believe you know me so well. What manner of man has shown you the true nature of evil?"

She crossed her arms and faced the window. The afternoon clouds had already moved in, increasing the wind and diminishing the daylight.

This was her opportunity to tell him of their first meeting. A time when he looked adoringly at his betrothed, Catherine. A time when her innocence nearly cost her her life and his integrity outweighed any potential scandal.

But what would telling him gain her? Other than having him lament the many losses he'd suffered since then.

"My father gave me to a...a man in exchange for this man's silence." She tried to keep the emotion from her voice but her father's betrayal bled like an open sore in her heart.

"Was it this man or your father whom you feared?"

"I feared the man he gave me to. Evil of the purest kind lives in this man's soul. But it was my father who hurt me the deepest."

"Was that the man who gave you those bruises?"

"Yes."

"Did he rape you?"

Vivian gazed at the village down in the valley. Was it only a few days ago she was down there defending the master of this manor?

"I do not know the answer to your question. I was not a virgin when he took me. I had given my virginity to a boyhood sweetheart I'd hoped to marry. I thought that once this evil man knew I wasn't pure, he would not pursue me and I could marry in peace."

"What happened?"

"My father took me directly from my sweetheart's arms. I had no choice then but to go with this horrible demon. I prayed throughout that intimacy would draw out his tenderness. Instead I saw the true character of his savagery."

She drew in a breath, swallowed the collecting sob. "He did not remove his clothes, not even his shoes, as he stripped me bare. When his caresses became pinches and his kisses became bites, I ceased my pleas."

"But he didn't stop."

"Perhaps I could have escaped him before it happened, but I told myself I was being punished by God. And so I forced myself to withstand it."

"Punished?"

She lifted her eyes to his anguished gaze, stunned at the transformation of a man dangerous one moment to a man shattered in the next.

Vivian nodded. "For disobeying my father. But mostly, for my birth."

Chapter Eighteen

Lord, how she missed London.

Catherine walked through the streets of the small village, a white lace parasol firm in one hand. There was not much here to see save for a dress shop, baker shop, a church at the far end of the main street and a few other odds and ends.

It was obvious no one was used to seeing a woman dressed such as she with the stares she attracted today. Either that, or they wondered about her stay at Silverstone Manor. Lord knew, she thought herself half insane for staying there.

She simply had to get out of that house. Being inside the crumbling walls and dusty furniture was bad enough, but then to have Charles in such a foul mood made it all the worse.

Martha scurried to keep up, a package dangling from each of her arms.

So far no one in this village could tell her any more about the manor or Charles than she already knew. They knew even less about Miss Suttley.

"My lady."

Disgusted, Catherine turned from some boys creating a ruckus across the street to Martha. "Yes? Did you learn something at the tavern?"

The girl nodded. "One of the maids remembers her from the night she arrived."

Catherine led them to an alley, then tucked them in a

private location on the side of the General Store. "What did she say?"

"Not much, I'm afraid. Only that Miss Suttley hailed from the south, from a small village in the Cotswolds."

Nothing she didn't already know. "Anything else?"

"Her father is a baron. Lord Whistle...Whistle-something. I can't recall the rest."

Catherine stabbed the pavement with her parasol. So far, Miss Suttley and Charles kept their secrets too close to their hearts. There had to be an opening in their armor. Somewhere.

She glanced beyond the buildings to the hill at the far end of the horizon. Silverstone Manor stood like a hideous gargoyle overlooking the village. She didn't know how the villagers put up with it. You'd think they'd expect more, want better from their lord. Instead, they all whispered with excited repulsion of what must go on inside those walls.

How little they all knew. There was nothing to fear in that house except for the scurrying of mice and the multitude of spiders.

Catherine turned back to Martha. The poor girl appeared paler each day. Apparently she was not taking so well to the countryside. "Tell me again what you've learned from the servants of the manor."

"Very little, my lady. They do not like to speak to me."

"But you must have something to tell me."

The girl adjusted the packages she was carrying. Her large eyes loomed over an occasionally pretty face. Today, the sun had brought some color back to Martha's cheeks, but the pallor still lurked beneath.

"I told you one thing of note yesterday, my lady. There is a gentleman who comes in and out of the servant areas. His hair is yellow, like yours, and he wears spectacles."

"Yes. You said he was young, the same age perhaps as Lord Ashworth. Have you learned his position at the manor?"

"No, my lady. But I do believe he is high-born. He has glanced at me a time or two but not spoken directly to me."

The sun broke through the clouds, lengthening shadows and warming their skin. Catherine opened her lace parasol and shielded her face.

A high-born man living in the manor, working as a servant. Of course, when the master himself is shoveling dirt, what else could she expect? Catherine resisted the wry smile on her lips. She could not bear to have her husband act that way. She was raised to mingle with the best of society. What would they think of the disrepair of the house or the unseemly actions of its lord?

She sighed. "So this is all you have for me then? A mysterious man, born of gentry, but whose position within the house is unknown."

Martha's lip trembled. "I do—do wonder about something else, my lady."

"Go on."

"The cook said a name once or twice I did not recognize."

Catherine arched a brow. "Could it be the man you just spoke of?"

"I thought so at first. But then he said the name too. They speak it until they remember that I am there, then everyone grows silent."

Another secret hiding amongst the cobwebs and dust. "What is the name you've heard?"

"Harry."

"Hmm, interesting." Catherine grinned, suddenly feeling better. The fact that the household staff would immediately stop their conversation when learning a stranger was about was a good indication they had much to hide. This was just the news she was seeking.

Immediately upon their return to the manor, Catherine would seek out Charles and test him with some provocations. Then later tonight she would find the spectacled man with yellow hair.

Everyone had a price.

ᙖ

Martin quieted the rage swirling like rotten ale in his gut. He knew coming here would be a mistake, and it would not be the last he made today. But he could not leave any place unchecked. He would find Vivian. And she would regret her unwise plan to abandon him.

The three-story brownstone house loomed larger as he approached. Unlike many of the residences in the area, this one was not alive with guests and revelry. But what could he expect at the home of an ill woman.

Martin knocked on the door, uncertain what to expect, but prepared for anything. The successes he'd made through the years had come from his ability to think quickly and react efficiently. There had been few people who crossed his path and did not end up serving him in one way or the other.

A stern, white-haired butler answered the door.

"Lady Ethington, please." Martin held out his card. "Tell her I am a dear friend of her cousin, Lord Whistlebury."

The man's nostrils flared. "Lady Ethington is at her country home."

Martin clenched his jaw, held his anger.

"But her daughter is here. I will see if she will receive you." The butler took the card and disappeared into the recess of the house.

He waited in the grand foyer, calming himself with the pleasant aroma of cut flowers. Priceless objects glimmered in alcoves, sparkled on tabletops. Easily, he could pocket several expensive items and re-supply his cash. He needed as much as possible for the house he planned to build. The architect's figures had come in higher than expected.

First, the bride. Then, the house.

"This way, please."

Martin followed the butler to a blue wallpapered room, where a black-haired woman sat upon the couch. His gut clenched, chest constricted. Vivian? He looked closer. No, this woman had blue eyes and a stouter build.

"Mr. Crawford. Please, have a seat."

Martin sat across from her. He licked his lips. New prey. Every woman he faced was a new opportunity. His appetite did not distinguish between age or hair-color or build. Every woman had one thing in common. And that was all that mattered.

"I am Miss Blake. My butler tells me you know of our cousin, Lord Whistlebury."

Martin resisted his snort. He knew much more about that man than anyone should know. Somehow he doubted the family was aware of Alfred's sexual tendencies.

"He is a good friend of mine, yes. I apologize for arriving at your home unannounced such as this, but I am searching for his daughter."

Miss Blake's eyes lit up. "Oh, Vivian! We played together as children. In fact, she stayed with us during her first London season."

He grinned. Finally, he was making a measure of progress. "Ah, yes, and that is why I believed she may be staying with you now."

The girl cocked her head in confusion. He liked the way her neck gleamed like alabaster in the light. She would have a pretty red circle if he were to bite it.

His cock stirred.

"Vivian is not here this year. I have not seen her at all. Is something wrong?"

Martin swallowed. "I'm sure all is well. I heard she was in London and wanted to surprise her. I thought to try here first."

"Oh, it is a shame then." She stood and looked down at his

card. "I will gladly tell her you inquired about her if she were to stop by."

Now that would not do at all. "I would rather surprise her myself. Would it be possible to send a messenger alerting me of her arrival?"

Miss Blake grinned. "Oh, but of course."

She led him from the parlor back to the main foyer. Martin stared at the back of her neck, at the brief glimpse of skin on her back. He could not have this one. He was smart enough to realize that. But he could have the fantasy of her crying beneath him.

She stopped at the door. "I do hope she shows, Mr. Crawford."

He raised an eyebrow as the corner of his lip curled. "As do I, Miss Blake. As do I."

Chapter Nineteen

A cool blast of air swept through the room. Vivian looked up from the book in her lap to the tapestry at the far end of the room. It dropped behind Harry.

"What are you doing here?" She glanced to the side door, the one leading to Lord Ashworth's lair. She hadn't heard him moving about in there yet but that didn't mean he wouldn't be back soon.

Green eyes rounded, the boy stepped toward her. A twinge of sadness lurked within them, though he blinked it away as he got closer. "I came to tell you something."

Vivian lifted a brow. "And you couldn't knock on my regular door?"

"I'm not supposed to talk to you, 'member?"

"Ah." She patted the footstool at her feet. "Well, what is so important?"

"First, I must be truthful." His gaze flitted away but then came back determined. "I was outside that day in the rain."

"What day?"

"When you went crawling under the bushes. I was watching you but then I thought you'd find me." He sniffled. "Then the storm came and I hid."

Her heart broke a bit. "I was very worried someone was hurt."

"But I really wanted to see what you were doing. And then,

well, I was afraid you'd see me."

She brushed a finger along his cheek. "Thank you for telling me now so I won't always wonder. Was there something else you came in here to let me know?"

His face brightened. "The egg you brought back has hatched!"

She smiled, relief flooding through her. She hadn't checked on it in days. Once it was moved into the kitchen, a discomfort came over her when she went into the room. The servants stopped what they were doing when she entered, even stopped speaking. It got to the point that she hoped someone was looking after the egg and focused her attention solely on the garden.

"Have you been looking after it for me?"

"I check on it every day. And now it's come out!"

"Well, we'll have to give it a name, won't we?"

"I think it's a girl."

Vivian smiled, resisting the urge to brush his hair from his eyes or trace her fingers over his many freckles. "Harry, would you care to name the duckling?"

Suddenly solemn, he nodded. All along he must have been hoping she would offer him that privilege.

"Go on then. What will you call her?"

He looked at his feet, twisted his fingers. "I want to call her Mary."

"Mary? Not Fluffy or Princess?"

He lifted his gaze, staring straight through her with an intensity no boy his age should possess. "Mary was my mother's name."

"Oh." Vivian could think of nothing else to say. Her heart ached for the sadness of his words, for the loss he endured. She knew nothing of his mother or what this woman meant to Lord Ashworth. But it was clear that her son wanted to honor her in the only way he knew how.

She rose from her chair and pulled him against her. He leaned into her then wrapped his arms about her waist.

He sniffled. "She's dead, you know."

"No, I didn't know. I don't know anything about her. But you can tell me about her if you like."

Harry stepped back from her and shrugged. "Maybe later."

"Certainly."

He climbed up onto the stool and crossed his legs. "Where are your mother and father?"

Her throat tightened. "My mother is staying with a friend, keeping her company. My father..." She looked down at her hands, remembering the sting on her palm when she'd slapped him. She could accept the horrible things he did to her, the things he forced her to endure. But she could not tolerate what he had done to her mother.

"Where is he?" Harry was looking up at her expectantly.

"He—he is back at home, I suppose."

"Oh. Do you have any brothers or sisters?"

"No."

"Neither do I. Want to see something?"

Vivian nodded.

Harry opened his mouth and pushed his tongue through the opening where his two front teeth were missing. "Now watch this." He twisted his tongue and it did it again.

She smiled. He certainly had a way of lifting her spirits. "That's quite impressive, Master Harry. You are very talented."

He beamed. "Do you want to come see the new baby? Cook is having a time trying to find something to feed her."

"Baby Mary should be okay without food for a few days. After that, tell Cook to give her some beetles and grass."

"Why don't you tell her when you come downstairs? I can show you how pretty she is."

Vivian gave in to the impulse, and brushed her fingers through Harry's hair. "You're not supposed to be talking to me, remember?"

He frowned. "Papa is being so silly."

She sat beside him on the footstool. "What is his concern, Harry? Do you know?"

The boy shrugged a shoulder, looked away from her. "He thinks someone will take me away from him."

Vivian's breath caught. Why would Lord Ashworth believe that someone would take away his own son? Did it have something to do with his talk of being a monster?

A door slammed. They both lifted their heads.

"I think your father has gone into his bedchamber. You'd better go."

Without hesitation Harry leapt up and hurried over to the secret passageway. Before slipping behind the tapestry, he turned back to her. "Can we visit again?"

She wanted to tell him that it was a bad idea. That she feared Lord Ashworth would truly send her away if he learned of their interactions. And yet, she also longed to spend time with the boy, to give him comfort and peace.

Besides, he was the only sign of hope for this house.

"We'll find a way. Now go take care of little Mary."

He gave her a toothless smile and disappeared.

Rage seethed inside Ashworth, twisting and snapping like hapless branches caught in a tempest. He ripped off his jacket, then his shirt. Then, bent and yanked off his shoes.

He wished he had brandy but the only drink was his nightly potion, sitting on his table as a final salvation.

Ashworth spun away from it and instead stared into the fire, bracing his palms on the mantle. The red and yellow flames popped, licking their way up the stone.

The heat warmed his face, fueled the blaze already aflame in his blood.

It was enough that he'd endured the agony of having to tell

his son about his mother's death. For days, he'd relived what he could recall of that night. Even now his stomach cramped at the memory of waking up on the floor of Mary's room, blood covering him, a knife shimmering in his outstretched hand. When he sat up and looked toward the bed...

Ashworth swallowed the bitter taste of bile surging up his throat. Had he truly killed her and not remembered? He squeezed his eyes closed, trying to recall what happened before he fell unconscious, but he could only recall screams and the distant sound of crying.

Sweat collected on his forehead, dripped down his back. But he did not move. Instead, he breathed in the hot air, tasted soot and despair.

Catherine had come to him in the grand hall tonight, just after he'd come down from telling Harry good night. He could tell from the twinkle in her eyes, the smug grin, that she was up to no good. And sure enough she wasted no time in making his life a worse hell. Rumors had reached her ears, she said, rumors of the manor's secrets.

Ashworth growled, wiped his forehead with the back of his arm. He yearned for a swift ride upon Demon's back, one fast enough to burn through the agonizing frustration in his veins. But darkness had descended along the slopes of Briarfell and he'd not chance injury when Harry needed him.

He clenched his fists. But more than Catherine, it was Vivian who tortured every fiber of his being. How he wanted her. At times the urgency swelled in his blood, crashed against his groin and drove him mad with desperation. He had to force himself to resist lifting her skirts and driving himself into her.

He glanced back at the night table, to his escape. However, his gaze was drawn to the side door, where light glowed beneath the wood.

He yearned to cross over that threshold but forced himself to remain by dropping in a nearby chair. He was riveted to the shadows passing by in her room.

Was she in that thin nightdress, her pink nipples poking through the fabric? Was her hair unbraided and wild about her shoulders? Did she truly long for him the way he longed for her?

Ashworth swallowed. His erection throbbed against the trouser buttons, begging for freedom. He brushed his fingertips across the rise, a tingle raced down his legs.

He was mad. A beauty was in the next room, freely giving what he so desired and here he sat touching himself. If only he could believe she truly wanted him, that she did not offer herself to further her purpose. She knew how badly he needed release. Would she stoop to using that feminine power to bring him to ruin?

Still, he licked his lips, thoughts of her hands on his staff. For so long he'd wanted. For so long, he yearned to free the power at his groin.

He stared at Vivian's door, his fingers brushing over his erection the way she had done it the other day. It was far more thrilling when it had been her hands on him.

A shadow fell across the light and then a quiet knock.

Ashworth stilled. He wiped his forehead, thrust a hand through his hair and sprawled across the chair. She would not see him weakened.

He cleared his throat. "Enter."

The door squeaked open and Vivian slipped inside the room. She wore a pink robe, loosely hanging over her white nightdress. Her hair was undone, just as he hoped, and spread across her shoulders.

The sight of her slightly dimpled chin and succulent lips dried his mouth. How he missed kissing them!

"My lord." She stepped forward. "I have something I feel the need to discuss..." Her voice died away as she spotted the swelling in his trousers. She swallowed. "Perhaps...perhaps I should come another time."

Ashworth raised a brow, curled his lips. "This is a perfect

time." Only in her loveliness would his anger and frustration dissipate.

Vivian gently nibbled her lip, took another step forward. Her gaze raked over his legs then up to his bare chest. "I-I heard you moving about in here and wanted to discuss...I don't like the idea of keeping certain things from you..."

She lowered herself to the chair opposite him, her back straight, her jaw tense, but her eyes burned with a raw hunger. The robe slipped from her shoulder, allowing him to see her breasts more clearly. A nipple peeked through the soft cloth.

A jolt ricocheted through his body. His tongue itched to taste her. He shook with need.

He would wait. Tonight he would determine if this was a planned seduction or if she truly desired him, scar and all.

She blinked. Her cheeks flushed to a most pleasant hue. Her fingers twisted the fabric at her lap.

"Go on." He smirked, actually enjoying seeing her discomfort. She so often presented herself in control, sure of herself and the situation, that this unease rather delighted him.

She studied her hands. "I believe this would not be the best time to have this discussion."

Ashworth acted on impulse. He dropped to his knees before her. The scent of honeysuckle swirled into his bloodstream then cast him on a river of pleasure.

Vivian's eyes widened, her lip trembled.

He ran his hands up her thighs. "I'm willing to listen, Miss Suttley. Unless you would rather do something else at this moment."

Her breath caught. Her muscles tensed beneath his hands. Slowly, her eyelashes lowered.

How he hungered to kiss her. If he went there, all control would be lost. Instead, he lifted the hem of her clothes, then trailed his fingers up her calves.

She whimpered.

He continued along her silken skin, over her knees and up the tops of her thighs. Vivian arched her back, her nipples straining against the nightdress.

Ashworth swallowed, clenched his teeth. Fire scorched his blood.

He reached the flare of her hips and rubbed his thumbs around her waist. Vivian threw her head back, her mouth parted.

Lowering his hands to the soft fluff of hair, Ashworth bit back a growl. She wiggled, tightened the muscles in her bottom, lifted her hips up toward him.

He wanted these clothes off of her. He wanted to see her naked, spread before him. As in his study, intense lust rose up and choked him, compelled him to slide her toward his waiting desire.

Her words from his study echoed in his brain: I prayed throughout that intimacy would draw out his tenderness. Instead I saw the true character of his savagery.

Was *he* a savage, like the monster who took her?

Ashworth sat back on his heels, his hands slipped out from beneath the fabric.

Vivian opened her eyes, stared at him. Passion made her gaze bright, but could he trust her intentions?

"Why are you here?" his voice was raw, husky with desire.

"I told you. I wanted to discuss a matter with you."

He lifted himself to the other chair again. "No. Why did you stay when you knew my intentions?"

She blinked. "Your intentions?"

Ashworth raised an eyebrow and glimpsed down at the outline of his erection.

"Ah." This time she grinned. "As I have told you before, you torture me."

"How do I know you are not truly seducing me, hoping that by finding your way into my bed, I will grant you the marriage you seek?"

Amazingly, she laughed. "I will admit to you that was my intention at the start. But now..."

He drew in a ragged breath. "Now?"

"Now I find myself having the most alluring dreams. I find myself melting in your embrace, aching for your kisses, desperate for your touch."

"What of your experience before?"

Vivian lowered her eyelashes. "I have told you that I am not a virgin. My maidenhood was lost to a young man who wanted to marry me. I'm not sure I truly experienced pleasure with him, but neither was it an unpleasant encounter."

"And what of the other man, the one who hurt you?"

"'Tis true that he assaulted me in a variety of painful ways, but he did not ever penetrate me. His true possession, he claimed, would come after we were officially wed."

She lifted her gaze again, searched his face. "Since the moment you first kissed me, my body has not been the same. My blood flows hot, my skin yearns for your touch, wicked thoughts plague every waking moment."

His entire body trembled. Could it be true? Could she actually desire him?

His chest tightened as he recalled the last few times he'd enjoyed her treasures. Would he ever be able to have her or would his gruesome visions destroy everything?

Chapter Twenty

Ashworth watched, breath trapped within his lungs, as Vivian stood from her chair. Her eyelashes lowered as she slipped the robe off her shoulders, letting it drop to a pink puddle at her feet. She stepped closer.

The scent of honeysuckle eddied from her skin. He breathed in deeply, filled his blood with her feminine aroma.

His flesh pulsed in a dangerous rhythm.

The corners of her mouth turned upward as she untied the ribbon at her neck. Was she was stripping herself naked?

Ashworth clenched the armrests of the chair. "Miss Suttley...Vivian..."

She raised a finger to her mouth, shushing him. Her nightdress slipped down one of her arms, exposing a pink-tipped breast. He licked his lips.

Vivian came up before him and stopped like a Greek goddess at his command. His eardrums whooshed with a frantic heartbeat, his veins scalded with heat. The urge to snatch at her hips jolted through him. But if he stroked her now...

Her fingertips touched his legs, sending a shiver up to his groin. He gasped as she lowered to her knees on the floor.

"Vivian, what are you—?"

His words died away at the sight of the smooth curve of her shoulder gleaming with the fire's blaze. Dancing flames reflected in her dark eyes. His mouth grew parched.

Weightless hands smoothed up his thigh.

Ashworth caught his breath, held it tight. If he but let it go...

Strong fingers enclosed around his erection.

"Faith, Vivian!"

His head fell back, eyes closed. Her motivation for seducing him was lost to the whirling sensations, lost to the pulsing ache in his chest. He needed her touch. Needed it in so many ways.

The restrictive pressure against his arousal was suddenly gone and then her fingertips brushed his bare flesh.

Ashworth clenched his teeth, gripped the armrests until he thought they would break with his strength. Her soft, feathery strokes sent tremors to his toes. His hips lifted from the chair.

Moist heat.

He snapped his head up. Looking down he saw the top of Vivian's hair. Oh God! His flesh jerked, his head buzzed.

And his stomach twisted, anticipating the visions. He tried to push her off but she only sank deeper. Ashworth groaned.

"Vivian, no..."

But then her tongue swirled up and around, flicking the tip. He could not stop her now. No, not yet.

Sinking his hands into her mass of dark hair, he clenched his muscles, watching her take him in fully then pull back. She licked, suckled, kissed. He'd not...not since that one time...he would lose himself in her luscious mouth.

Her tongue darted and tasted, dampened and pressed.

The tell-tale shiver burst from the base of his spine. His sac tightened.

Ashworth pulled her head up and away, then grabbed his staff. He moaned, shuddered, as hot fluid spurted and landed on her nightdress.

She lifted her gaze to him, smiling. The sight of her hungry eyes sent him plunging forth.

He cupped her jaw with both hands and yanked her face to his. Capturing her warm mouth, he thrust his tongue between her lips the way he ached to thrust his shaft between her legs. He tasted himself on her, stirring the passion brewing once again at his groin.

Ashworth pushed at the fabric still on her shoulders and the gown slid down to the floor. He cupped her breasts, weighed them, massaged them, flicked the point with his thumb.

She sighed, still on her knees.

He pulled back, bracing himself for a haunting vision of dripping blood. But there was nothing but the beautiful sight of this naked beauty. No marks, nothing to mar the perfection of her skin.

Relieved, Ashworth flicked his tongue over the pink nubs. Her whimper mingled with the frantic beat of his heart.

How he wanted her. How he wanted to do things to her, make her cry out in ecstasy, make her burn for his fulfillment.

Again, he moved back, waiting for horrible noises and images to destroy the moment.

"What is it?" her quiet, husky voice sent tingles down his spine.

"I..." He could not tell her of the visions. Not yet. She would think him mad.

She touched his knee. "Do not believe I feel horror or shame. Yes, I'd questioned my reactions to you, wondering how I could yearn for your touch when I was repulsed by another man's."

"I do not repulse you?"

"No, you do not. I have known true monsters, my lord."

How was she so certain he wasn't one?

Ashworth pulled her up and gathered her into his arms. He didn't know what compelled him to offer her such comfort, but nothing had ever felt more right.

She curled up into a ball, her warm body pressing up

against his hips and chest. Eddies of contentment swirled through his bloodstream.

Other than cuddling Harry, Ashworth had never held anyone like this. He'd never enjoyed a woman's silky hair spread across his shoulders, the curve of her hip against his waist, the gentle swell of her breast upon his chest. Her honeysuckle scent soothed him more than any nightly potion, her warm breaths heated him more than any fire.

Almost without thought, he kissed the top of her head.

She sighed and angled her face up to him. Eyes, lost like a moonless night, beckoned to him. Desire still burned within their depths, but something else struck a knife through his heart.

Something resembling love.

Vivian sighed. She could stay here all night, listening to the rhythmic beat of his heart. Lord Ashworth—no, after all this, he was now Charles to her—held her with such power, such tenderness, that all unpleasant thoughts were erased from her mind. He was her cocoon. She was sheltered, protected.

He glanced away from her, breaking the connection which had lifted her heart.

She stared at the scar which had marked him a monster. It ran from his eyebrow to the top of his lip. He was lucky his eye had not been damaged in the attack.

But what was the attack? What happened to cause such mark on his face? Would he ever trust her enough to tell her?

Vivian reached her fingers to it. Touching his marked cheek reminded her of caressing her mother's, the bumpy skin of healed burns. Both her mother and Lord Ashworth carried the horror of another's soul, lived each day with the reminder of anguish and confusion.

He slackened as her finger stroked the line. This mark had a connection to his soul, something that gave him life, yet kept him hidden in his self-made prison.

On impulse, Vivian straightened her back and pressed her lips to his face. Her tongue traced the groove down his cheekbone, slowly, as if she wanted to taste each nuance of his skin.

Charles shivered, groaned. Instantly his flesh hardened against her thigh.

When she reached his lip, he opened his mouth, devouring her. Vivian closed her eyes, surrendered to the swirling sensations in her veins. Heat pooled between her legs, nipples tightened then sprang to life.

Uncomfortable, she lifted her leg and straddled him on the chair. His arousal pressed insistently on the swollen nub of her desire. Instinctively, she rubbed against it.

Charles tore his lips away from her. "Vivian, do you know what you are doing to me?"

Fire blazed through her blood, edging her onward. She pressed, lifted, stroked. Tingles shot from her groin down to her toes.

"Please..." Her eyes drifted half closed. Flames danced behind him, creating a demonic halo about his head. It didn't frighten her. No. No man from hell could create such an intoxicating rush at her core.

Gasping, she leaned forward, her nipples scraping across his chest. A surge of wetness flooded between her legs, dampened his hard flesh.

Charles groaned, his lungs rumbled with the primal sound. He gripped her hips, pulled her harder against him. He rose up to meet her thrusts, massaged her in just the right spot. A band constricted across her lower belly. Any moment she would burst.

Her breath caught as his tongue lapped the curve of her neck, swirled upward to her ear. "I want...I have to be in you. *Now,* Vivian. Do you understand?"

But she couldn't stop.

Gripping his powerful shoulders, she slid herself up and

down the edge of his erection, nearing the peak of intense pleasure. She moved herself over him, ready to find completion with his fulfillment.

Then strong hands grabbed her bottom, lifted her, and pulled her away from the sweetness of release.

"No!" Her cry rang out in the room.

Charles held her shoulders, forcing her to stare at him. She saw stark hunger in his eyes, the barest thread of restraint. And something else. Fear.

"You—you don't want it to be this way." His breathing was labored, erratic.

Vivian shook her head. "How it happens matters not. I just want you inside me."

For the briefest moment, he closed his eyes. Trembling, she stared at his hard jaw, sensual lips, his scar. "You are afraid." The whispered words escaped her lips.

Instead of denying it, Charles nodded. His silver eyes opened, anguish burning in their center. "You do not know what I see each time I touch you. Whenever you make my blood burn."

She brushed the damp hair from his forehead. "Tell me, my lord, so that I can help to heal you."

He sighed. "I don't know that you can."

"I can but try. But you must let me in first."

His lips thinned but he did not answer. He kept his secrets so close to his heart, so dark within the depths of his soul that it was no wonder he could not break free of them.

He must learn to trust someone, to break his silence.

Despite the rampant heat coiling in her blood, Vivian slid off of him.

"Where are you going?"

The vulnerability in his voice made her pause. But then she continued over to his bed, where she pulled off the blankets and dragged them over to the fire.

Vivian could feel him watching her as she bent and spread the blankets out, clearing away stools and books to give them enough room. When it was ready, she laid upon it and tapped the space next to her.

"Come join me."

The muscles in his chest and arms rippled as he stood from the chair. Her gaze lowered to his flat stomach and the trail of hair that led to his arousal. It poked through the undone buttons of his trousers, magnificent and breathtaking.

Charles pushed the remainder of his clothing off and stood naked before her. The flames glistened along the fine hair covering his skin. Long, powerful legs lowered to the blanket. Then he was beside her. It took every degree of willpower she possessed not to caress him.

"Why are we here?" He asked the question as if he truly didn't know the answer.

"I want you to take me. Here, by the fire. But first..." She rose up on one elbow, forcing a lusty gaze away from desire's salvation. "First, we will exchange secrets."

A mighty war raged within his blood.

Ashworth wanted nothing more than to enfold this naked woman against his skin, sink his swollen flesh inside her willing heat. An explosion waited impatiently.

And yet foreboding seized every nerve ending. The screams, the blood, the nightmare that possessed him each time he grew aroused. Was he a murderer? Would he kill another lover?

"Well?" Vivian raised her eyebrows.

Her dark hair curled around a breast, encircling it like a moat surrounding a mighty castle. He resisted the urge to brush it away.

"Shall I go first?"

First? Hadn't she already brought him to release with her succulent mouth on his body?

"I'll tell you my secret, then you tell me yours."

Ashworth swallowed. The fire heated his back, made him thirst for drink. Brandy would do especially well about now.

"Why?" the word came out as a croak. "Why must we talk about secrets now?"

Vivian grinned. "I realize you may have other things upon your mind." A quick glance at his erection made her blush. "But I also do not want these moments to be destroyed by your actions, by whatever it is that comes over you when we touch."

He tensed. "You think by me telling you about it, that it will disappear?"

"It's possible."

No. He'd not tell her of the horror he remembered, of what he feared he did not remember. Perhaps this was his punishment for such heinous crimes, to be forever restricted from a woman's love.

Ashworth rolled over onto his stomach, his arousal pressing painfully against the blanketed floor. He stared across the room to the long curtains fluttering with the evening drafts.

"I may have done something monstrous, something too horrible to detail. That's all I will tell you on it."

Vivian sighed. "Very well. I have many of my own secrets to share, ones that are too painful to speak of and bring into the daylight."

Throat suddenly tight, he glanced over at her. "You mentioned punishment for your birth. You could explain that."

"I could, but I will save that for another time. A time when you will be willing to give me more of yourself."

More of himself. What did she want of him? To give his heart? He was felled by love once. But that woman did not believe in him enough to trust him. She did not love him enough to see past the physical imperfections.

Nay, he was given Harry to raise as a son because God knew he would never have his own. Love, marriage, blood heirs—none were a part of his future. Vivian must understand this.

"What we may do here tonight will not change anything. I still will not marry you."

She blinked and for the briefest moment he thought he saw a shadow of sadness, but it may have only been the reflection of the fire. "I understand that."

She lifted her chin. "The secret I will tell you is why I originally came into your bedchamber tonight."

Ashworth turned back to the curtains again. There were small holes in the fabric and the bottom edges were frayed. Threads swirled about as if they were knotted strands of hair gusting in the wind.

Vivian scooted closer to him where her warm breath fanned over his arm. "I've met Harry."

Chapter Twenty-One

His heart stopped. He must not have heard her correctly.

Ashworth sucked in a deep breath, forcing calm through his bloodstream. He went to great lengths to keep Harry hidden, to protect him from outside influences and prying eyes. Even the boy's clothes came in packages all the way from London.

Vivian's fingers brushed his shoulder. "Did you hear me? I have met your son."

His throat closed in, stomach pitched. He tried to fight it, but he could not keep the rage from rising up and exploding.

"He was to stay from you!"

"Yes, he told me that." Her voice was soft. Steady. Damn her.

Ashworth turned to glare at her. A dark curtain of hair fell across her face, covering one of her eyes. "Then why did he not obey?"

She lifted a shoulder. "Curiosity?"

His heart pounded, mouth dried. "He knew what could happen if he spoke to a stranger. He would not have come to you on his own."

"What, my lord? What would happen? What do you fear? Why is the poor boy forced to endure his life within these walls?"

"He would be outside if you had not come here!"

Vivian blinked. Her face paled. The firelight caught a

shimmer in her eyes, but no tears fell. "I am glad to hear that he does have the opportunity to be in the sunshine. However, that does not explain what you fear will happen if a stranger meets him."

He could lose his son. And he couldn't allow that.

Someone out in that outside world might know the identity of Harry's real father, someone could believe Ashworth murdered the boy's mother. They might take him away. A new wife may not accept Harry as her own son. He must keep him hidden.

Ashworth swallowed, but his throat burned. It was as if a blow had been delivered to his gut. "I have my reasons, Miss Suttley."

She sighed. "Well, he is delightful, intelligent and desperate for a mother."

He sprang up to his feet, blood churning in an angry frenzy. "I know my son."

"The egg I brought from the lake has hatched. Harry named the duckling Mary, after his mother."

His mother, Mary.

Would this misery ever end? How much worse could the night get? Oh God, Catherine. She had mentioned something earlier in the evening about rumors and secrets of the manor. Did she too know of Harry?

He leaned forward, his hands gripping the back of a chair. The fire blazed before him. It heated his skin, intensified his pain. Harry was the only thing he had in this world. He would do anything—anything—to keep him safe.

"Go, Miss Suttley. This night is over."

"No."

His jaw tightened. "No? I've asked you to leave my room. Return to your bedchamber."

"I'll not let you push me away again."

Ashworth swung around and found her standing on the

blankets, hands on her hips. Naked.

He gulped. Nay, he could not let her beauty, his desperate need for fulfillment, sway his purpose. He must banish her. From his room. From the house. From his life. She was ruining him, unraveling him. Everything had been perfect, safe, secure, until she came into his life, demanding he marry her.

"How did you know of me? Why did you come here?"

She raised an eyebrow. "I told you I came here to hide myself."

"You ran from one marriage to another with a stranger?"

Her lips twitched. "I have my reasons."

He crossed his arms. "You'll not tell me."

"I revealed one of my secrets already. You have not shared one of yours."

His laugh was cold, short-lived. "Why bother? You find out my secrets on your own. Now, go on. The night has ended between us."

Vivian lifted her dimpled chin. The firelight danced across the pink tips of her nipples, the smooth plane of her stomach, down her long legs. "I will not go. You must force me from your presence."

His pulse jumped. The stubborn wench. He would not let her rule him.

Ashworth strode to the blankets, swept her into his arms and started for the adjoining door. But something happened in those few paces. Her warm skin melted against his. Her soft hair swept over his arm, tickled his ribs. Her tantalizing breasts pressed upon him, her smooth bottom brushed atop his limp flesh.

A ribbon of honeysuckle slipped over his skin. She licked circles on his shoulder blade. Swirls and warm moisture, just like her mouth on his shaft.

Suddenly, he was rampant.

He bowed and took possession of her mouth, sucked her

tongue with ferocious power. She wrapped her arms about his neck, holding onto him as if he were her life-force.

His flesh awoke, her bottom swayed across the tip. Liquid leaked out the top. He must have release. Now.

"Vivian, I..." His voice trailed off as he stared into her bottomless gaze. No hesitation, no doubt, nothing forbidden clouded her eyes.

"Yes," she murmured. "Oh, yes, please."

He didn't want to do it this way the first time. The first time in nearly eight years. But he could not control the wild urges in his blood. Head buzzing, pulse frantic, he could only think of his hardness deep inside her warm channel.

Ashworth released one arm from under Vivian and pulled her legs around his waist. No foreplay, no affection, no worshipping. Only the primal need to be as one.

"Now. Oh, God, now." Her voice broke.

Leaning her back against the tapestry, Ashworth thrust her hips downward and impaled her on his desperate arousal. Glorious, tight moisture welcomed his plunge. Vivian gasped.

He closed eyes, afraid to see visions, afraid to see disappointment in her gaze.

Lust, nearly a decade in the making, swelled, expanded. He thrust her down on him again. And again. Nerves prickled under his skin, sweat dripped down his face.

"Vivian..."

"Don't stop. No, not yet."

But he couldn't stop the mounting ecstasy. It soared like a monstrous wave. Cresting...

He grabbed the smooth cheeks of her ass, lifted her high on his arousal and slammed her down again.

Knees weakened, legs trembled.

She moaned in his ear. "I—I never knew...yes, more..."

Then a splintered cry and Vivian's sheath convulsed around his flesh. Her spasms shattered any restraint he had left.

Years of denial and wild desperation exploded. He drove himself into her again and again, then shouted into the still room. At once, he was numb and euphoric, satiated and delirious.

Ashworth gulped in mouthfuls of air. Then, the reality of what just happened slammed through his chaotic brain.

He dreaded opening his eyes. He could not stomach seeing a terrifying vision of Vivian covered in blood. Even more, he could not witness the discontent in her eyes. Vivian had told him of what occurred the last time a man was intimate with her. She spoke of how the act lacked gentleness, tenderness. He had not sought to her needs or tried to please her. He used her body for his own purposes.

Ashworth had just done the very same thing. He had not cradled her in affection, or revered her body with gentle caresses. He was selfish, thoughtless. Not much better than the man she'd run from.

Looking past her to the tapestry, he slid her off of him and set her on the floor.

"My lord?" Vivian's fingers swept across his jaw. "Why won't you look at me?"

Ashworth turned away. His knees still shook from the intense climax, but he held himself steady and crossed the room. He scooped up his nightly potion and swallowed it in a gulp. "Go," he said over his shoulder and prayed she would not refuse or argue as she had done before.

"You still will not let me in."

Why did she want to be let in? What was there to see but a man who could not control his impulses? A man who lacked the ability to show tenderness and vulnerability. A man who hid himself away for fear the rumors and nightmares may be true.

"I'll not ask you again." Still naked, Ashworth climbed into his bed and covered himself with a thin blanket she had left behind.

He heard Vivian gather her clothes and pad over to the door. "You cannot know the truth unless you seek it."

Then she vanished into her room and left him to suffer in the haunted silence.

Chapter Twenty-Two

Martin did not know where else to search for Vivian, but he did know how to relieve the raw lust prowling in his groin.

Despite being away for so many years, the dirty streets of St. Giles had not changed in his absence. He walked through the smells of waste, emotion surged into his blood. Fury, desperation, anguish. All merged into a hard knot at the base of his throat.

The deeper he walked through the alleys, the dimmer the light became. People shuffled by him, some giving him odd looks, others ignoring him completely.

He knew these people. Knew what it was like to live like this, to not know when the next meal would come.

Martin turned the corner and a group of ragged children raced past as they chased an animal. A rat perhaps? Those predatory rodents grew as large as dogs around here.

He stopped. There it was.

On the corner, beside a twisted dying tree, stood the home of the only woman he ever loved. His gut pitched.

He lifted his chin and crossed the street, stepped over garbage. He had to see it. The room, the memories of Mary, something must be left behind.

"Evenin', sir. Somethin' I can offer ye?"

Martin stared as a woman emerged from the shadows. The evening light cast her hair in red, her lips in rosy plumpness.

His heart skipped a beat. "You look just like her."

She stepped forward. "Like who?"

"Mary." He nodded toward the door. "She had red hair and lips begging to be kissed."

The woman, probably not yet twenty, still had enough innocence to blush. "I remember her. 'Twas just a girl then."

Martin looked from the whore to the tiny window, as if he expected Mary to glance out it. "She's been gone a long time."

"Aye. Can't forget the night she died."

Rage and grief rose up to choke him.

As much as he loved Mary, he could not make her his bride. She had lived here too long, never gaining the proper education or the acceptance of society. She could never become the wife he needed.

A small hand settled on his arm. Martin glanced down to see the whore smile up at him. "I have a room just down the row."

He nodded at her. The restless urgency of his encounter with Miss Blake hadn't dimmed. Neither had his gnawing rage over Vivian.

"They say it's haunted." The girl pointed to Mary's door as they passed. "Her spirit lingers there, looking for her killer."

"So they never found who murdered her then."

She shrugged. "Never found the baby neither."

Martin stopped walking, his lungs tight.

The baby.

Heat flushed up his neck.

Again, the mention of Mary with a baby. But it couldn't be possible. No.

If Mary had a baby, it must have been another lover's and it was no wonder she didn't want him to know. Perhaps the one who was with her that night. That man—his supposed friend—lied to him about lack of experience. He must have been seeing Mary for months, a year at least, to get her with child.

His hands fisted. Black spots swam before Martin's eyes. He should have killed Ashworth that night while he had the chance.

The whore stepped around a sleeping drunk and opened her door. "Ye comin'?"

Martin glanced back up the row to Mary's door. That bitch. That stupid bitch. She shouldn't have crossed him.

He clenched his jaw, wiped the sweat from his brow. Fury seethed in his blood, swirled through his heart, and plummeted to his groin.

He turned back to the girl, and stared her down until she had to look away. Mary paid for her indiscretion. Vivian would be next. Then he'd deal with Ashworth once and for all.

Catherine adjusted the neckline of her evening dress as she spotted the rear stairs. Charles was in another of his moods tonight, barely speaking at dinner and then drowning himself in brandy. He took no notice of her attributes, despite how often she tried to catch his eye.

Damn it, he did love her once. He whispered his desires in her ear as they danced, trembled as they kissed. Now he was nothing more than a shell of a man, a self-pitying eccentric, who pretended to have an engagement with a baron's daughter.

She swallowed the anger rising in her throat and climbed the stairwell to the servants' quarters. For two days she had failed to catch a glimpse of the yellow-haired gentleman Martha mentioned. Tonight she would seek him out.

The wind swept against the house at this late hour with its unyielding intensity. She hoped to find most servants abed, other than the one she needed.

The hall was dark, save for the flickering candelabras along the walls. All doors were shut. How would she determine which room belonged to her quarry?

Catherine slipped past an alcove with stuffed chairs and tested the first door. She knocked gently, not even certain what she'd say when someone opened the door.

But there was no answer.

With a small twist, she opened the door, peering into the shadowed darkness. The partial moon cast splintered light upon tables, chairs, bookshelves, and desks. This was not a bedchamber.

She entered the room and quickly shut the door behind her.

She found writing tablets and novels. A globe and several maps. This was a schoolroom!

But for whom? Was there a child here? Could it possibly be the Harry the servants spoke of?

Her stomach tingled with excitement. If Charles had a son, and had gone to such great lengths to hide him, he would be willing to do anything to protect that secret.

Catherine had had enough of this manor, of his indifference. Despite his unspent wealth, her patience was running low. As a widow, she may not have the best pick of the eligible peers, but she would not suffer at Silverstone for much longer. She would find his secrets, she would blackmail him with them, and then she would return to London as his wife. In name only.

She noticed a door along the far wall, one that must lead to either the child's room or the teacher's room.

Catherine sashayed around the desk, chair and scattered tables. A light glowed beneath the door, bringing a smile to her lips. Certainly a child would not be up so late. And if a gentleman were here speaking to the servants, his duty would most likely be as a tutor.

Perfect.

It would be polite to knock before entering, but what if he refused to let her enter? She must put aside all thoughts of proper etiquette and be daring.

She sucked in a deep breath and turned the knob. Light from the room spilled onto her, making her blink. She saw a yellow-haired man on his bed, spectacles perched on his nose while he read a book on his lap.

The man did not move as she clicked the door shut behind her. As she took a step closer, she could see that his eyes were closed. He had fallen asleep while reading.

Catherine studied the man, as something about him seemed familiar. His age must be close to her own and yet there was something in the lines on his forehead, the grooves around his eyes, which made him appear years older.

She was nearly beside him when he startled awake. Blue eyes widened beneath the magnified glass. His face paled. "Dear Lord, Catherine?"

He knew her name! She bent closer, inspecting the sharp corners of his chin, the slash of his cheekbones.

"My word, is that you, John Hughes?"

John had been a close friend of Charles during their school days and after. In fact, the two of them and that other lad, Martin something, were inseparable at times. It wasn't any wonder that John would follow his friend here. Yet, was their friendship worth giving up a future in society?

John scrambled off the bed, clearly distraught at not only her presence in his room but probably for his blunder in calling her by name. She grinned. It was most comforting to be in the position of power.

"You know I've been here," she said as he pulled a shirt on.

"Get out." His back was to her but she could hear the sharp edge in his voice.

"But I've been so bored here. Now I've found an old friend."

He turned to glare at her. "I am not an old friend."

Catherine leaned against the wardrobe. "But I was almost married to your best friend."

"Almost."

"So, you are bitter at my snub as well."

At that, he raised an eyebrow. "Actually no. I never wanted him to marry you. I was quite relieved when you broke off of the engagement."

"Oh really?" John thought she wasn't good enough? Or perhaps he wanted her for himself. She wasn't above certain things to get information she needed.

She glanced down at the swell of her breasts, then caught his gaze. "I am available again."

John laughed. "No, I think not."

Catherine gasped as her blood curdled into a rage. She marched over to him, hands on her hips. "You tell me what a man your age is doing out in this God-forsaken excuse for a house instead of finding himself a wife."

He shrugged. "I have my reasons."

"Do you?" She nodded toward the schoolroom door. "Would it have anything to do with a child here? Perhaps one by the name of Harry?"

He flinched. She could see he tried not to, but he couldn't stop the shock at hearing the name. So she has been right. A boy named Harry lived here. But who was he?

"So Charles asked you—paid you handsomely I'll wager—to come teach this child. He wanted someone he could trust, not an outsider."

John crossed his arms. "I've asked you to leave."

"Why are you hiding this? Why is Charles keeping this boy a secret?"

"You'll not get your answers from me."

She glanced about the room, noting the worn dresser and scuffed floors. "Your loyalty is touching and yet is this really what you want? You live like a servant, not a gentleman."

"I don't need worldly goods."

"You should have joined the clergy then and yet here you are."

John removed his glasses and set them on his bedside table. "Here I am, for reasons which you will never know."

"It must have something to do with that boy."

"Go back to your room, Catherine. Go back to London. There is nothing here for you."

"Perhaps. But I do enjoy a good mystery, don't you?"

"I enjoy solitude and privacy, just as Lord Ashworth does."

She snorted. "You mean loneliness and isolation."

He rubbed his eyes. "There is nothing more for you to learn tonight. I beg you to let me retire."

Catherine lifted her chin and gave a careless shrug. "You realize, the more one tries to hide something, the more curious others become."

John's face contorted. He snatched her arm and pushed her to the door. "Take up your questioning with Charles. I am merely in his employ."

Catherine yanked herself free. "You can be certain that I will do just that."

Vivian surveyed the landscape. The garden was just as she hoped it would be. Just the right amount of shade trees, flowering bushes and hints of color to bloom next summer. Charles had replaced the diseased plants without ever speaking to her about it.

Of course, he'd said very little to her in the last few days. She swallowed against a tightening throat. Charles had completely withdrawn from her again.

Her nipples ached with memories of that night, of his fingers pressing into her hips, his arousal deep inside of her.

Vivian brushed the dirt from her hands. If Charles would not tell her his secret pain and if he saw no reason to send Lady Wainscott away, then why continue to stay? She'd finished the bloody garden, as she promised.

A gnawing in her gut forced her attention to the upper windows. Harry.

That little imp had burrowed his way into her heart already. He snuck through the secret passageway each evening to tell her about the progress of the duckling. He brought books for her to read. He stole cookies for her to relish. Harry did not tell her whether his father had stopped visiting him recently, but the attention the boy showed her had increased tenfold.

A breeze gusted, bringing the scent of rain. Vivian gathered her gardening utensils and headed back for the house. She didn't know what she would say to Charles when she found him, but speak to him she would.

His silence, Lady Wainscott's smug glares and the looming presence of loneliness had become more than she could stand. Could she possibly find refuge elsewhere?

Vivian glanced again at the top windows, where a face pressed up against the glass. Her heart wrenched. The solitary gargoyle jutted from the roof just above. Together the lonely pair seemed an odd match in this isolated manor.

She straightened her back and slipped inside the warped rear door. Before turning left and heading up the staircase, the two locked doors on the right caught her attention.

What was down there? Who was the man who'd emerged from that door?

She tested one handle and found it locked. But the second one startled her by turning freely. The door opened to stairs dropping off into darkness. But when she peered in further, a faint glow of light beckoned from the deep.

Curiosity overtook any apprehension and Vivian slowly descended the steps, making sure to shut the door behind her. Surprisingly no creaks or groans marked her footsteps.

At the landing she could make out several rows of shelves. A few scattered bottles lay covered in a thick layer of grime. Spiders stretched their webs across the empty rows, waiting for unsuspecting victims. A wine cellar.

Vivian breathed in the damp, dusty air that tasted as if it had been trapped for a thousand years.

The light she had seen glowed beyond a stone archway. She must find Charles, end this miserable awkwardness between them. And yet, that light summoned her, drawing her forth as if a rope were tied about her waist.

Vivian gasped as she entered the next chamber. This room held more playthings than she could count. Rocking horses. Balls. Jacks. A train set. They littered the walls, as if she'd stepped into a toy store. Puzzles. Soldiers. Drums and a horn.

Dear Lord, this must be a playroom for Harry. Perhaps for days when the weather was frightful. Or, for when company arrived and his father must hide him away.

Tears collected in her eyes. Harry was such a happy boy, one of mischief and delight. Why did Charles keep him in this isolated manor, far away from others who might love him?

She'd seen enough.

Vivian straightened her shoulders and crossed under the archway toward the stairs.

The light vanished.

Darkness dropped around her like the shroud of a heavy blanket. Vivian fought for air, reached her hands out to feel for something. Anything.

She could see nothing. Not her fingers before her face, not shadows against the wall.

Fear rose up her throat and lodged into a sob.

Her heart stopped as a noise creaked behind her. Something stood at her back, breath warm on her head. Powerful hands clamped onto her arms.

Vivian struggled, but she was held firm, her skin bruised with a ferocious power. "Re—release me!"

"Get out of this house." The monster spoke to her, words murmured deep with hatred.

She smelled a man's soap, a hint of sandalwood. Dear God,

could this be Charles? "Who—who are you?"

He wrapped one arm about her shoulders, yanking her back against his chest. The other hand closed about her throat. "Go or you will never see daylight again."

His fingers tightened, slowly cutting off her air supply. Bright spots swam before her eyes. She started to struggle but found it useless.

Her mother. Harry.

Their faces, voices, smiles rose up in her mind. She had to see them again. They needed her. She needed them.

Vivian stomped the heel of her shoe back, connecting with the foot of the man behind her. He howled, his hands falling away from her body.

She stumbled forward into the blackness, anywhere away from his reach.

"Damn you, bitch." Pain increased the loathing in his voice, though the words themselves were no more than a whisper. "Mark my words. If you do not leave this place, I will kill you."

Vivian held her breath, her whimper, and remained still, lest he make a move for her again.

Finally, he let out a low growl and she heard him retreat into the back chamber. Sounds of toys being crushed under foot and items being knocked over followed his withdrawal. The noises grew dimmer as he somehow made his way farther into the depths of the cellar. Then, there was nothing. Another secret passageway must have helped him to escape.

Vivian stood in the utter darkness as her pulse roared in her ears, the taste of unshed tears flooded her mouth. She tried to remember the layout of this first room but she could not. Her only focus had been the rows of empty wine storage and the many spider webs. Once she had seen the light and chamber of toys, she had not paid attention to anything else.

She trembled. Had it been this cold before? Would there be a chair in her path?

Vivian took a step forward, her hands before her as a shield. She walked in the abyss of a moonless sky, with no stars to guide her, no sensations to orient her. She took a few hesitating steps and found nothing in her path. In fact, nothing marked her course for several strides.

Then Vivian's toe banged on a hard object. She stumbled then fell forward, landing on her knees. The stone floor jarred and bruised her bones, eliciting a cry of pain and outrage.

Tears burned in her eyes as she turned over onto her bottom and pulled her legs up to her chest. Vivian huddled into a ball and rested a cheek on sore knees.

She'd been buried alive in a tomb, forced to endure petrifying darkness.

Where no one could hear her scream.

Chapter Twenty-Three

Ashworth felt like a bloody idiot. But when he saw Catherine heading down the long hallway, a smirk on her lips and a gleam in her eye, he had to escape. His male pride suffered but he could not tolerate her voice, her snide comments, her goading questions.

He took two steps at a time down the rear stairwell. Catherine would never come down these steps, which were caked with mud and adorned with fluttering cobwebs.

He stepped onto the worn stone floor, where drops of water collected before the warped door. The door Vivian often used to access her garden. The door which had remained closed until she arrived and demanded it opened.

Vivian.

An anchor weighed in his gut.

For the past three nights he had thought of nothing but her luscious body over his, her legs wrapped tightly around his waist. As it had then, his flesh hardened. Even without watching their union, he could imagine it in his mind, feel it along the hardness of his staff. He'd hoped that one incident would have cured him of this desperate need, but he only craved more. More.

Shame and guilt snaked through his bloodstream and he clenched his hands into fists. He hadn't thought of her needs, hadn't given her the adoration she deserved.

He was a fool. A wretched, tormented, lascivious fool.

"Charles?"

Damn. Catherine must have seen him nip down that stairwell. She still stood at the top, possibly debating whether to dirty her dress by attempting to descend them. It depended on how important it was that she confront him.

"Lord Ashworth. Did you come down this way? Answer me, please."

Like bloody hell he would.

Ashworth glanced about him. He had four choices. Go back up the stairs and face the witch. Go out the back door and into the yard, where she would most likely follow him. Or go through one of these other two doors. One led to the old kitchen he had shut down when he had the new one built. The other led to the wine cellar, where Harry played when the weather was too unpleasant.

Her footsteps moved away. Still, he snatched the lamp sitting on an ancient table in the corner and lit it with the matches from the drawer.

The handle to the door was unlocked. John and Harry must be in the schoolroom instead. It didn't matter. He could easily lose himself in the shadowed rooms for an hour. Hell, he'd even been known to put together a puzzle or two.

Ashworth entered the stairwell and closed the door behind him, locking it carefully in case Catherine chose to follow.

"Is—is someone there?"

Was that raw, desperate voice from Vivian?

His heart shuddered as he bounded down the stairs. The light extended on a few feet before him. Was she down here in the pitch darkness?

"Miss Suttley?"

"He—here, my lord."

Her voice shook.

Ashworth swallowed, maneuvered around an old sofa and table and found her drawn up into a ball on the floor. The light from the lamp stuck long shadows across her face, tearing at his soul. Her shining eyes resembled a lost, frightened child. Alone. Bewildered. Vulnerable.

An impulse ached to pull her into his arms, but he forced it away. It had been several days since he had spoken to her. Damn if he didn't fear her reaction to what they'd done.

He set the lamp down upon the table. "Are you hurt?"

She shook her head but didn't rise.

"What are you doing down here, Miss Suttley? And in the dark...?"

"My curiosity call—called to me. A light had been burning when I arrived..." Her voice trailed off but one of her hands rose up to her throat.

Her curiosity. If given the opportunity she'd turn over every stone in the yard, open every book in this house, disturb every half-dead soul. "What happened to the light?"

Vivian glanced away, unwilling to tell him what transpired to leave her in such a state of distress. No matter. He was here now and she could go.

"Come." He held his hand out to her. "Stand. Now you can see your way back."

She accepted his hand and rose from the floor. The fear which had previously stolen over her vanished with the lift of her chin. "I still wish to speak with you. Is there somewhere else we can be alone?"

Why would she seek him out? To berate him for his shameless lack of tenderness? To call him on his avoidance of her presence?

"Follow me." He led them up the steps and down a back hallway to an antechamber of the unused great hall. With only one heavily draped window, the room was nearly as dark as the wine cellar. He lit a small lamp.

Vivian immediately lowered herself to the sofa. "Sit." She pointed to the open spot beside her. "I don't care for you towering over me like that."

Had he not been so ashamed he would have refused her demands. But, as it was, his body craved being close to her. Even if the inches separating them seemed like miles.

Ashworth lowered himself to the sofa. It was impossible not to brush his leg against hers. The contact spread warmth through his joints and a jolt of desire to his groin.

"You've been evading me." She brushed a stray hair from her face, dark eyes shining like polished onyx. "While I'm beginning to realize this is something you do, I want to tell you that I will no longer stand for it."

"But—"

"Please do not interrupt. If you want me gone from your house, I am prepared to leave. The garden is complete and yet Lady Wainscott remains."

His lips flattened. She was angry. He could hear it in her clipped words, see it in the tenseness of her shoulders. For so long she refused to leave, refused to release him from the chaos she created. Now after his quick and urgent taking of her the other night she was ready to walk out the door.

An ache widened in his chest. He was an arrogant fool who could not admit when he'd been in the wrong. Ashworth lifted a shoulder. "I do not love the Countess, nor do I intend to cater to her needs."

Vivian did not blink. "Then why is she still here?"

Because she was stubborn and determined and...and he had no real reason. Other than to remind him what happened when he fell in love. Catherine reminded him of what could happen if he gave his heart to Vivian. He would not say that, of course. Instead, he shrugged carelessly. "Why make her go? It gives me pleasure to see her fume in defeat."

Her midnight eyes widened. "You let her stay to amuse yourself with her emotions? Is that what you do with me?"

Hell, he wanted Vivian to stay. "Yes." But he did not enjoy fooling with her emotions. "I mean, no." She was not Catherine, but she was a woman. He'd learned how easily they changed their minds.

She crossed her arms. "I will no longer be your false betrothed. You once offered to give me coins to find another place to go. I will take that offer and make my way to another hidden location."

Heat flared up from his gut. His ears burned. "You can't go yet."

Vivian raised her brows. "Oh, can't I?"

She couldn't just depart like this. She wouldn't go when he demanded it and now, when he wanted her to stay, she insisted on leaving. Bloody hell, he controlled what went on in this manor. "You'll not go until Catherine leaves."

"I promised to stay until the garden was complete. And it is."

"What about Harry?"

"Ah, now you are willing to let me play with him?"

A vein throbbed on his forehead. "He won't stop talking about you. He couldn't bear it if you left him."

"What about you, my lord?" Her voice lowered. "Could you bear it if I left?"

At one time he could not tolerate it if she stayed. Now he wasn't so sure the nightmares weren't worth her presence.

He had to be a man and admit to his failings. Admit that he used her body for selfish release.

"I..." He stood and partially turned away, staring into the darkness. The soft glow from the lamp embraced them in an intimate cocoon. Ashworth cleared his throat. "I will tell you that I am sorry for the other night."

"Sorry?" Her voice squeaked.

"For what happened in my bedchamber."

"That is unfortunate. Because I am not the least bit sorry."

Vivian knew he wasn't remorseful for what happened

between them. She remembered the way his eyes squeezed closed, the look of utter ecstasy in his upturned lips. How could she not know what those primal groans meant?

He'd found rapture that night. And so had she.

Her breasts ached for his hands, mouth yearned for his kiss. Whether or not she remained here at Silverstone Manor, Vivian was out to find pleasure. While she still could.

Charles turned back to her, the light spreading across his cheek. His scar appeared deeper, wider in these shadows. His eyes looked more hopeful than she'd seen in a very long time.

He thrust a hand through his hair. "But I...overtook you."

She scooted to the edge of the couch. Her nipples twinged, pebbled. But he was still too far from reach. "I needed you as desperately as you needed me. I thought I might die from the longing if you had exiled me to my bedchamber."

"Vivian, you spoke of how your first time lacked tenderness, how the other man did nothing to bring you satisfaction."

She gazed up at his long, lean figure. This time it pleased her to have him towering over her. Her blood burned. "And it was so. But you are not him. My body has craved your touch almost since the day I arrived."

He took a step closer and Vivian smoothed her hands down his hips. "I am no virgin."

Charles moaned at her caresses. "I feared I was the same as the man you had run from."

She leaned forward and rested her cheek into his pelvis, where his flesh instantly hardened against her. "You are a man who has made me wanton with desire."

He dug his hands into her hair. "I..." His voice softened, like the whisper of an angel. "I don't want you to think I am a monster."

Vivian turned her face and pressed her lips to the strained fabric of his trousers. The spot between her legs dampened as she remembered the taste of his flesh in her mouth, the stark hunger in his gaze when he yanked her away. For all his might and prowess, he was only a vulnerable man when faced with the most ancient of needs.

His hands swept down her shoulders to under her arms and he pulled her to stand. "Not today." He started unbuttoning her dress. "Today we give you bliss."

Vivian licked her lips, recalled the dream she had of being out on the lake. Her mysterious stranger kissed her inner thighs, pressed his lips against her mound, sunk his tongue into her core. He tasted her until the sweet tension broke and rocked her into reality.

She whimpered.

He lifted her chin, nibbled at her lips. "So you like my idea." Hot hands found her breasts and freed them of the restrictive clothing. "You want me to fondle you, kiss you, taste you."

If he touched her in just the right spot now, she would be lost to the heavens.

Instead, she took in a deep breath and unbuttoned his pants.

"No." The word trembled with raw hunger. "Not yet."

But Vivian continued until his trousers were loose. She pushed his clothing to the floor, allowing his magnificent flesh to spring free into her hand.

"Vivian...I—I can't...not if you..."

"Tonight is not the night to be leisurely." She kicked off her petticoats and undergarments until she stood naked before him. "I want to prove to you that what happened the first time brought me as much pleasure as it did you."

She led him to the couch and pushed at him.

Charles lifted a brow. "You want me to sit?"

Vivian nodded. She watched as he removed his shirt, her gaze drawn to the massive expanse of his chest. Every muscle perfect and powerful, from the firm curve of his jaw to hard planes of his stomach. From the tight roundness of biceps to the strength of his feet. Every feminine part in her body rose to attention, cried for his mercy.

He was glorious, breathtaking, wild and fierce. And she yearned for him like she never would another.

He lowered himself to the sofa and spread his arms across the back. His erection rose upward, as if daring her to act upon it.

Vivian moved close to him, her pulse violent. But first she unraveled her braid, knowing how much it aroused him to see her so undone. His breath snagged as she combed her fingers through her hair then swept it over her shoulders.

"It shines like the still waters of Briarwater at midnight."

She smiled at his flattery. "Someday I would like to return to Briarwater." Hovering over him, Vivian straddled his legs. "I would like to take a small boat, you and I, and row out to the middle under a brilliant, starry sky."

He sighed. "Yes."

She bent low, brought her lips close to his. "Take me hard and fast as you did the other day."

He blinked, gulped.

"This tension inside me must be broken. I've not the patience for slow adoration." Her hands gripped his powerful shoulders, already slick with a sheen of sweat.

Hot fingers clamped onto her hips. "Are—are you ready for me?" Desire and dread mingled in his shadowed eyes.

"Why did you close your eyes last time? Don't you want to watch us?"

His lips thinned, nostrils flared. "Vivian, I want to watch more than you will ever know. But I cannot. I fear..." He would say no more.

Those bloody secrets! She would force it from his lips somehow. He would tell her what kept him so hidden behind crumbling walls and untrue rumors.

Vivian lowered herself until her aching dampness rubbed against the tip of his arousal. Charles moaned. His eyelids drifted closed.

She sank down on him and whimpered with the amazing sensation of fulfillment. She could stay here forever, connected to him.

His hands rocked her back and forth, pulled her up and down his shaft. She watched his cheeks turn ruddy, his lips part. But his eyes remained shut.

Using the strength in her legs, she lifted herself up and held still.

"Down, Vivian... keep moving."

She pushed his arms away. "Not until you look at me."

Instantly, he squeezed his eyes. "No. I'll not."

She sank down, tingles raced through her legs until her toes curled. Her tension tightened, bringing a gasp to her lips and a powerful yearning to her nipples.

But she forced herself to rise. "Look at me."

Charles clamped his jaw, but refused her command. "Do not force me to do this, Vivian. I want pleasure too."

Damn him! What did he see when he gazed upon her? What terrible vision turned him away?

Vivian slid down once again on his erection. This time, she moved her hips toward him, stroking her sensitive nub against his hard flesh.

He threw his head back. Damp curls clung to the strained tendons on his neck. Vivian brought her lips to his skin, licked the salt along his muscles.

Groaning, he grabbed her breasts, kneading them, circling the peaks with his thumbs.

She rocked on him, rising, twisting, pressing. She pushed the tempo, suckled his ears, plundered his lips.

The tension rose between them, the air thick with their

desperate need for release.

He buried his face into the curve of her shoulder, nipping her skin with a gentle tease. "Vivian...oh, Vivian."

The bubble expanded deep in her core, widening, ready to burst. She wanted...oh Lord, she needed...

No, she would force him to share this moment with her. Vivian rose up one last time, her restraint put to the test. "Look. At. Me."

She cupped her hands around his jaw, the evening whiskers a sensual tickle on her palms. "I will not leave you. No matter what."

"Nay, Vivian." His husky voice spoke of hunger.

"Either tell me what you fear or open your eyes. Else you will not find relief within me."

The entire room stilled, paused into immobility. Even in the dim light she could see the struggle upon his face, the wincing of his closed eyelids. Any moment now she expected him to push her off, choosing frustration over confession, disappointment over courage.

Her leg muscles throbbed from the position she held, her heart drummed deep within her ribs. The need for relief was so intense, so strong, an urge rose to bring her fingers to the wetness between her legs.

Instead, she swept her hand along the slick skin of his hardened flesh, reminding him of her presence. Of what he would miss should he choose the familiar comfort.

Charles stilled her hand. "Can't you understand? I want to envision your beauty, not see you as...as repulsive."

She pressed her lips to his ear. "You can control what you see. Believe that you will see beauty and you will."

"I don't...can't believe you."

"Then I go." She pulled back and lifted her leg away. It pained her to do so. Not just for the passion she craved with him but the trust she hoped he'd give her.

"Wait."

Vivian paused, stood before him. A cool breeze blew across her damp skin. The light dimmed and flickered.

Charles drew in a deep breath and straightened his shoulders.

His eyes snapped open.

Chapter Twenty-Four

There was no blood.

Ashworth stared at Vivian's brilliant eyes, her succulent lips, dimpled chin. His gaze moved lower, down her smooth shoulders, over her rose-tipped breasts, along her shadowed stomach.

His pulse quickened. He saw nothing marring the triangle of hair between her long, shapely legs.

Oh God, had the curse been broken?

Her hand reached out and brushed his jaw. "What do you see, my lord?"

Ashworth swallowed, his mouth suddenly parched. "Beauty."

She traced a line down his scar. "You trusted me. Believed me."

Deliverance swept like a crisp river through his bloodstream. He'd been freed. No more sights of blood, no more visions of death. Perhaps the nightmares too would be gone.

He grinned, brushed his fingers over her tempting peaks.

Her breath hitched. She still wanted him. How he planned to fill her....

Ashworth pulled her closer to him, buried his face between her breasts. She smelled lightly of sweat mixed with honeysuckle. He licked his way down her skin, tickled her navel with his tongue.

His flesh hardened again.

"I want to taste you, Vivian. I want to see...nay, lick, every inch of your supple skin."

"I want," she swallowed, "I want that, but I need...I'm so tight..."

His lips curled. "Tight?"

She straddled his legs again. "I must have release. Soon."

Ashworth grabbed the round cheeks of her bottom, his voice low and husky. "You still want it hard and fast, Vivian?"

She bit her lip, whimpered.

In an instant, he flipped her onto her back, lying her along the couch. Her face flushed, eyes half lowered, as he nudged himself between her legs.

"You are beautiful. And you are mine."

Ashworth thrust himself deep. Her wet heat enveloped him in glorious rapture. She wiggled beneath him, rose her hips up. Her need for release was far more desperate than his. He plunged in over and over, wrenching cries from her lips as her head twisted from side to side.

Her nipple tasted of heaven, sweet and luscious.

"Please!" She grabbed his hips, pulled him deep. "More!"

He reached his hand between their bodies and flicked her swollen nub with his fingers, even as he continued driving into her soft flesh.

"Oh...yes!" Her head dropped back and her channel convulsed around him in divine spasms.

He'd intended to still, to let her have her moment. But he couldn't withhold the surge rising up from his core. Ashworth plunged into her moisture again and again. Surely he would die if he stopped now. Die if he didn't find release.

Tingles raced down his spine, then exploded in his groin.

His groans echoed off the chamber's walls. He collapsed onto her, physically and emotionally spent. "Vivian...you don't know what you have done for me."

Her breath was warm in his ear. "Are you a changed man?"

"You have set me free. I don't know how but you've done it."

"No." She brushed the damp hair from his forehead, her own breathing shallow. "You have believed in yourself. Perhaps now you can tell me what you would see."

Could he? What would she think of his gruesome visions? Of his shocking story of waking up and finding a whore covered in blood and a knife in his hand?

His gut twisted, saturating his mouth with a bitter taste.

Ashworth slid out of her. His breathing was still erratic, his pulse still frenzied, but he could not reveal his horrifying secrets.

"Don't go."

But he was already pulling his clothing on. "I'll find Lady Wainscott and ask her to leave. Her presence has become too unsettling."

Vivian's eyes penetrated through the soft glow. "You ask her to go because it upsets me?"

He shrugged, uncertain which answer she hoped to hear.

"Does that mean you intend to marry me?"

Ashworth forced himself to continue his dressing, forced himself not to flinch. "You don't know me. Don't know what I'm capable of."

"Then tell me."

"Nay."

"You are afraid I would leave you? Not accept you?"

He didn't know what he feared by telling her. Could he trust her? What if she found a way to take Harry from him?

She wouldn't want him anyway. Could she possibly love him despite the truth? He snorted. He once thought Catherine loved him too.

Vivian stood and searched for her underclothes. He watched her firm bottom as she bent over to sort through the jumble of fabrics on the floor. He could observe her all day, gaze at her while sleeping, stare at her as she gardened.

She continued dressing in silence, only releasing a heavy sigh as she braided her hair. Now completely recomposed, Vivian lifted her chin.

"I'll not be your mistress, my lord. As much as I need to remain in hiding, I cannot sacrifice my honor." Along with determination in her eyes, he could have sworn he saw something akin to dread. "If you find you still cannot marry me, then I...I will go."

Ashworth spun away from her. His throat stung as if he'd swallowed a mountainside of thistles.

How could he marry her? Despite being absolved of the visions, he was not pardoned from his possible participation in a killing. He suffered enough raising Harry under that chance, but the sight of his son never caused ghastly images.

What if those hauntings returned? He could not sleep in his wife's bed, nor fill her belly with his child.

And if she left the manor? His son would wail at her loss, the garden would once again fall into a hopeless tangle, the room next to his would house only spiders.

And he would feel dead. Just as he had before she'd arrived.

So Charles thought he could avoid her.

Catherine turned the corner down the dimly lit hallway. She would not return to London a failure, with her tail tucked between her legs. How hard could it be to convince a lonely, wealthy eccentric to marry a beautiful woman of proper society? Who else would be willing to have his name?

The oft-dirty Miss Suttley?

She laughed and rounded another corner. The girl, despite being a baron's daughter, was not prepared to be a viscount's wife. Obviously, she too was out to use Charles. But her reasons were vague.

Catherine would make them known. She would not allow that girl to take her man away.

The ancient wooden door she sought loomed dark at the end of the hallway. Outside it a glass of clear liquid rested upon a tarnished silver platter. Ah, a perfect greeting.

The tray in one hand, she knocked.

Shuffling noises behind the door and then it swung open.

Catherine couldn't withhold her gasp. Charles stood in only his breeches. His bare chest gleamed in the low light, hard angles and dark shadows. She never realized the strength in his shoulders or arms, the leanness of his stomach.

Something stirred deep inside her center. She had not been with a man for far too long. And her husband never looked like this.

Charles sighed. "Catherine. What are you doing here?"

She gathered her wits and held the tray up. "You called for a drink?"

His silver eyes stared at her, penetrating her. The spot between her legs ached, dampened.

He took the tray. "Thank you. Good night."

She refused to yield that easily. "You have avoided me."

"For good reason, I am certain."

"I tire of these games. Do what makes the most sense."

He set the tray down up his night table. "Yes, I plan to."

Her heart pattered. She untied the string of her robe, letting it fall open to reveal her thin chemise. "Take me tonight, Charles."

His lips curled as he crossed his arms. "I thought I revolted you."

"I-I have overcome that." She ran her fingertips over the hard muscles of his arm. "I want you. I want to marry you."

He remained motionless. "You want me to return with you to London? Host balls at our home? Father your children?"

Catherine struggled to keep the smile upon her lips. She could deal with those issues later. Right now she needed to hear that he would take her, that he would clear her of her late husband's debts. "Kiss me and I will do whatever you like."

"Whatever I like? Tell me I have your word on that."

He glanced her over. A tingle raced through her bloodstream, weakening her knees.

Right now her need was so great she would agree to anything. Perhaps she would even want him in her bed each night, bringing her pleasure such as she experienced right now.

He yanked her close, knotted his hand in her hair. She gasped, pressed her breasts against his chest. "Your word, Catherine."

She angled her face, lowered her lashes. "Yes. Anything you wish. Just kiss me."

His warm mouth touched hers. Catherine opened her lips to him, welcoming his tongue with a fervor of need. She melted against him, rubbed her aching spot on his leg. His tongue stroked hers, reminding her of a man's arousal deep within her.

She grasped his hair, pulling him in further. The need for release rose up, causing pain at her nipples, hunger at her flesh.

Charles kissed her hard, almost violently. His large hands rested on her shoulders as if he were ready to shove her away at any moment. She wouldn't let him.

Catherine thrust her hips against him, captured his jaw in her hands, and suckled his tongue as if it were plunging within her feminine center. The crest of her passion rose to a pitch.

She yanked on his fingers and placed them over her breast. With his slightest touch, she climaxed.

Waves of release shuddered through her. She was so dazed, Catherine didn't realize Charles had thrust her away until she nearly fell against his bed.

Catching her breath, she watched as he stood motionless

before the fireplace. He forced a hand through his hair. His face betrayed nothing as he turned to face it. He must have felt passion for her. That episode must have brought out some desire.

She gathered her composure and walked over to where he stood. "When will you tell Miss Suttley to go?"

He did not make a move that he heard her.

"Have her pack her things at daybreak."

"Miss Suttley is not going anywhere."

Heat from the fire crept up Catherine's legs. Her elation of a few moments ago dimmed. "You have no reason for her to remain here if we are to wed."

"We are not to wed, Catherine."

Her pulse charged. "Look at me, damn you!"

He swung around, his lips twisted into a snarl. "You gave me your word you would do anything if I kissed you."

"I did. You mentioned living with me in London. Having your children. How can that not mean you will marry me?"

"You said you would do 'anything'. It is you who interpreted it to mean that."

She narrowed her eyes. "What are you telling me, Charles?"

"*You* are to leave Silverstone at dawn."

Rage choked her. "Y-you are sending *me* away?"

"Yes. Go back to the wretched hole you crawled out of."

"But what about our kiss?" Her lips still tingled.

Charles crossed his arms and shrugged. "It meant nothing. I felt nothing."

"You can't send me away." She stomped her foot. "I will not go without a marriage contract."

"I can have you forcibly removed."

Catherine stifled her scream, her gut burning with the agonizing rejection. Damn him. Damn that Miss Suttley. She'd find a way to force his hand, she'd find...

Ah, how could she have forgotten?

She lifted her chin. "You have no alternative but to choose me."

He did not blink.

"I know your little secret."

His lips tightened, but he said nothing.

She smirked with glee. "He goes by the name of Harry."

Chapter Twenty-Five

The struggle to keep his face impassive required more strength than he could have imagined. Ashworth fought the dread welling up his throat. She knew about Harry. But how she found out or what exactly she discovered he must ascertain. He must not let fear or rage take control.

"Tell me, Catherine. What is it that you know about Harry?"

She moved closer to him, stood within an arm's reach. But he wouldn't touch her again. "I know that he is a child who lives here under your roof. You have hired your friend, John Hughes, to tutor him."

Was that all she knew? She was not aware of the connection between Harry and himself? Or that the boy was taken from Mary Yeardley's flat?

Ashworth nodded. "Yes, you have found out that truth."

"Who is he? Is he your son?"

"Did you not learn these answers on your own?"

Her nostrils flared. "John would not tell me more."

"So then you know nothing other than I have a boy living here."

"You keep him a secret. There must be a reason for it."

"But that would be none of your business."

"Damn you!" She slapped his cheek.

The sharp sting spread across his jaw. Fury blazed through his veins, wild and reckless. He grabbed her arm and shoved it down by her side. "You'll not control me, Catherine."

She twisted but could not free herself. "Go to hell, where you belong."

He narrowed his eyes, bared his teeth. "That I may. But your actions are not much holier than my own. Vanity. Lies. Deception. Manipulation. What won't you do to get your way?"

Her porcelain skin mottled with red. "You'll regret refusing me. I'll see to it that you meet your ultimate downfall."

He raised an eyebrow and released his hold. "Now, did I seek revenge on you when you refused me?"

She shrugged. "That was your mistake."

Ashworth didn't answer as Catherine made her way to his door. She grasped the handle then looked back at him. "Your nightmares are only beginning, I promise you that."

"Be gone at daybreak."

But as she slammed the door, his gut knotted. He could not shake the feeling he had just chosen Vivian over his son.

No, he must believe that Catherine would find nothing about Harry, no one to connect him to the murder in St. Giles.

And now that one woman was leaving, he must turn his attention to the one remaining. Could he finally convince Vivian to leave him to his seclusion or did he long for her to remain here forever?

☓

Vivian stared at the calm surface of Briarwater. She could not believe she was here. Nor could she actually believe that Lady Wainscott was gone. She and her maid had taken their things and left before breakfast a week before.

Charles had not spoken much to her in the days that followed and now he was again in one of his silent moods. It was surprising that he'd offered to take her and Harry out on a boat if the weather held.

A quick glance at the sky told her they would not have more than a few hours to enjoy the shifting sunlight and warm breeze.

Harry, squeezing her hand tightly, bounced up and down as his father pulled the rowboat closer to the dock. The boy's red hair gleamed brilliantly against the blue waters. His eyes were alive and bright as the swaying trees.

With the boat secure, Charles helped her in, his hand warm and familiar. Her heart sped at the contact. She took a seat, the boat rocking as Harry clambered on board and settled beside her. Finally, they were all seated and set out upon a brief journey.

Of course, this was not what she had in mind exactly when she told Charles of her desires. No, she wanted to be here under a starry, midnight sky. She wanted his hands upon her, his mouth tasting her.

"Look!"

She smiled at Harry's exuberance. Perhaps this was better. The boy had not been permitted here before. He told her on the walk that he had not gone farther than Silverstone's borders.

"I see a turtle!"

Vivian followed his pointing finger to a clump of branches and leaves floating on the water. Sure enough, a large turtle sunned himself upon the oasis.

She lifted her gaze to the boy's father. He wasn't looking at them, but staring out at some unseen point, lost to his thoughts and troubles. "I think he is enjoying this."

Charles did not answer. He continued rowing, unaware of what lay behind him or the direction they headed.

Harry clutched her hand. "Did you see it?"

"Yes. He was magnificent."

"Why isn't Papa looking?"

"I don't know. He must have much on his mind."

Harry bounced in his seat and finally turned to her with

questioning eyes. "Maybe he is thinking of that lady in the fancy dresses."

"Lady Wainscott?" Had Harry met her too? Had he gone through the endless secret passageways and spied on her?

"She's gone now. Maybe he misses her."

A vice gripped her lungs, stole her breath. Vivian never considered that the Countess could have left on her own accord. Maybe Charles had not dismissed her from the manor, maybe she departed and he now grieved for her loss.

Vivian swallowed. "Did you ever talk to her, Harry? Tell me the truth."

The child shook his head. "No. She scared me a little."

She squeezed the boy against her but watched his father. He'd removed his jacket and now rowed in only his white shirt. It billowed in the wind then pressed against the solid angles of his chest.

She wanted to touch that chest, allow her fingers to smooth the dark curls on his stomach. The last two times they'd been together, they had not been given the time for exploration. Suddenly, she missed that. Suddenly, she wanted it more than anything.

Vivian reached forward and tapped his knee. He focused on her, startled. "We've nearly gone to the other side."

Charles glanced behind him then dropped the oars. "I suppose I had not been paying attention."

"We saw a turtle, Papa. You missed him."

"Well, then, we shall turn around and find him again."

Relief tugged at the corner of her lips. Finally he had come around and joined them in their adventure. And yet his eyes still held his secrets. Ones she feared she would never learn.

After finding the turtle and spotting several species of birds and curious fish, they headed back to the dock.

"Papa," Harry said, as they neared the shore. "May I come down and have dinner with you and Miss Suttley?"

"Will you be joining me for dinner, Miss Suttley?"

She lifted her gaze to his predatory stare. She was unable to determine if he wanted her there or not, if he longed to have the Countess return or was glad she had gone.

His hooded, unreadable eyes breached her sheltered soul and plunged her under his spell.

Vivian could do nothing but nod.

"It is settled then." He offered his son a smile. "We will ask John to join us tonight and all dine together."

John must be the man she heard speaking several times, the one she assumed to be Harry's tutor.

After they'd gotten off the boat, Harry scampered up ahead, pulling flowers and chasing after squirrels.

Charles took her arm. Warmth spread into her heart then flooded the remainder of her body. "Wear one of your new dresses tonight."

His request surprised her. With Lady Wainscott gone, who was left to impress?

They climbed the slope of Briarfell, the breeze much cooler than earlier. Up ahead, Harry crouched to inspect something on a moss covered rock.

A weight seemed to press on Ashworth's shoulders. "I slept very little last night."

"You did seem rather distracted on the boat."

Charles stopped her with his arm, but his eyes revealed nothing. "I have decisions to make. Ones that affect you."

Her pulse trembled, ice trickled into her bloodstream. Was she the next to go? Would a pouch of coins rest on her pillow when she returned from dinner?

"Come see!" Harry waved to them from his position.

Charles left her and lowered himself beside his son. Vivian stared at the two of them. One with hair the color of fire, the other a warm brown. The love between them was obvious, deep, unbreakable.

An ache burrowed beneath her breast. Who was she to come into their lives and disrupt it all? She'd arrived at Silverstone an unwelcome outsider. Had she become any less foreign to them?

Vivian had been a desperate fool when she burst into this manor demanding to marry its lord. Now she knew better, knew more what she wanted for her future.

She didn't want to be wedded to a stranger for the mere sake of his protection. She wanted affection, tenderness, devotion, trust. Damn it, she wanted love.

And no matter how intensely she may arouse Charles's passions, it was clear he did not love her.

Vivian chose a dress of emerald green, with lace piping around the neckline and little bows at her waist. It had been so long since she wore something so fancy she actually felt foolish. Especially being in this dark house where the only things that shined brightly were spider webs catching the occasional sunrays.

Charles turned from speaking with another man when she entered the dining hall. His silver eyes widened, the corners of his mouth curled.

He nudged the man, John she assumed, and raised his eyebrows. Her cheeks flushed, a mixture of embarrassment and annoyance. She was not one to enjoy being put on display. Her father could never understand why she'd rather be out in the fields or tromping through mud instead of going to balls.

Martin had made it clear that she would not appear any less than a lady at all times as his wife. He'd literally ripped off the plain linen dress she wore that one night, telling her the others would meet a similar fate.

Her throat tightened, eyes burned. What if she had not run? What if she had not heard of Viscount Ashworth and his supposed need for a wife? Would her belly already be growing with Martin's baby?

A small hand tugged on her fingers. "You look very pretty, Miss Suttley."

Vivian smiled. Leave it to Harry to shake her from her fears. "Thank you. And you are quite handsome yourself."

Charles came around, Harry's tutor in tow. "Mr. John Hughes, may I present Miss Suttley, daughter of Lord Whistlebury."

His formality surprised her, but not nearly as much as the icy gleam in John's eyes.

He took her hand and kissed it. "Miss Suttley."

She nodded, searching for that coldness again but it was gone. Perhaps she had imagined it completely. "Mr. Hughes."

Charles clapped John on the shoulder. "This man has been a friend of mine since school days. I couldn't have been luckier to have him move out to Silverstone with me."

John's cheeks brightened, suddenly making him appear the most pleasant man in the world.

Dinner progressed well enough, making Vivian almost sorry she had avoided it for so long. It certainly wasn't the same to dine alone in her room. Then again, this company was infinitely better than what she had to face before.

They talked about Harry's schoolwork, his love of animals and nature. Harry gave everyone an update on the baby duck's growth and how well she was eating her meals. There was mention of the weather, the snows arriving in a few months, and the cold, dark nights. All topics were light, frivolous.

No one asked her where she'd come from, who she'd left behind, or if she ever planned on returning.

None of them seemed to care of her past, of who she was and what made her the person she'd become. Life in this manor transformed its inhabitants. They had become lost, hollow. Each of them avoided a pain in their past, an aching memory which bound them to these stone walls and kept them from the rest of the world.

None of them were truly living.

Charles stood, gulped his wine, then called everyone's attention. "Before we partake of dessert, I have something to say."

Vivian held her breath, her nerves tingling. She knew not why she waited with such anticipation on his words. Perhaps it was that a final decision was being made. She would no longer exist in limbo, caught between his secret need to send her away and his burning desire to have her stay.

"Yes, Papa?" Harry squealed.

He smiled at his son, the scar curving like a bird's feather. "Miss Suttley has been here with us for a few weeks now. She has created a garden and created havoc. She's withstood the disrepair of this house and a bully's taunting. She's made friends with spiders and ducklings alike."

Charles turned his attention back to her. He stared across the table, his hooded gaze drawing her in. Suddenly, there was no one else but the two of them, no dishes or candles between them, no sounds, nothing but his lips close to hers.

"Miss Suttley..." He cleared his throat. "I want you to be my wife."

In an instant she was back in her seat, at the far end of the room, Harry and his tutor on either side of her. The sounds of dishes clanged in her ears. The smells from the last course assaulted her nose.

She clutched the arms of her chair, unable to think, unable to speak.

Harry leapt from his seat and jumped up and down. "I'm going to have a mama, I'm going to have a mama."

When she glanced at John, his face was white. But he smiled at her and lifted his glass. "I think this calls for a celebration. Why don't I see if Cook has any of her special tarts?"

"Well, Vivian, have you nothing to say?"

To say she was stunned would undervalue her true feelings. She had been certain he would ask her to go in the morning. Certain he would be more than ready to have his manor, his life, return to the way it was before she arrived.

She blinked at him.

Charles grinned, his eyes dark with hunger. "Perhaps you would care to discuss it later. In private."

Vivian nodded. That was it. She needed time to think, to sort out the unsettled gnawing in her gut. Marriage to him was the very thing which brought her here. The sole reason she refused to leave. She should be leaping as Harry was.

Instead, his proposal gave the same cavalier impression as the rest of the conversation. As if he'd just mentioned that trees in the yard needed pruning. He didn't ask her, didn't say he loved her, just declared what he wanted.

But how could she be his wife when he would not open himself to her? How could she live here forever when she knew nothing about his past or what brought him to this circumstance?

"Here we are."

John entered the room followed by a servant girl carrying a tray. He placed a dish before her. "First we serve our newest member of the family."

She stared at the tart before her, the aroma of apples and currants pleasant, yet nauseating. Her appetite was gone, stolen by shock.

When all had been served, the girl disappeared. Harry dove into his dessert without taking a breath. The others ate too. She just stared at her plate.

"It's Cook's specialty," Charles said between mouthfuls. "You must take a bite or two."

Vivian nodded and took a taste. The warm apples and sugar melted on her tongue, but there was a bitter trace afterward. It tasted as if Cook had added the wrong spice to the ingredients. No one else seemed to notice or mind.

John lifted his eyebrows. "Well, do tell, Miss Suttley. How does it rate?"

Too polite to make a complaint, Vivian took two more bites then set down her spoon. "I cannot eat another bite. This dinner has been most wonderful."

She watched the three of them clean their plates, Harry beg for more, and her wine cup refilled. But she'd had enough wine already, for a sudden tiredness pressed down upon her. Her stomach, already shaky from Charles's statement, twisted and burned.

"I think..." she rubbed her temples. "I think I need to lie down."

"Vivian, are you ill?"

The flickering candles in the room glowed unnaturally bright, searing her eyes. She must get to her bedchamber.

"Pl-please, excuse me."

She pushed back from the table and tried her best to make a dignified retreat and not to stumble from the room. She made it down the long hallways, up the grand stairwell, and down the passageway to her room.

Dizzy and nauseous, her door but a few steps away, Vivian sank against a wall. Voices and random moments spun and collided in her brain.

You have set me free. I don't know how but you've done it.

I want to make you my wife.

If you do not leave this place, I will kill you.

She dropped her head to her knees, swallowing the bile slithering up her throat. Oh Lord, she'd not grown ill from the wine or the sudden turn of events.

She'd been poisoned.

Chapter Twenty-Six

Martin climbed into the rented carriage, his jaw throbbing from endless clenching. Dowager Ashworth had done nothing more than turn her nose up at him and walk out of the room. Bitch.

His mother had not been any more help. In fact, she was becoming more and more useless to him.

"21 Grosvenor Square," he told the driver.

However, his lovely widow friend he'd met at that ball had truly been a fountain of information. Now that he had a child to locate, as well as Vivian, he needed as much of her help as possible.

He would find this child everyone seemed to know about, the boy who could be Ashworth's son. And his once friend would pay for the betrayal. What better way to draw the man out than by kidnapping the boy? The boy who should be *his* son. He just had to find that coward.

Martin sat back in the seat and watched the wealthy homes of London speed past. He'd live here one day, or close to it. He may not ever have a title but he could amass the income to buy his way into elite society.

He needed Vivian. Honestly, his widow lover could provide him with more of what he needed to further his goals. She had the class, the title, the home. But then she would have the control. And he would not stand for that.

No, Vivian would do just fine. He'd already claimed her as

his own, marked her with his teeth and hands. She was young, beautiful and naive.

"21 Grosvenor Square," the driver announced, pulling the carriage to a stop.

Martin stepped down into light rain. "I shall return in thirty minutes."

He'd not fail at this house. She must have the answers he sought, for he knew no one else to contact. Ashworth's friend, John Hughes, had vanished several years ago and his family would no longer speak of him. All other friends had lost touch with the Viscount.

He banged the heavy knocker. Only Catherine, now the Countess of Wainscott, could have some idea of where Ashworth had gone. And perhaps if he had a child along with him.

The butler led him to the rose-colored parlor. Martin did not sit but waited by the enormous fireplace, inspecting the brass figurines and crystal vases.

Ashworth would have married Catherine had he not decided to visit Mary that night. Bloody fool. He lost his bride, place in society and disappeared into hiding. All for a sample of Mary's talents.

The sound of rustling skirts drew Martin's attention. He looked over his shoulder to see Catherine, still exquisite these many years later. Her golden hair shimmered, her skin pure and unblemished. She was one of the marble statues in the main foyer come to life.

Her sharp hazel eyes and amused grin made the hair on his neck rise. "You do not seem surprised to see me."

"I'm not."

Martin moved closer, the scent of lavender filling his senses, arousing his groin. "Then perhaps you can tell me why I am here."

Catherine pointed to a chair. "Won't you sit?"

"I prefer to stand."

"Fine then." She lowered herself to the sofa. "You could only be here to ask me information about Lord Ashworth. You must assume I know of his whereabouts."

Martin curled his lip. "Perceptive, Lady Wainscott. I'm impressed. Now tell me why it is that I seek him."

"It has something to do with that whore, of course. Weren't you the one who introduced them?"

Martin clenched his hands into fists, his pulse quickening. He detested when Mary was called a whore. Yes, she earned her coins that way, but what other way was there on those streets? And, yes, he'd introduced Ashworth to her, but he never expected them to betray him. Or to have a child, by devil! The child that should have been his!

"Her *name* was Mary Yeardley."

She raised an eyebrow, lips twitching. "But of course."

"So tell me, Lady Wainscott, do you know where Ashworth resides now?"

"I do."

Relief buzzed through him. "You can provide me a location?"

"I can. In fact, I could take you there myself should I care to return. But I don't."

"Return?"

She nodded, bitterness in her eyes. "I was there not so long ago, you see. Spent several weeks in that awful disaster of a manor. I've never been happier to be home."

Martin sat. This was even better than he expected. "Tell me then, who was there with him? Or does he live alone?"

"Charles wants the world to think he is there alone, but others are there, hidden behind walls and secrets."

"Who? Who else is there?"

"Well, there is someone there you know. John Hughes."

So that's where John disappeared to. He left London, his

family, his chance at his inheritance to be with Ashworth in the far countryside? What the hell for? Perhaps Ashworth had a fascination for his own gender like Lord Whistlebury.

Catherine chuckled. "I see you are confused. I was too, believe me. But he is actually in Charles's employ."

"As what?"

Her eyes lit up. She was clearly enjoying this conversation, as if she had nothing better to do than divulge all of Ashworth's dirty secrets. Luckily, he was just the right person to hear them.

"John is there as a tutor."

A flood of viciousness rushed through his system. So, he'd been right. The baby had been Ashworth's. Their treachery had gone on longer than he realized, long enough to give them a child. Betrayal of the worst kind.

He swallowed to keep his fury in check. "A tutor, did you say?"

Catherine shifted in her seat, smoothed out her dress. "Unfortunately, I know nothing more than there is a boy there by the name of Harry. I know not his age, nor what he looks like."

"Harry, eh?"

"So, Mr. Crawford...Martin. I have given you the information I know. Now you can tell me what it is you seek from Charles."

This time he was the one who laughed. "I seek exactly what you told me."

"About the child?"

"Yes."

"Why would you care about this boy?"

Revenge. The boy was proof of Ashworth's ongoing affair with Mary. He'd pay for his reckless act. What better way to destroy the man than to take his child away? That child would be Martin's in the end.

The energy of regaining control filled him with a sense of power.

Martin inhaled a deep breath, tasting Catherine's lavender scent. He licked his lips, briefly perusing her buttermilk skin. Ah, the bright and beautiful marks he could make upon it. "Tell me, Lady Wainscott, why did *you* go out there to see your former love?"

Her nostrils flared. "I'd rather not discuss that."

"Because he refused you?" He snorted. "You rejected him first."

She eyed him coldly. "I had good reason. He did not."

Martin shrugged, stood. He didn't care of their relationship, of their pathetic inability to repair the past. He only cared about getting to Ashworth's lair.

"Thank you for your information. Perhaps I could be of service to you."

"Yes, actually." She rose to her feet. "I'll give you directions to his manor. Are you headed there directly then?"

"Yes. I'll leave tomorrow."

Catherine smirked. "Well, then, perhaps there is something you could do for me after all."

He stared at her neck, her bosom, his heart racing again. "What could that be, my lady?"

"Not me." She lifted her pretty chin. "Set your paws on the woman Ashworth claims is his betrothed."

"Ah, so there was a reason he snubbed you."

"I have found myself someone much more worthy. The Earl of Middleborough has asked for my hand. I am much more blessed with this match."

Martin led the way to the foyer, where the butler retrieved his hat. "Why have me bother with this girl then? Is it that if he won't have you than he can have no one?"

She scribbled notes on a scented sheet of paper and handed it to him. "The reasons are mine. Just cause him misery. Get rid of her, I don't care how."

He chuckled, excited at the possibility of retribution on Ashworth by taking away two of his loves. "I'll see to it that the lowly chit is no longer good enough for your beloved Charles."

Catherine laughed. "That lowly chit claimed to be a baron's daughter. But she behaved and dressed no better than a shop worker."

Martin paused, his nerves suddenly taut. Could it be...? "Did you say 'baron's daughter'?"

"Yes, so she claimed."

He held his breath. "Her name?"

"Miss Suttley. Why? Do you know her?"

He should have experienced relief. Finally, he knew where Vivian was. Instead a squall of violence gathered in his bloodstream. That bloody bastard had taken both Mary and Vivian from him. While Martin wasted all this time in London, chasing lies and vile memories, Vivian was in his enemy's manor. Ashworth had probably soiled her by now.

He stormed out of the house, down the steps into a downpour. Rage consumed every piece of his soul as he climbed back into the carriage.

Vivian didn't end up at that remote manor by accident. No, she overheard Martin say how much he despised the viscount, how he'd hoped he never saw the bastard again. It was the perfect place for her to run from him.

He forced a smirk upon his lips. He'd be there soon. And then there would be hell to pay.

For everyone.

"She's here, milord."

Ashworth ran over to Pinkley, who stood guard, like an impenetrable sentinel, over the slumped figure of Vivian.

Heart hammering, Ashworth sank to his knees next to her.

"Vivian. Please, what's happened?"

She whimpered. "So tired."

He scooped her into his arms, pressing her close to his chest. Pinkley scurried ahead and opened her bedchamber door. "Bring up some tea."

"Aye, milord."

Ashworth nudged aside the bed curtains and laid her on the bed. Her face was pale, eyes somewhat sunken. "Was it the wine?"

She blinked haunted eyes at him. "I-I should tell you something."

He brushed his fingers across her lips. "Shh, tell me later, after you have rested."

"No, you must understand. I have to tell you now."

Wind gusted against the walls, quickening drafts through the room. Vivian's lips trembled.

"You are cold." He stood, removed her shoes, and pulled the blankets over her. "You must get well soon. We have a wedding to plan."

Her frigid fingers gripped his hand. "I...I am not so certain there will be a wedding."

His breath lodged in his throat. Dear Lord, she didn't think she would die, did she? "You will recover from this. It will pass."

She managed a smile. "Yes. I am already feeling improved."

There was a light knock on the door. "The tea, milord."

Ashworth retrieved the tray. His rapid pulse belied his calm exterior. How could she not want to marry him now? It was her lone reason for remaining here, for driving him mad with chaos and pleasure. She refused to leave, refused his peace. And now that he'd offered it to her, she refused to accept it?

Concern transformed into ire.

He turned to see her up on an elbow, a slight color returning to her cheeks.

"I have offered you what you sought those weeks ago. Now

you do not want it?"

"I came to you in a panic, desperate for a solution."

He crossed his arms, clenched his jaw, but said nothing.

"But things have changed. I have changed. I want more than just this isolated manor and your name."

"Those were the reasons you stated. Now what do you desire? A fancy house? Trips abroad? Servants to attend you?"

Her eyes narrowed. "No. I want to feel fulfilled, have my heart filled with joy."

"You are saying I cannot give that to you?"

"You will give nothing more than your body."

Ashworth bristled, then dared to ask the very thing he feared. "You want love?"

Vivian sat up and swung her legs over the side of the bed, fervor returning her strength. "It isn't only love. I want trust, devotion, courage. You won't give me those either."

Bloody hell, she was rejecting him. Just as Catherine had done. She couldn't accept him as who he was, she insisted he become something else. Why couldn't she understand that some secrets were better left unsaid?

He was tempted to walk out, drown himself in brandy and sleep until the next sunset. But he would not let her pity him. Instead, he walked over to where she sat upon the bed and stood above her.

"Do you want adoration along with my desire and lust?"

She lifted her chin, her seductive eyes melting his indignation. "I know that you bring me desire. I cannot be near you without my blood humming for your touch."

He traced a finger down her throat, across her shoulder. "I need you, Vivian. Like your garden needs the rain. Like the flowers need the bees."

She rested her head against him. "I know that, my lord. But you don't realize you need more, not only—"

Ashworth would not let her say more. He captured her lips

in a kiss. She tasted of the wine, of sweet apples, of intoxicating honeysuckle.

She leaned back, pulling him down with her.

Liquid heat erupted in his veins. He nibbled on her mouth, licked the curve of her ears, cupped her breasts. By God, she would make him whole. He could not rest until she made him complete.

Vivian smoothed her finger down his scar. "Cherish me. Make me believe you cannot live without me."

Ashworth lifted his face, grinning. "I can easily show you—"

No!

The blood had returned! Bile rose up his throat, choked him.

He leapt back, scrambled from the bed.

"What is it?" She came after him. "It's happened again, hasn't it? Tell me what you see."

He spun away from her, overcome by anguish and misery. He thought she'd cured him of the curse. But it wasn't gone. Would he never be free from it?

Without looking at her, he headed straight for his adjoining door.

"Don't you leave me!"

He didn't stop, but as he went to slam the door behind him, Vivian pushed her way into his room. "I won't let you run this time."

He glared at her, bracing himself for the visions, but only determined beauty stared back at him. "Don't you see? I am not healed. I am still the monster I've always been, haunted by memories too painful to speak of."

"Speak of them and they will be less painful."

His fingers closed into fists. "If it is that easy, then you do it. Tell me your secrets."

She gazed at him, her eyes narrowing. Finally, she sighed. "All right then. I will, but you must promise to tell me what you dread. I will not let you rest until you've done so."

He could scarcely breathe for the fear of the memories, the fear of Vivian's reaction, the fear that he was, in fact, a murderer.

"Promise me. Please."

Unable to resist the tenderness in her gaze, he nodded.

She lifted her chin. "My secret that I've not wanted to tell you is that ever since I've been in this house I have felt in danger."

"Danger?" The Monster? Had the rumors actually come to pass on her?

"One night I was assaulted in the hallway—"

"Assaulted?"

"I don't know who it was but a man stopped me, frightened me. And then the other night, while in the cellar, he was there again."

The Monster only came out during the lost hours of the night when Ashworth drank his potion, not at other times. "What happened then?"

She crossed her arms, leaned against the wall. "I was looking at the toys down there and the light went out. He came up behind me in the blackness and..."

"And?"

"He terrified me. Told me to leave this house or he would kill me."

It could not have been him. He'd not been near the cellar room that day until he'd found her in the dark. But why would she invent a story like this? "No one here wants to kill you."

Her icy glare suggested otherwise. "And just now, after dinner, it wasn't the wine that made me ill. I was poisoned."

Even if he wandered the halls at night, Ashworth certainly did not accost Vivian in the cellar or poison her food. "Vivian, no one in this manor would want to hurt you. They've all been told to keep away from you."

She pressed her lips together, inhaling a deep breath. "You don't believe me."

"I cannot."

She struggled within herself, her face flushing, nostrils flaring. But in the end, she grabbed his hands and gripped them tightly with her fingers. "Regardless of whether you believe it or not, that is what happened. I have told you a secret I have carried, now it is your turn."

His stomach burned, twisted. She was like a bloody hound on a bone, damn her. Damn women. Why could they not leave well enough alone?

But he'd promised. "I...I don't recall everything. The night was a blur."

She pulled him down to the bench at the end of his bed. "Tell me what you do recall. What happened that night? Who was there?"

He clenched his teeth, he still didn't want to tell her. But she was insisting. Demanding, even. Hell, she'd never given up on him the whole time she'd been at the manor. If he couldn't trust her with this story, how could he ever have any type of a marriage with her?

"I was in the room with a woman named Mary."

"Mary."

He nodded, but would not look at her. Could not bear to see if she recognized the name as Harry's mother. He could not see if the disappointment she held for him lingered in her gaze.

"I was to marry Catherine soon and I, well, I had not been with a woman before. I needed...I needed guidance."

"Go on."

"A friend of mine had told me about a...a woman he often visited. I went to see her."

"This was Mary."

"Yes. We shared the night together. Everything was fine and then later, afterward, I got dressed and went out back to relieve myself."

Vivian leaned in toward him, her warmth comforting. "What happened while you were gone?"

Ashworth gulped the hot grief of tears in his throat. "When I came back in there was a man beating her. He was the same friend, the one who told me about her. He was screaming she had betrayed him."

"Did he kill her?"

He shuddered, swallowed again. "No, although when I wrestled him away from her I thought she was dead. But after the man left, she stirred. I ran over to help her as best I could."

"So you might have saved her life."

If only. He broke from Vivian's grasp and strode to the fireplace, where he paced. "She was bloodied but not as injured as she appeared. In fact, Mary was furious with me for not coming to her aid sooner. She claimed I was a coward, that I wasn't good enough for her."

He stopped, stared at the weak flames. "Before I realized what she was doing, she found a knife on the floor and started swinging it at me."

"It wasn't the intruder who slashed you? It was Mary?"

He nodded. For a long time he couldn't even recall the actual moment when his face was cut. Little by little the nightmares brought back the truth. But it was the rest of the story he never could remember.

"I fell backward from the pain. I heard crying, I thought it was her until I saw a bundle move inside a box."

"Harry?"

"Yes. But as I reached for him..." Ashworth's breath shuddered, as he remembered reaching for the torn blankets. He was so close, just a bit more of a stretch and...

"But then Mary hit me on the head with something and knocked me into oblivion."

"Oh goodness." Her voice was closer now, almost within

arm's reach.

"When I awoke later, I was still on the floor." He gulped, winced. His gut burned and cramped. "On top of my outstretched hands was the bloody knife Mary had used to attack me."

She gasped.

"I looked on the bed..." Ashworth squeezed his eyes closed but the image was entrenched in his brain, forever frozen into nightmares and gruesome visions. "Mary was on the bed, stabbed repeatedly, her dead eyes staring at the ceiling."

"Oh, my lord." Her voice broke, tearing at his soul.

"Harry's mother was dead. And I do believe I killed her."

Chapter Twenty-Seven

It wasn't true.

Charles did not kill Harry's mother. She knew it, sensed it in her bones, breathed it in her lungs. This man was not a murderer. He'd saved her that long ago day.

But the look on his face was pure agony. Guilt, horror, wretchedness. "If it were not for my dear friend John, I don't know how I would have made it through each day."

He stripped off his dinner coat, undid several of the buttons on his shirt. Sweat glistened on his face. But he would not look her in the eyes.

"Each time I feel passion for you, your beautiful face turns into the ghastly image of Mary's." He stopped, swallowed. "All I see is blood, death."

Vivian took a step closer, the low fire warming her feet. "But it did not happen in the cellar. Did it happen the first time, over by the tapestry?"

Charles leaned against the mantel, hung his head. "I refused to look at you directly, afraid I'd see it. I don't know the answer, but I am guessing it did not happen."

"So if it did not happen downstairs, but did otherwise, then maybe there is some other cause."

"Nay. It must have something to do with my desire for you. I am being punished for what Mary and I did. And for her death."

Vivian began pacing the room. She didn't believe it. There was something else. "Maybe the bedrooms? No, then you would have seen it that first night."

"Stop, Vivian. There is no point to it. I am doomed to live this way. The scar, the nightmares, the visions—they are all my penance for my sins."

"Your sins!" She wrapped an arm about a bed post. "I don't see how...wait, it's the bed. Each time you have had those visions, we are either on the bed or touching it."

"The bed? What would that do with anything?"

"Didn't you awake to find Mary on the bed covered in blood?"

He leveled his silver eyes at her. "Yes, but, what does that do with my horrible visions?"

"Your mind connects any bed with death. Perhaps now that you've spoken of your secret, the connection will be gone."

Hair fell across his eyes. "I am cursed, Vivian. Cursed."

Wind and rain whipped at the window, thunder rolled in the distance. "You are not cursed. You are not guilty of murder."

"How do you know?"

"Because I know you."

He crossed his arms, turned away.

"I also met you once, long ago, and forever more you were my hero."

He glanced back at her. "Met me? When?"

"It was a garden party at the Duke of Whilhemshire. I was but a girl then, perhaps twelve. I longed to see the exquisite gardens and the Duke himself offered to show them to me."

He gasped. "That was you?"

Vivian nodded. "I barely noticed his brief touches, and his constant compliments were music to my ears. At the time, I didn't understand why you tore yourself away from your beautiful betrothed and demanded the Duke leave my side."

"He was a lecher of the worst kind." Charles hung his head. "I'd heard the rumors and when I saw him with a young girl—you—I noticed the way his gaze roamed over you and his hands touched you inappropriately."

"You risked your reputation for me that day. I was but a stranger to you and yet you had yourself expelled from the party just so that I would not be harmed."

"A distant niece of his was found raped and dead months later."

"I know. Don't you see, Lord Ashworth, you saved a stranger from potential tragedy. That is not a man who could kill another."

He turned away again.

"A man who would murder would not reach for a crying baby. He would not then take that baby back to care for." Vivian let go of the bedpost and walked toward him slowly. "A man who would murder would not live his days in torment over the possibility of it. He would not resist falling in love and being vulnerable to keep others away."

She stopped before him. "You are no murderer, Lord Ashworth. Someone else did it and left you to take the blame."

His gaze held her, eyes shining. She could see he wanted to believe her, wanted so desperately to be rid of this horrible burden. "But who? Who would do this?"

"Could it be the first man? Perhaps he came back to finish the job?"

"I don't know. Maybe. But I truly believed he thought she was dead already when he ran off."

"What was this man's name?" Thunder boomed overhead, wind gusted at the glass.

"Martin Crawford."

Oh Lord.

This is what had come between them. And it was that loathing which brought her here, a place he would never think to look for her.

It made sense that Martin would beat Mary like that. Even enough to kill her. But would he have gone back to check that the deed was done? Or would someone else have slipped in there?

Charles sank down into a chair. His hair scattered about his face, wild and unruly. He looked like a little boy, alone and lost and frightened. Not at all like the monster he claimed he was.

"You cannot find an answer." His tone was almost accusatory, as if he thought she could not solve his long-suffering problem. "I held the knife."

"That doesn't mean—"

"When I drink a concoction Pinkley brings me at night to relieve me of my nightmares, I do not remember anything." He stopped, glanced away. "It is possible my memory of that night in London is gone too. I may have killed her."

"But why?"

He lifted a shoulder, stared into the fireplace. "For retribution for what she did to my face? I don't know. But she was dead when I fully awoke."

"I will not believe it."

"Then who, Vivian?" He gripped the arms of the chair, his voice rising to an unfortunate anger. "You tell me who else may have done this and I will feel absolved of my demons."

Her mind scrambled, searching for any clues. But all she knew was that someone in this manor tried to kill her. Could it be the same person? Was it possible that the two circumstances were related?

Wait. If the two were related—Mary's killing and her own death threats—then there must be a commonality among them. Someone, other than Charles himself, who was in both locations.

"How long have you known John? You said since your

college days, yes?"

"Yes, why?"

"Because he could be the culprit. He knew you during this episode with Mary and he is here in this house."

His eyes widened, cheeks flushed. "You think he killed her? You think he is trying to kill you?"

"He could have come through the secret passageways to spy on me, or frighten me."

"You know about those?"

She nodded. "It makes sense, don't you see?"

"It most certainly does not! John has been my friend for nearly fifteen years. Why would he do something like this?"

"You would have to ask him that question."

"No, I won't, because it isn't true. Why would I trust my son to a man who could murder? Why would he allow me to suffer like this over Mary's death?"

Disappointment tensed Vivian's muscles. He would not even consider the possibility, not look past the comfort he knew to recognize a new belief. He'd rather believe such a terrible thing of himself than to give thought to anything else.

She lifted her chin. "You do not believe that John could have a hand in any of this?"

"No."

"Do you believe that my life has been threatened?"

"I—I don't know why you would lie about it, but..."

Her shoulders slumped. "But you see no reason to trust me."

"I'm sorry, Vivian. There was no trouble here before you arrived, no death threats, no horrible visions when I looked at someone beautiful. Only the nightmares, which I cured with laudanum."

"That may be true, but there was also no life. That garden was no more lifeless than any of you. How can you see what you are missing if you do not let another in? How can you appreciate the rain if that is all you know?"

Her chest tightened, throat stung. "I resurrected that garden, brought beauty back into this house. But all of you, save for Harry, want it returned to dullness. If your vision is as bleak as the weather here, then I am not meant to remain."

He stared at her, lips pressed tight, scar glowing deep.

Since he did not reply, she continued, making up her mind as she did so. "I was willing to live here, willing to chance those threats against my life if I knew I had you to protect me. But you cannot protect what you do not think is in danger. Without your trust, there is no marriage."

"So you are leaving Silverstone?" His voice was empty, devoid of any emotion which would tell her his true feelings.

"Yes, I'll go at daybreak." She turned, walked toward the adjoining door. With each step, her heart prayed he would stop her. But each stride brought nothing but the sting of tears to her eyes. And when she finally reached her room and shut the door, there was nothing but silence. The wind, the rain, even the thunder had ceased.

The next morning, despite having only a few brief hours of sleep, Vivian packed the clothing and items she brought. She longed to say good-bye to Harry, to tell him that her going was none of his fault. But she feared he might convince her to stay. As much as she cared for him, she could not live here without his father's love.

Pinkley and the groomsman came to her room to carry down her trunk and other small bags. Mrs. Plimpton handed her a basket of warm scones and other pastries. As she followed the men through the hallways and down the staircase, no one said a word.

Servants she had never before seen lined the walls, watching her go past as if she were the queen herself. Only John, who stood at the bottom of the stairs, smiled at her.

"Safe travels, Miss Suttley."

She nodded, looking for an evil gleam in his eyes but saw no emotion whatsoever.

Vivian reached the main foyer. She turned at the door to the numerous faces behind her. They did not speak, just watched her out of curiosity, as if they may never again have a woman among their midst.

She wanted to say something, but nothing came to mind. None of them had become her friend, sought her out or made her stay more welcome. Too loyal to their master or too entrenched in habits of poor etiquette, they had left her to find her way much of the time. And now she would find her way somewhere else.

Charles had not come to see her go. As was his way, he avoided anything too painful.

She nodded at Pinkley and he opened the door for her. Vivian stepped out into the misty early morning, a chill seeping into her lungs.

Sighing, she started down the steps into the fog. A carriage waited to take her to the village. But at the bottom, a man in the mist blocked her path. Her heart quivered. Charles?

"Good morning, Vivian."

Oh God. Martin.

Ashworth raced after his son, down the main stairwell. He'd thought about telling the boy after Vivian had gone, but it didn't seem fair. Harry would want to say good-bye.

But now the boy ran around the house looking for her. He'd slipped inside the secret passageways and Ashworth could not locate him.

Sighing, he walked past the staff of the manor. They lined the railing as if to watch a parade go past. All looked away as he strode past, save for John, who shrugged.

The front door stood ajar as Pinkley and the coachman wrestled with Vivian's belongings. "Outside, mi'lord."

Ashworth nodded at Pinkley and steeled himself for his last sight of Vivian. He had decided not to attempt to change her mind. What she wanted from him he could not give her. She would never understand that. She'd never been faced with that kind of horror, with the sickening realization that it could have been at her own hands.

But he should at least say good-bye, offer the coins he'd once promised her.

A struggling sun had begun to burn through the morning fog. He could see two figures down at the bottom of the steps. From the distance, it appeared they were in an embrace.

Curiosity mingled with a tight jealousy. He bounded down the steps.

What he found at the bottom stopped him cold.

Martin Crawford stood with Vivian pulled against him, his face twisted into a sneer. One arm held her shoulders, the other hand clenched her wrists behind her back.

Vivian's pale skin revealed her fear, but blazing midnight eyes spoke of ire.

Ashworth stood before them, his heart in his throat. He forced himself to sound calm. "This is a surprise."

"Good morning, Ashworth. It seems I have found something of mine in your possession again."

Something of *his*? "You know Miss Suttley?"

Ashworth glanced at Vivian. She looked away.

Martin laughed. "So she did not tell you of our engagement. We are to be married, although she's no longer worthy to be my wife."

Temper pounded in Ashworth's ribs, his jaw tensed. "Vivian, is this man you told me about? The one your father gave you to?"

Her stare still off to the trees, she nodded.

"Did you know that we knew one another?"

Again, she nodded.

Martin rubbed his cheek along the top of her head. "She's clever, is she not? She heard me say how much I despised you, that I hoped I'd never again see your face. So, she used you to escape me."

Martin Crawford, the one man Ashworth most feared would find him. The one man who may realize that Harry was his own son. He hid so far away in these hills to keep Martin from discovering his whereabouts. And Vivian brought him right to them.

"You chose not to share *that* secret with me, Vivian."

She winced at the clipped fury of his words, biting her lip. Her eyes glistened with unshed tears.

"Lover's quarrel, is it?" Martin pressed his lips to her neck. "Then you should not mind if I take Vivian back with me. She has a lesson to learn."

"Miss Suttley! Miss Suttley!"

Ashworth turned at the sound of Harry's voice but could not stop the blur racing past him. "Harry, no!"

But his son had already latched himself onto Vivian's legs, attempting to pull her away from Martin. "Don't go, Miss Suttley. Please, don't go."

"By devil!" Martin's voice cut through the air. "He looks exactly like Mary."

"You knew my momma?"

Ashworth reached for his son, but not before Martin snatched him. Now the monster held both Vivian and Harry against him.

"You've ruined Vivian no doubt." Wild rage flashed in Martin's eyes, dangerous and unpredictable. "You took my Mary away from me. You had a son with her, a son that should have been mine! And he will be."

"You aren't my poppa!"

Martin snorted. "I should have been. I loved your mother until that man killed her."

"A monster killed her!" Harry twisted in Martin's grasp but couldn't free himself.

Ice crashed through Ashworth's blood, dimmed his sight, stole his breath. His brain scrambled for a plan. He had to get his son away from Martin. He had to save Vivian from a horrible fate.

Would he fail again?

"Let Harry go." He lifted his head at Vivian's distraught voice. "It is me you want."

Martin bent and grabbed her ear with his teeth. Vivian winced but refused to cry out. "I'll want you for a few nights, and after that it's doubtful anyone will want you. But I'm not letting the boy go."

Ashworth fisted his hands, spots whirled before his eyes. "Let them both go. It is me you want."

"Now that is an interesting proposition." Martin cocked his head. "But unless you have a pistol handy to shoot me down, I'll not be freeing either of these two. I will come back another time to deal with you."

Ashworth stood there, dumbfounded as Martin slowly backed toward the carriage. His arm was tight against Harry's shoulders. One wrong move and the life could be choked right out of the boy's throat.

He wasted time in deciding how to act. For each second brought Martin closer to the open door.

"No!"

In the moment it took Ashworth to realize the wrenching cry had come from Vivian, she had both kicked Martin and jabbed him with her elbow. The shock of her sudden attack loosened his hold on his captives.

Harry fell to his knees, then scrambled over to his father.

Vivian did not have such luck. Martin recovered and snatched her hair, yanked it back until her neck gleamed in the morning light.

Ashworth gave Harry a tight squeeze. Relief overwhelmed him only to be replaced with gratitude. Vivian saved his son. Now he must save her, no matter what the cost.

"Go inside, Harry. It is not safe for you here."

"But what about Miss—"

"Go now, son."

Tears streaking down his cheeks, the boy obeyed and went up the steps and inside the house.

Ashworth straightened and set his glare on Martin. "Now let Miss Suttley go. This fight is between you and me."

"Oh no. Vivian forsook me. And what's worse, she ran to you. A man who'd already betrayed me and killed the woman I loved."

"You'll not take her in peace. Pistols or the old-fashioned swords?" Ashworth would see this all end now. He could not live in fear of Martin finding Harry any longer.

"NO! I'll not let you die and leave Harry alone in the world." Vivian finally broke free from Martin's grasp and ran, not toward the house, but into the waiting carriage.

Her actions stunned Ashworth just long enough that Martin got a head start on him. By the time he'd reached the carriage, the door banged shut and the wheels lurched forward.

Vivian was at that devil's mercy. He remembered the bruises on her back, the tales of Martin's painful assaults. That man would abuse her until she could not move, he would bloody her until she lay near death. If she lived, she would never find love again.

His throat closed in tight. He'd not give up on her.

"John!" Ashworth raced back to the front door and yanked on his friend. "Come, we must go after her."

But John stood immobile, his eyes huge.

"Won't you help me stop the carriage? That bastard will disappear with her." He remembered Mary's battered and bruised body. "Possibly kill her!"

But the tutor, his friend, shook his head. "I want her to go, Charles. I don't want her here."

He terrified me. Told me to leave this house or he would kill me.

I was poisoned.

John? No, it couldn't be. Not his closest friend. Not the man who saved his soul, offered to help take care of him and Harry.

Ashworth swallowed the bitter lump souring his mouth. He hadn't time to dwell on John's unwillingness to help or reasons for wanting Vivian gone. He had to catch that carriage before it got too far down the hill.

By the time Demon was saddled, he feared too much time had passed. But he was able to push the stallion to a full run and reach the vehicle as it crested the hill near the village's border.

Heart thundering as loud as Demon's hooves, Ashworth pounded on the door. "Open this door!"

Much to his surprise and relief, the carriage slowed. Martin's insane need for vengeance or his irrational feelings of superiority must be more important than having his way with Vivian at the moment.

The door opened to Martin's sneer.

"No," Vivian cried behind him. "Please, this is all my fault. I never should have come to Silverstone Manor. I never should have brought this nightmare upon this house."

"We have unfinished business, your new lover and I." Her captor shoved her back from the door. "Wait for me here, I'm not through with you yet."

Ashworth slid from Demon's back, fury scorching his veins. "If you've hurt her again..."

Martin chuckled. "She's no longer your concern. She was mine first and she'll be mine again until I tire of her. Obviously, you weren't able to keep her." He stepped out of the carriage and slammed the door closed. "She *was* leaving you, wasn't she?"

Ashworth clenched his jaw, unable to dispute it. "Follow me."

He led them up a hill, but a cry stopped them before they reached the top. Ashworth swung around, heart lodged deep in his throat. "Vivian, no..."

She raced up the hill after them, eyes shining, hair in disarray. "Please, stop this madness."

Ashworth hurried down to meet her halfway, to meet her before Martin could get his hands on her again. "You must go back. Tell the driver to take you back to the manor."

"You mustn't fight him. What if he kills you? What will happen to little Harry?"

Without thought, he pulled her in an embrace, kissed the top of her hair, breathed in her essence. Like warm wine, contentment and peace soothed his nerves. "I won't fail."

She sniffled against his chest. "But—"

"I can't allow you to go back with that monster. I saw what he did to Mary. I won't let it happen to you."

"Martin won't play fair." She angled her head up to him, midnight eyes glistening in the morning light. "If you die because of me..."

"If I die, it was my time to go. This isn't because of you, Vivian. This is because of what happened seven years ago. I've hidden here because of this man, because of my fears. It must end."

"Enough!" Martin's shout startled them. "Do you intend to provoke my anger further?"

"Go to hell, Crawford," Ashworth yelled back, bringing a weak smile to Vivian's lips.

She caressed his chin with her fingertips, then traced his scar. Ashworth closed his eyes for the briefest moment, savoring the gentle strokes of his angel.

"You'll not stop this duel," she said softly. "Not even for me?"

He pressed his lips against her forehead, swallowed the tightness creeping up his throat. "I end this nightmare for you, for all of us. Go back, Vivian, I need you someplace you will not distract me. Look after Harry."

Rocks bounced down the hill, alerting them to Martin's descent.

Vivian wiped her eyes and stepped back from him. "I love you, my lord. You are no monster to me."

Without giving him the chance to respond, she turned and hurried down the hill to the waiting carriage.

Ashworth straightened his shoulders and began the climb again, passing Martin without uttering a sound. He led them to a nearby clearing, surrounded by trees on one side and a cliff on the other. There, his groomsman waited, a sword in each hand.

Ashworth reached for one. "We duel."

"To the death?"

"To the death."

Chapter Twenty-Eight

Ashworth had not touched a sword since London.

Martin stopped in the center of the field and raised his face to the faint sunlight. A gust of wind lift his hair. "You obviously think I cannot best you in this. You are wrong."

Ashworth joined him. "I want it over. The nightmare that began seven years ago must come to an end now."

Martin lunged for him immediately. Ashworth swung away, then returned with a strike of his own. They parried over the length of the field, at one point coming dangerously close to the edge of the cliff. But then Martin pushed his way back.

Ashworth sliced through the air, the tip of his sword catching Martin's arm. A cry of pain rang across the field as blood formed on the fabric.

"You bastard!" Martin charged, forced him to retreat. The ground was muddy, slippery as they fought.

Ashworth's pulse swelled and crashed in his head, sweat dripped down his neck. Only the sounds of their blades clashing echoed in the air. The sharp tang of blood saturated the senses.

"You killed her!" Martin's voice rose with depraved madness. "You took her from me, got her pregnant, and then you forced my wrath upon her."

He lunged toward Ashworth, who leapt back from the blade. In the process he slipped on the wet ground and landed on his back.

Martin stood over him, poised, hatred blazing in his eyes.

"No!" A scream rang out in the distance. They both looked over to see John running towards them. "Don't kill him."

"Well, well, John Hughes." Martin caught his breath. "Heard you'd become nothing more than a boy's tutor."

"Please don't hurt him."

"John, leave. This is not your concern." Ashworth started to rise but Martin jabbed the sword at his neck.

John struggled to breathe. "Why-why did you have to chase after her?"

Ashworth stared into a gaze ripe with perverse anguish. Obsession. "Why do you want Vivian gone?"

John yanked off his glasses. "I wanted Catherine gone. I wanted them all gone!"

Martin narrowed his eyes. "All?"

"I—I was in a rage. I followed Charles to that house, I saw him with that whore."

"Whore?" Martin's sword swung to John's neck.

While the other two were distracted, Ashworth slowly sat up. In a heartbeat, he shifted into a crouch.

"Yes, she was a whore. All women are. Conniving, heartless and wicked. They were all in my way."

All in my way.

Ashworth's breath lodged in his throat. Had it truly been John all along just has Vivian said? Could it be true?

"In your way for what?" Martin's sneer rang out through the fog.

"Charles is too good for them."

The sword slid down John's skin, drawing blood.

"Mary was better than him or any of those other wenches."

Despite the sharp blade, John actually laughed. "And yet you beat her."

Martin's face contorted in rage as he shoved John to the

ground. In an instant, he was on his chest. The sword lifted high to the sky, catching a glint from the weak sun.

Ashworth leapt up and knocked Martin off. "John, are you crazy? You're taunting a madman!"

But with the wild glare in those blue eyes, Ashworth suddenly believed John was just as mad.

"I want you to love me, Charles. *Me!*"

Blood pounded like thunder in his eardrums, yet he had to know the truth. All of it. "Did you take Mary's life?"

"She was nearly dead anyway. I just finished her off."

Softly. "Did you try to kill Vivian?"

Tears filled John's blue eyes. "Instead of sending her away, you asked her to marry you."

Betrayal crushed deep in Ashworth's chest. Shock made him immobile. John had been his only friend, his only remaining link to the outside world, and all along he'd been the culprit, allowing Ashworth to suffer the horrific visions, the terrifying nightmares, the loneliness. He had valued that friendship more than Vivian's trust.

"You killed Mary!" Martin's shriek came with the sudden flash of the blade. Before Ashworth could react, blood spurted into the air and a gurgle escaped from John's throat.

Ashworth rose up in a engulfing rage and charged toward Martin, knocking him over. The two of them rolled on the grass, wrestling, kicking, swinging punches. With each roll, each swing, they moved closer to the cliff's edge.

Pain swelled and crashed in Ashworth's bones, crackled in his skull, but the wrath did not lessen. He knocked Martin backward with a hard punch to the jaw.

A shriek split the air as Martin slipped. "I'm falling! I—I can't hold on." He clung to the edge of the cliff, terror frozen across his features.

"You do not deserve to live."

"Save me, please. I'll go, I—I promise." He squealed,

scrambled to clutch more grass and tree roots. "Hurry! I'm slipping!"

Ashworth stared down at the monster at his feet. How easy it would be to kick him off and send him to oblivion. He could free the world of one more devil.

A man who would murder would not live his days in torment over the possibility of it. He would not resist falling in love and being vulnerable to keep others away. You are no murderer, Lord Ashworth.

He had not killed Mary. In fact, he had tried to save her life after Martin's beating. He tried to save the baby's life before being knocked unconscious. He awoke with the knife in his hand because John had put it there.

All these years he'd carried demons which weren't his own. He believed the rumors the villagers told, would not dare to look at himself in the mirror. He thought he had been marked as a monster.

But Vivian had faith in him. From her first meeting as a girl to the moment she walked out the manor's doors, she had not feared him. She did not recoil from him. She wanted him. She loved him.

You are no murderer, Lord Ashworth.

He bent down and yanked Martin onto solid ground. "I did not kill before and I shall not kill now."

Heart heavy, eyes damp, Ashworth started toward to John.

Suddenly a vice tightened around his ankle, tripping him toward the hard ground.

Martin!

Ashworth twisted around, but the predator clutched harder.

"You took Mary. You took her child. You took Vivian. Now I take you!" Martin reached forward, murder blazing in his eyes.

Instinct lifted Ashworth's free leg and drove it forward with a hard thrust. The kick sent Martin flying backward. This time there was nothing to stop him from going over the cliff.

Shaking, Ashworth slowly rose to his feet. In a matter of minutes, two monsters were dead. Would Vivian still want the third?

೦ʒ

The kiss of early evening blew a scented breeze against Vivian's skin. She smiled and lifted her eyes to the stars emerging in the darkening sky.

She should be exhausted. But while everyone was still inside partaking in the revelry, dancing, and fun, she would rather enjoy the beauty of the evening. After being within Silverstone Manor's walls for several weeks, the sight of other houses and city lights was a welcome distraction.

"So, my lady, here is where I find you."

Vivian's heart melted at the sound of her husband's voice. He came up behind her and she leaned against his chest. "I needed fresh air."

"And I need you. Every day I need you more."

She squeezed his fingers. "I still find it hard to believe that we are here in London."

"No more than I. It's been almost eight years since I've left the manor. I had forgotten how many people there were in this city."

"I am amazed how well our mothers are getting along."

Charles laughed. "Yes, my mother can act a bit superior at first, but your mother's kindness warmed her up quite readily."

Vivian swallowed. There were still secrets between them. Despite their vows, neither of them had revealed their full truths. They had apologized, proclaimed their love, but they had not laid themselves completely bare.

She would change that now. "Walk with me."

She took his hand and led him down the rear patio steps

and into the yard. The sweetness of roses guided them to an iron bench among the swaying trees.

Charles sat next to her, his powerful legs pressing against her skirt. The sharp cut of his cloth emphasized his strength. Her mouth dried, anticipating tonight. Their wedding night.

But first, she would tell him everything.

"Did you notice my mother's face?"

Charles tensed, shifted. "I saw her scars, of course. Having such a face myself, I know what pain it might cause to be reminded of it."

Vivian peeled the glove from her hand and traced the line down his cheek. "Don't you see? This makes you who you are. Do you think you would still be the same man had that night never occurred? Do you think you would feel the same sensitivity and compassion if you had not been marked?"

"All I know is that it brought you to me."

She looked into his gray eyes, seeing tenderness and love. "And my mother's scars brought me to you, as well."

Vivian pulled her hand away and leaned her head upon his shoulder. His scent of sandalwood mingled with the heady perfume of roses. "When my mother came from France to marry my father, she was already pregnant. She had hoped she could hide it from her new husband, but he found out soon enough."

She watched a bird dart through the shadowed underbrush. "In his fury, he threw hot water at her, scalding her face."

"Oh, Vivian." Charles pulled her close.

"For some reason he stayed married to her, even claiming to all outsiders that I was his daughter. But we always knew he never truly loved me. And he proved it the day Martin Crawford came into our lives."

"You don't need to discuss this...not tonight."

"No, I must. I want you to know everything. Martin discovered my father in a compromising position. With another man. Bribery and blackmail led to me being exchanged for silence."

She tilted her head to look up at him. "And when I overheard some girls talking about an eccentric viscount in need of a wife, I thought nothing of it. Until Martin, drunk and unbearable, mentioned how much he despised you."

"We don't need to worry about him any longer."

"I know. I'm so very sorry I led him to you."

His silver eyes glowed in the moonlight. "It's all for the best. I am no longer half-dead, hiding myself behind my nightmares and my scar. And Harry is safe, happily being spoiled by two grandmothers."

She brushed her finger across his chin, hoping, waiting. "Yes, your son is safe and that's all that matters."

He sighed. "Harry is not my blood son. I truly believe he is Martin's son, but the fool was too blinded by jealousy and anger to realize it. You knew all this already, didn't you?"

Warmth filled her heart. "I figured it out the night you told me about Mary's death. You said it was the first time you'd seen her and yet mentioned Harry being there."

His lips curled. "You are most clever, my love."

"But not clever enough to unravel this mystery: why I had such sensual dreams from the night I entered the manor. Were they real? Did you sneak through the hidden passageways and lie in bed with me?"

"Perhaps." His eyes lowered. "I awoke several nights in dark hallways, my mind filled with lustful thoughts, my flesh aroused for you."

"But you don't know if you actually visited me."

"I am not certain, but I believe I must have. Everything I remembered from dream felt so real."

Vivian smiled. "Yes, for me, as well. So have we shared every secret lurking in our souls?"

Charles pulled her around to straddle his legs. Tingles

raced to her toes. "There are a few we have left to investigate."

"Oh?"

He nuzzled his lips against her neck, trailed his tongue along the length of her shoulder. "Tonight will be the night we take it slow. Tonight I cherish you."

Vivian bit her lip, heat blazing through her bloodstream. They had not been together since that evening in the wine cellar. Her nipples ached, core tightened.

She found his mouth and pressed her lips up it, his warm breath an intoxicating elixir. "I don't believe I can wait that long, my lord. You'll have to cherish me another night."

"Any night, anywhere."

She captured his jaw in her hands. "Perhaps now you'll take more kindly to strangers."

Her husband grinned, a devilish gleam in his eyes. "Only if she is an unconquerable baron's daughter, from a day's journey away."

Vivian grinned and captured his lips with her own.

About the Author

Leslie tends to obsess about the things she enjoys: writing, Gerry Butler, gardening, beading, Gerry Butler. She's been writing since high school, when *Wuthering Heights* inspired her to create worlds of dark heroes, brave heroines and stormy nights. Since then she's written tales of history and stories of the future (as pseudonym Jordanna Kay).

When she's not writing, gardening or beading, Leslie can be found either at her day job or being a slave to her three children. In her dreams, she is alone on a white-sand beach with only Gerry as her cabana boy.

To learn more about Leslie:

Visit www.lesliedicken.com

Send an email to leslie@lesliedicken.com

Follow her on Twitter: http://twitter.com/LeslieDicken

Friend her on Facebook:

www.new.facebook.com/profile.php?id=555317012

Friend her on MySpace: www.myspace.com/jordannakay

GREAT CHEAP FUN

Discover eBooks!

THE FASTEST WAY TO GET THE HOTTEST NAMES

Get your favorite authors on your favorite reader, long before they're out in print! Ebooks from Samhain go wherever you go, and work with whatever you carry—Palm, PDF, Mobi, and more.

SAMHAIN PUBLISHING LTD

WWW.SAMHAINPUBLISHING.COM

LaVergne, TN USA
19 June 2010
186604LV00006B/5/P